CRAVED

The Vampire Syndicate

REBECCA RIVARD

Wild Hearts Press

❧ I ☙

ZOE

TWO YEARS EARLIER

I exited the limo, squared my shoulders.

Bold. Take charge.

The moon was a hazy crescent in the indigo sky. Montreal's downtown was alive with humans enjoying the summer night. They carved a cautious path around me like minnows avoiding a shark.

The Tremblay Ice Princess was recognized everywhere.

I entered the chic little hotel, my bodyguard at my heels. The lobby was all wood and steel, the walls charcoal gray. My strappy red high heels tapped an excited, this-is-really-happening rhythm on the polished maple floor.

"Mademoiselle Zoe." The night manager's eyes widened. He hurried around the desk. "I'm afraid there's been a mistake. We don't have a record of your reservation. But don't worry, we have a lovely suite—"

"I'm here to see a guest." My tone said that was all the information he'd get from me.

"Very good." He jerked his chin at his assistant, who hurried to call an elevator.

"Wait here," I told the bodyguard.

I

Jean-Michel had been with my mother Victorine from the beginning, one of the vampires who'd come with her from France to found the Tremblay Syndicate. The wily old Frenchman was now a top soldier, slim, elegant and lethal as the silver stiletto strapped to my thigh.

He moved closer. "You're sure about this?" he asked in an undertone.

I stifled a sigh.

Jean-Michel did *not* agree with this midnight visit to Rafe Kral's penthouse. Not that I'd told him why I was there, but you can't hide much from a man who's guarded you since you were in diapers. I might be twenty-four, but to a vampire Jean-Michel's age, I was a half-filled page in a tediously long novel.

I stared at the elevator's floor indicator light, willing it to move. But it appeared stuck on the fifth floor.

"Kral isn't going to attack me in the heart of Tremblay territory."

"You can't know that."

I set my jaw. "Is it so hard to believe he likes me?"

"Of course not. But he's Karoly Kral's youngest son. He's been raised to believe the Tremblays are the enemy. Just because your mother and Karoly signed a treaty to end the blood feud doesn't change that. And now, he's in town to negotiate a joint venture with us. He has everything to win by seducing you."

I shook my head. I was saved from answering when the elevator doors opened—finally—and a human couple emerged, dressed for a night out and so wrapped up in each other they nearly bumped into me.

Jean-Michel moved to block them. "Watch your step."

The woman looked at me and whitened. She elbowed the man.

"*C'est la Princesse Zoe,*" she said in a stage whisper that I didn't even have to be a vampire to hear.

"*Désolé,*" said her companion. "We are truly sorry." He curved a protective arm around the woman and hurried her out of the hotel.

I stepped inside the elevator and pressed the button for the ninth floor. I turned to face Jean-Michel, whom I'd instructed to stay in the lobby.

He folded his arms over his chest. "Damn it, Zoe. He's using you."

I narrowed my eyes. The old vampire might be the closest thing to a father I had, but when all was said and done, he was my bodyguard, not my conscience.

"Maybe," I replied. "Or maybe *I'm* using *him*."

The doors slid shut, blocking his disapproving frown. My breath came out in a whoosh. I raised my hands and shimmied in a happy little dance that would've shocked Jean-Michel.

Zoe Tremblay didn't do human emotions. I was the Ice Princess, the cool, controlled and marginally-less-vicious version of my mother.

Who was on her way to get naked with the son of my mother's bitterest rival.

The floors to the penthouse ticked past. In the elevator's stainless-steel doors, my face seemed all eyes except for a slash of red lipstick. The flirty little black dress showed off my toned arms and legs, and my hair was in a sleek dark knot at the base of my neck, exposing a tasteful amount of throat.

I smoothed my hands down my skirt. I knew I was beautiful. I was a vampire, after all.

But Rafe Kral had his pick of the sexiest women on the globe, vampire or human. Everyone wanted a piece of him and his two older brothers. The dhampir sons of a vampire father and human mother, they were nicknamed the Kral Dark Angels, the supernatural world's heartthrobs. They even had their own hashtag.

Rafe was the youngest. The charmer. The cocky, bad-boy Angel that men wanted to be—and women just wanted. To a man like that, my vampire beauty was nothing special.

The elevator stopped. I swallowed over the golf-ball-size lump that had lodged itself in my throat somewhere between the first and ninth floors.

You can do this.

Bold. Take charge.

The wood penthouse door was reinforced with silver to repel vampires. I rapped on the doorjamb so the silver wouldn't burn my knuckles.

Footsteps sounded. I straightened my spine. The door opened, and Rafe's lean, powerful frame filled the doorway. Behind him, tiny lights glimmered in the penthouse's deep blue ceiling so that he appeared silhouetted against a starry night sky.

My breath snagged.

He was so...much. A god of a man with inky black hair that curled around the kind of face you see on the cover of men's magazines, and a body that was all wild, wolflike grace beneath a soft white sweater and jeans.

"You came." His cheek creased in the lopsided grin that had launched a fan club devoted to his smiles.

My stomach lurched.

That grin promised something hot, forbidden, all-consuming. Something I craved with every cell of my being.

I smiled slowly back. "Invite me in, Rafe." A tongue-in-cheek poke at human superstitions, because vampires don't wait for an invitation.

His fingers closed around my arm. He drew me into the penthouse foyer. Our bodies brushed. An electric jolt shot to my core, and just like that, I was wet for him.

As a dhampir, his senses were as sharp as mine. His nostrils flared and something dark and a little dangerous ignited in his eyes.

He closed the door and pulled me up against him. I stumbled in the high heels, but instead of steadying me, he let me fall into him, my breasts against his chest.

I slanted him a look from beneath my lashes. "Well, hello to you, too."

His lips came down on mine. His tongue drove into my mouth with a hunger that awed and excited me. He tasted of wine and something primal, male.

I moaned and buried my fingers in his hair, scraping my fingernails down his nape.

An approving growl. "You want me," he said against my mouth. "Say it."

"Mm." I nibbled on his lower lip.

"Say it." He lifted his head and stared down at me, his eyes so dark, they were almost black, like strong espresso. "Say you came here tonight because you want to be fucked."

I moistened my lips, trying to get my bearings. I was new to this. I hadn't expected games...or whatever this was. When I'd pictured us having sex—and I'd been thinking of it a lot in the two weeks since we'd met—I'd pictured sweet, hazy, romantic. Wine and low music and a soft bed, not this hard wall of masculinity pushing me up against the wall and kissing me senseless.

"Say it, Zoe." He kissed his way down the side of my throat, nipped my earlobe.

Heat spiraled through me. My mind was still catching up, but my body was definitely on board. My lace panties were soaked; my breasts heavy, sensitive.

He touched his teeth to my throat. Not biting. His fangs hadn't lengthened. But it was a threat just the same.

This wasn't a game to him.

The threat wasn't physical, not in the sense that I was in any danger. But he *was* trying to dominate me.

And I liked it, more than I should've. I was the vampire, the powerful pureblood. But my knees felt wobbly, my insides like warm, sweet honey.

My head fell back against the wall. "Yes," I rasped.

"Yes, what?" he said against my throat.

"Yes, I want you."

He gave a hum of approval and bit the cord of my neck. Just hard enough.

Oh, yeah. I dug my nails into his shoulders.

His fingers closed on the straps of my dress. He jerked them down, baring my breasts and trapping my arms against my sides.

The only thing covering my upper body was a sheer red bra with a delicate lace trim that matched my panties. He stared at my breasts with that hot, hungry look. Beneath the filmy material, the tips hardened.

I curled my fingers into my palms, itching to cover myself. Vampires are naturally lean, but the women still have sex-kitten bodies. Not me. I was all angles and planes.

But because I wanted to cover myself, I didn't. Instead, I stared back. Daring Rafe to be disappointed.

He didn't even notice. His focus was all for my slight curves.

"Damn," he breathed, cupping my breasts through the bra. "You're beautiful."

I made a small sound of disbelief. "No, I'm not," I said, then winced.

Great, Zoe. Why don't you point out your other flaws, too, like your knobby knees and your pointed chin?

"Perfect." He rolled my nipples between his thumbs and first fingers. "They're perfect." His eyes met mine. "*You're* perfect."

He lowered his mouth to give each furled point a hard suck through the bra. I squirmed against the wall—and let myself believe, just a little.

Because maybe to this man, I *was* perfect. Not Victorine Tremblay's too young, too soft, never-quite-enough daughter.

His fingers were on my back now. The bra came undone, and he pushed it out of his way so he could keep kissing and licking my breasts.

I was desperate to touch him. I wriggled my arms free and sank my fingers into his silky curls.

His mouth continued down my abdomen until he was kneeling on the floor. Catching my skirt in both hands, he pushed it up to my waist—and blinked at the stiletto strapped to my thigh.

"Kinda old school." Rafe caressed my leg over the thin nylon sheath. "I like it. I bet you know how to use it, too."

"Of course," I said, insulted.

"You don't need this with me." His fingers went to one of the straps holding the sheath in place. He glanced up, giving me a chance to object.

I didn't say anything. It was a test, and we both knew it.

Trust was the most precious commodity in our world.

Still holding my gaze, he released my skirt to remove the sheath and set it on the floor.

I'd never felt so naked, even with the skirt covering my thighs again. The hair on the backs of my arms raised, and my heart sped up to an almost human rate.

Boom...boom...boom.

I reminded myself that the blood feud had been over for nearly a decade. Things had progressed to the point where Victorine was considering a joint venture with the Kral Syndicate—a casino on the Canada/United States border—the joint venture that Rafe was in Montreal to negotiate.

But that didn't stop me from recalling the feud's height, when Kral assassins had made multiple attempts on my life.

"Relax." He lifted my skirt again, hands warm against my hips.

His breath sucked in. The lace panties didn't conceal much more than my bra. He eyed my mound with the same intent scrutiny he'd given my breasts. Heat licked up my spine, like he was already touching me.

He touched his mouth to the spot right over my clit and blew, a hot stream of air that nearly made me jump out of my skin.

My thighs tensed. I brought my hands back to his head. "More. Right there."

"You like that?" He waited for my eager nod before doing it again. He followed that by tonguing and kissing my clit through the panties.

A big finger slid beneath the gusset and inside my sex. "You're so wet. So ready for me."

"Mm." I tried to pull him closer, but he resisted.

He'd been holding up my dress with his free hand, but now he looked up. "Hold up your skirt. And don't let go."

When I obeyed, he made a guttural sound of approval. "Damn, Zoe. You look fucking sexy."

I swallowed. I felt so vulnerable, standing there with my legs spread and skirt bunched up around my waist. But I also liked how much Rafe seemed to like it.

Then I forgot everything but him as he pressed another kiss to my swollen, sensitized flesh. Inside my sex, his finger did wonderful, wicked things.

My pelvis rocked up. I moaned and dug my fingers into the thin material of my skirt. "So good...so good." I was speaking in French now. "*Si bon, si bon.*"

"Take it, sugar." He released me long enough to drag the panties down my legs. I lifted one foot so he could pull them off. Before I could kick them off the other foot, his hot mouth was on me, the panties still hanging around one ankle.

In between kisses and licks, Rafe kept talking. Sexy, dirty talk that made my whole body tighten.

"Gods, I love how you taste. So...perfect. Like a good girl gone bad. I'm going to do this until you come, and then you're going to beg me to bury myself deep inside you so you can come that way, too."

He carefully inserted a second finger inside me, stroking my inner walls. Heat surged up my spine, sparked behind my eyelids.

"Beg me, Zoe. Tell me you want more."

I was so wet, so primed for him. The whole scene was so erotic. Me wanting to touch him but not being able to because I was holding up my skirt. The wall against my back. The man kneeling at my feet but clearly in total control.

"Please. More. I—"

Was that broken voice mine?

Then Rafe did something with his tongue that had me groaning. It was too much sensation. I tried to catch my breath. Tried to slow down, to savor every delicious feeling.

"Come for me," he said, and nipped my tender, over-stimulated clit.

Sparks exploded behind my eyes. My inner muscles clamped around his finger. I moaned his name and shot over the edge.

My legs felt as unsteady as a toddler's. I slid down the wall, but Rafe caught me and wrapped an arm around my hips, keeping me where I was.

He gave a few easy licks, giving me time to recover, before

removing his fingers from me. He sucked them clean with a wicked look up at me.

My chest heaved. I regained enough strength to stand on my own. "That was—"

"Shh." He shaped my hips and thighs with his hands. Teased my calves with his fingertips. Slid a finger into my left sandal to caress my instep. "Don't talk. Just enjoy."

He kissed his way up my body until we were face to face again. "Now," he said against my lips, "let's get this dress off you."

Boom. Boom. Boom.

It took me a few seconds to realize that this time, it wasn't my heart that was pounding, it was the door. The knob rattled.

"Zoe?" said Jean-Michel, low and urgent. "Victorine's here. In the hotel."

My stomach dropped.

Rafe bit out a curse.

"Coming." I released my skirt and dragged the dress straps up over my shoulders, but I'd forgotten about my bra. I swore and fumbled to disentangle it from my bodice.

"Hurry," Jean-Michel said from the other side of the door. "She's on her way up."

Rafe growled. "Give her a fucking minute."

He spun me around and pulled the dress down so he could refasten the bra, then set the straps back on my shoulders. The panties were a lost cause.

"Lift your foot," he muttered and jerked the panties over my sandals. He stuffed them in his pocket and rose to his feet.

"Open up, damn it." Jean-Michel rattled the doorknob again. "She'll be here any minute."

I dragged a shaky hand over my head. "I'm sorry," I told Rafe. "I don't know how she found out I'm here."

"Hey. Whatever happens, it was worth it." His crooked smile slammed into my heart with the force of a fist.

Regret filled me.

It's just sex. Yeah, he'd made me feel beautiful, wanted, but we both knew it couldn't be anything more.

I snatched up the stiletto and its sheath and turned to face the door.

Bold. Take charge.

"Don't worry," I told Rafe. "I'll tell her I—"

"Go," he said at the same time, pulling open the door. "I'll stall her."

Jean-Michel took my arm and nodded at the fire exit. "This way. We can take the stairs."

The elevator pinged. The doors opened and a trio of black-suited men spilled into the hall—two enforcers and Étan, my mother's current lieutenant—followed by my mother in one of her trademark scarlet dresses.

Jean-Michel swore under his breath. He released my arm and stepped back.

Victorine took in the stiletto and sheath in my hands. Her mouth thinned into a harsh red slash. "I'm sure you can explain."

A sick panic closed my throat.

She knew exactly what Rafe and I had been doing. With her vampire senses, she could smell the hot, dark scent of sex emanating from us both.

But she wanted to force me to admit it.

"I—"

"Not you." She sliced a look at Rafe. "Him."

He gave an easy smile and spread his hands. "There's nothing to explain, really. I invited the princess up here to go over the final details of the joint venture."

Victorine drew herself up to her full height. "Do I look stupid?"

"No." His smile turned rueful. "Look, I'm sorry if I broke some unwritten rule. But don't blame Zoe. This was all my doing."

"Oh, I don't doubt that for a moment." She flicked a finger. Étan and the enforcers flowed forward in a black triangle, taking Rafe with them into the penthouse. With a snap, the door shut behind the four of them.

I rounded on my mother. "He's done nothing wrong, damn it. I'm here because I want to be."

Her hand slammed into my throat, shoving me against the wall.

Jean-Michel drew a breath. "Victorine..."

"Quiet," she hissed and he subsided. "You *slut*." She shook me by the throat like I was a naughty kitten. "You think I'd let you risk getting pregnant by a Kral? And a dhampir, yet?"

I knew better than to fight back. She was twice my strength and ten times more ruthless.

"I'm sorry," I said as best I could past the bruising grip she had on my throat.

From the penthouse came the thump of flesh against flesh, and a stifled groan that I knew had to be Rafe.

My stomach contracted.

"I trusted you." Victorine shook me again. "You were supposed to get close enough to make sure he didn't try any tricks. Not let the bastard seduce you."

She set me back down. "You're weak. Just like him—a dhampir." She shook her head. "Maybe I should let you have each other."

My gaze slid to the side. *Maybe you should*, whispered the bold, happy Zoe.

But that was crazy talk. We both knew she'd never let me go. Not her only spawn.

"I'm sorry." I schooled my face to show no more emotion than my cramped, stunted heart. "It won't happen again."

She jerked the door open. Rafe was on his knees, the vampires looming over him. Étan had my panties in his hand. He threw them in Rafe's face with a feral growl, followed by a vicious kick to his ribs.

Someone moaned. I didn't know it was me until Étan's head snapped around.

"Well?" Victorine asked me. "What do you have to say to him?"

Blood trickled from Rafe's temple. His left arm dangled at his side; the wrist bent at an unnatural angle. He looked up at me and attempted a smile through his bloodied lips. "Sorry."

Do something.

Étan sneered. "She doesn't need your apology, dhampir." In the past few years, the hundred-year-old vampire had shot up the hierarchy to become Victorine's most trusted man, but this was the first time she'd allowed him to speak for her.

Rafe growled. "I wasn't talking to you."

"No?" Étan hit him open-handed. Rafe's head snapped to the side. An enforcer grabbed his broken arm and twisted it further.

I lurched forward. "*Enough*."

My mother's arm shot out, blocking me. "Think," she hissed. "You're a princess. My only spawn. And he's a dhampir."

I opened my mouth. Shut it.

Speak up for Rafe, and I'd lose everything. Rafe might be a syndicate prince, but he'd never be good enough for Victorine. Vampire spawn didn't mate with dhampirs, especially vampires as high in the hierarchy as me.

And recently, my mother had said she was considering promoting me to lieutenant.

Rafe could never be more than a guilty pleasure.

Victorine lowered her arm. "Well?"

Rafe's eyes burned into mine. Seeing me for the hypocrite I was.

I had to force myself to hold his gaze.

"I was just playing around." The words tasted bitter on my tongue. "I wanted to see if you lived up to the hype. You didn't think I was serious, did you?"

"No." His mouth wrenched to the side in a grotesque imitation of his famous grin. "I didn't think you were serious."

Victorine stepped inside. I couldn't see her face, but I suspected it wore a satisfied smile, the kind a cat wears as it eyes a cornered mouse.

I had the bad feeling we'd played right into her hands.

I dug my nails into my palms hard enough to draw blood. Because if I didn't, I was going to attack my own mother.

The enforcers snapped silver cuffs on Rafe's wrists. The smell of burning flesh filled the air. His face contorted, but he didn't make a sound.

The door closed. A quiet but definite click that echoed in my head like a slam.

My chest constricted.

Rafe would survive. Victorine was too smart to stake him. Take out one of Karoly Kral's sons, and the Kral Syndicate would come after us with everything they had.

Bold. Take charge.

Yeah, right. I closed my eyes, so disgusted with myself I could barely breathe.

"Let's go." Jean-Michel nudged me forward.

I walked down the hall. Shoulders back, spine straight, and shame like acid in my stomach.

❧ 2 ❧

RAFE

THE PRESENT DAY

The July sun shone hot and bright on Montreal's swanky Crescent Street. I exited the metro, put on my sunglasses, and glanced into a shop window, checking my glamour.

Yep, I looked just like another American tourist. A short, stocky tourist in a Disturbed T-shirt and running shoes.

I didn't dare travel the city in my real skin. The Tremblay vampires would be taking their day sleep, but every syndicate included a few dhampirs like me, vampire-human mixes who could move about during the day.

I wasn't even supposed to be in Montreal. I'd warned my father that sending me to Canada was a bad idea. After Victorine's men had finished with me, the prima had told me that if I ever touched Zoe again—if I even breathed the same goddamn air as her daughter—she would consider it an act of war.

But Father had somehow learned the real story behind my abrupt departure from Montreal two years ago. Not from me, that was for damn sure. All I'd told him was that the negotiations for the joint venture had fallen through because the Tremblays had imposed too many conditions.

"Use a glamour on the daughter," he'd said. "Or that famous charm of yours."

I'd shrugged a shoulder, but my gut had churned with humiliation. I'd replayed that scene in the penthouse a thousand times in my mind. I'd thought Zoe and I had something real, something bigger than the Kral/Tremblay blood feud.

I was wrong.

"I was just playing around."

Father had insisted I try. My brother Zaq was being held prisoner somewhere in Paris, and Father suspected Victorine was behind Zaq's abduction, that she'd formed an alliance with Slayers, Inc. to take out me and my two brothers.

If so, it was my fault. I was the one who'd fucked up by messing with Victorine's precious only daughter, putting not just myself, but Zaq and Gabriel at risk.

And I was the only one who could fix this. Because despite what Zoe had told her mother that night in the hotel, the princess had a weakness for me.

A weakness I intended to exploit—if I could just *get* to the woman.

I'd spent the last couple of days working my few contacts in Montreal, trying to find out something, anything that would help Zaq.

I'd bribed, pleaded, threatened. But nada. I hadn't even found any proof tying Victorine to the slayers.

Meanwhile, my brother was wasting away in a cell somewhere in France. Chained in silver and being fed on by a vampire.

Crescent Street was full of humans enjoying the warm summer afternoon. They strolled past Victorian brownstones and a few out-of-place high-rises that shot like weeds above the field of trendy boutiques, galleries, and restaurants. I joined the crowd, matching their plodding, window-shopping pace until I reached a high-end chocolate shop.

Inside I was greeted by a blast of cool, chocolate-scented air. My quarry, Felix Fortin, was waiting on a pair of tourists. A bilingual native of Montreal, what Felix didn't know about the city's residents —vampire or human—wasn't worth knowing.

I waited until the tourists took their chocolate and left, then locked the door behind them.

Felix started to object. I removed my sunglasses and shed the glamour.

"I need some information."

Felix blinked rapidly. He was a Kral informant. He knew exactly who I was, although he didn't look happy to see me. "Of course, m'sieur. How may I help you?"

"I'm looking for Princess Zoe."

He darted a glance at the locked door and smoothed down his white chef's coat. For a man who spent his days making candy, he was damn scrawny, with lanky limbs and a nervous, high-strung energy.

Or maybe it was me making him nervous.

"*La Princesse* isn't in the city," he said.

My back teeth clamped down. I'd figured that much out for myself. "Then where is she?"

Felix edged backward. I relaxed my jaw and reminded myself to be charming.

But I didn't feel charming.

Two years since I'd last seen Zoe, and the anger was still fresh, raw.

Two years since Victorine's thugs had tossed me onto a jet out of Montreal, broken and bleeding and bitter as fuck.

Two years since I'd sworn never to get played like that again.

Now, Zaq's kidnapping had changed everything.

I had to get to Zoe.

But she'd apparently gone to ground. Burrowed into some Tremblay lair.

I'd been searching Montreal for her since Thursday. Today was Sunday, and all I'd discovered is where she *wasn't*.

Not in her family's mansion in Old Montreal. Not at the Tremblay Vampire Syndicate's downtown headquarters. And not at any of the usual society parties.

You'd think Zoe knew I was looking for her, but that was impossible. I hadn't gone anywhere without my glamour. If Victorine found out I was in Montreal, my life wouldn't be worth the pack of cigarettes Felix was nervously fingering.

I dredged up an engaging smile, the one that usually had humans falling all over themselves to please me. "Think, Felix. You must have some idea of where she is."

He shoved the cigarettes back into his coat pocket. "*La Princesse* spent the last week on her family's private island."

"What's the name of this island?" I dropped any pretense of charm.

Fuck charm.

I was blood-hungry—I hadn't drunk in days—and on edge. Each day I wasted trying to find Zoe was another day Zaq spent in captivity.

"Isle de Minuit." Fear emanated from Felix in sour waves.

I took a calming breath. Felix wasn't the problem here.

"Midnight Island? That's northeast of here, right?"

I'd heard the Tremblays owned a private island. Hell, they probably owned more than one. My family did. But last I'd heard, Zoe had been living with Victorine in the Old City mansion. Maybe she'd finally asserted her independence from the vicious two-hundred-year-old bat.

Felix bobbed his head in a jerky nod. "*Oui*. On the Rivière des Mille-Îles. The Thousand Islands River. But the only way to reach the island is by a private causeway owned by the Tremblays."

I set a stack of large bills on the counter. "How do I get to her?"

Felix licked his lips and eyed the money like he wanted to grab it and run. "You can't. The causeway is guarded twenty-four/seven. The only other way to reach the island is by boat, and there's an electrified, silver-reinforced fence around the entire island. You could take a chopper, but the guards would have you surrounded the moment you landed."

"There has to be a way."

"I'm sorry." He spread his hands. "There's no way on or off

without the Tremblays' permission. You'll have to wait until the princess returns to the city."

"That's not good enough." By then, Zaq could be dead. I reached for the money.

His fingers closed over mine. "Wait."

I snarled and showed my fangs. Felix snatched back his hand.

I waited a few beats, then nodded. "Go ahead."

He shot another anxious glance at the door. "The Crimson Ball. It's the big party the prima throws for Princess Zoe's birthday every year. But you can't attend without an invitation."

My skin prickled and my heart picked up speed.

I pushed the cash at him. "July twenty-fifth, right?" That summer two years ago when Zoe and I had first met, preparations had been underway for her birthday ball. Not that I'd been invited.

"*Oui*. In the Tremblay Chateau ballroom."

"Which is on the damned island."

And July twenty-fifth was Thursday. Four nights from tonight.

I shoved a hand through my hair and stared at the shop's black-and-white checkerboard floor.

I had to attend that ball.

"If that's all, M'sieur?" Felix attempted to shoo me out of the shop.

"Who prints the Crimson Ball invitations?" I tossed more cash onto the marble counter.

"Please." His Adam's apple bobbed. "They'll kill me. Or make me a blood slave."

"The name." I shoved my face into his and put the force of compulsion into my voice. "*Now*."

Felix's thin face contorted as he fought the urge to speak. But he gave me the printer's name.

"Good man," I said. "Now forget I was ever here. You never saw me. You didn't speak to me. As far as you know, I'm not even in Canada. Got it?"

"I never saw you," he repeated, eyes glassy. "Never spoke to you. You're not even in Canada."

Leaning over the counter, I tucked the money into his pocket behind the cigarettes and called on my glamour. It shimmered over me like a magical paint job. My curly black hair straightened and turned dirt-blond, my chin sprouted a wispy stubble, and my body seemed to shorten and thicken.

I helped myself to a box of chocolate truffles. "*Á bientôt, mon ami.* It's always a pleasure doing business with you."

❧

The print shop was fifteen minutes away on a narrow cobblestone street in Old Montreal.

And it was closed on Sundays.

I glared at the carved wood "*Fermé*" sign. I could break into the shop, but all the invitations would have been sent out by now. I'd have to return tomorrow.

I headed back to the Latin Quarter, resigned to holing up another night in my rented apartment.

At dusk, I gulped down a bloody steak. Outside, the party-loving Montrealais were out in force. They packed the restaurants and bars of Rue St. Denis and overflowed into nearby streets, including the one beneath my third floor window.

I stared out at them, edgy and hungry despite the steak. Itching to go out hunting. But the Tremblay vampires would be out, too, prowling among the humans.

I turned from the window and reached for the truffles. The scent had teased my nostrils all afternoon, rich and dark and sweet. I opened the box and froze, staring at the truffles like they were tiny hand grenades.

I'd grabbed a box of Zoe's favorite candy.

Chocolate and alcohol are the only human foods a pureblood vampire can tolerate. During the casino negotiations, we'd usually taken a break around midnight for chocolate and a glass of blood-wine.

And each night, Zoe ate the same thing—a dark chocolate salted caramel truffle. Slowly, with an intent expression that had made me want to drag her onto the conference table and do dirty things to her.

It was the only time she'd let on there was a real person behind that unsmiling exterior.

After a few days, she'd started playing up to me when no one was looking. Running her tongue over her lips. Making little hums of satisfaction. Licking the chocolate and caramel from her fingertips.

Things had progressed from there. We'd managed to steal away from our respective security and spend an hour alone at a hole-in-the-wall pub. The time flew by, the two of us absorbed in each other.

Zoe had told me she envied my being the third son. "No pressure," she'd said.

"There's pressure," I said. "Maybe not what you get as Victorine's only spawn, but it's there. People are always watching, waiting for me and my brothers to fuck up. Especially me. I'm the 'face' of the Kral Syndicate."

She'd tilted her head. Her silky black hair slid forward over one shoulder. "Would you walk away from it if you could?"

"Nah. I don't mind being the face. What sucks is people believing that's all I am—the jet-setting playboy *face*. I'm a damn good negotiator. The nuts and bolts of business bore the hell out of me, but I like the challenge of putting a deal together."

She nodded. "So few people bother to look beneath the surface. And you *are* a damn good negotiator. I report to Victorine each night, and I can tell she's impressed, even though she'd never admit it."

Our eyes met—and I felt *seen*, like Zoe had looked beneath the cocky, fun-loving surface to see the real Rafe, the one who was doing a kickass job at keeping things calm and moving forward at the negotiation table.

Panic flickered across her face. "I'd better go." She pushed back her chair and come to her feet.

"Wait." I threw some cash on the table and rose as well. "I'm leaving in a few days. I want a real date with you."

She shook her head. "I'm sorry. I can't."

I moved closer, fingered a lock of her hair. "Please."

In the low lighting, her hazel eyes gleamed gold. She moistened her lips, and my stomach tightened. She was going to refuse.

But she'd said, "All right. Your hotel. Tomorrow at midnight. But just us. No bodyguards."

"I'm in the penthouse."

"I know," she said.

Gods, I'd been an idiot.

I slapped the lid back on the chocolate box.

I'd thought Zoe was interested in me, Rafe Kral—but she'd just wanted a walk on the wild side.

Monday afternoon found me back in Old Montreal. This time, the print shop was open, but the crablike, gray-haired man who presided over its dusty interior refused to forge me an invitation to the Crimson Ball, even when I offered him a stupid-high sum.

I sighed. I didn't want to waste magic on compulsion, but I dug deep and let my vampire into my eyes. "You *will* make me an invitation."

A half hour later, I left, invitation in hand, after first wiping his mind of any memory of my visit.

My next stop was an exclusive men's shop to buy a tuxedo and shoes for the ball. When I exited the shop, I was smiling, a dark excitement seething in my blood.

Ready or not, Princess. Here I come.

A shocked look from a woman in a business suit told me I'd let my glamour waver.

Hell. Stress and hunger were making me sloppy.

I amped up the glamour and ducked into an entrance to the metro. I joined the crowd of commuters riding the escalator down to the Underground City, a large, brightly lit warren of shops and restaurants connected by subways and underground passages to the city above.

You had to hand it to Victorine. The Underground City was a vampire's idea of paradise. Humans might believe they'd designed this city below the city, but to me, it was proof of how deep the Tremblay Prima had sunk her scarlet claws into Montreal. In how many other large metropolitan areas could you go to work, watch a movie, buy a beer or a baguette, attend a concert or even go skating —and never go above ground?

I elbowed my way onto a metro car and stood with my back to a window, the garment bag over one shoulder, the bag with my new dress shoes in my other hand.

The car lurched into motion. I was surrounded by humans, warmed by the summer sun. Their salty-sweet scent filled my head. Some of the women wore summer dresses or tiny, throat-baring tops. Hell, as blood-hungry as I was, even the men in tank tops were tempting.

I stared over their heads, trying not to see all that smooth, bare flesh.

Five days I'd gone without blood. I didn't even dare buy blood-wine for fear of drawing the Tremblay Syndicate's attention. Instead, I'd made do with rare meat.

And each time I used vampire magic, I grew weaker. Powering a glamour, traveling in the shadow dimension, compelling information from humans—they all took energy.

If I didn't feed soon, my magic could fail at a crucial moment. But I couldn't risk it; vampires have a sixth sense about these things. Even if I lured a human back to my rented apartment, there was a chance that a Tremblay vampire would sniff her out and realize a stranger had fed from her.

My stomach growled. I swallowed, tried to ignore it.

The blood craving raised its seductive head.

Feed. Just a taste...

The metro stopped. A few people got off, but even more shoved their way on. A young woman in a red tank top and capris sank into the seat in front of me.

My mouth watered. I zeroed in on the side of her neck and the blood I heard pulsing through her carotid.

It would be so easy to cut her from the herd, lure her into one of the Underground City's convenient dark nooks.

I wrenched my gaze away.

Get control of yourself, damn it.

I could almost see my father's lieutenant, Tomas Mraz, shaking his square blond head. Mraz never let me and my brothers forget we were dhampir, that we were weaker physically, with less control over our magic. That to compete in the vampire world, we had to work our asses off.

The metro jolted back into motion. I braced my feet apart and tried not to stare at the pretty human, but her scent wafted around me, warm and so, so sweet.

My nostrils twitched. *Feed.*

I clenched my jaw and thought of Zaq.

Aboveground, the bars and restaurants of Rue St. Denis were packed. People spilled out into the sidewalk tables, sipping beer or nursing soup-bowl-size cups of coffee. Through the open doors came the jangle of music overlaid with laughter and rapid French.

I turned down the street that led to my rented apartment. I was nearly there when I received a text.

I glanced at the screen, surprised to see it had come from my father. He'd gone dark when he left for Paris. He suspected we had a mole, someone high in the Kral Syndicate hierarchy who was feeding intel to the slayers. He'd ordered both me and my brother Gabriel to keep communication to a minimum.

But Father had attached his personal code, so I knew the message was legit.

Go home. The woman is of no use to us.

Disappointment stabbed through me. I didn't want to leave Montreal without seeing Zoe, even if it was just so I could tell her to her face what I thought of her.

But that was selfish. Father wouldn't have called me back to

New York if he didn't have new intel about Zaq. Maybe he needed me somewhere else.

Will do, I typed back, and picked up my pace.

I hadn't flown directly to Montreal—that would've been suicide. The Tremblay Syndicate would've been on me like fleas on a dog. Instead, I'd taken a flight to Toronto and rented a motorcycle for the five-hour drive to Montreal. If I was lucky, I could catch a late flight out of Toronto and be in New York a little after midnight.

Right before I reached the brownstone, my phone pinged again. This time it was from Gabriel.

You are needed in New York ASAP.

I frowned. The code was Gabriel's, but it appeared to come from the number my father had just texted me with.

The hairs on my nape stirred.

The phone pinged again.

You there?

I hurriedly typed a response. *G? That you?*

Of course.

Suspicion crawled up my spine. Something felt off. That wasn't how Gabriel talked—or texted. He'd say something like, *WTF—who else could it be, you ass?*

Only five people in the Kral Syndicate had access to my current phone number: Gabriel; my father, Karoly Kral; his lieutenant Tomas; and two high-ranking enforcers. All trusted members of Father's inner circle.

I was beginning to think the first message hadn't been from my father, and I sure as hell didn't believe the second had been from Gabriel.

Suspicion turned into full-blow alarm. I turned off my phone, shoved it into my pocket and kept moving past the brownstone, zigzagging downside streets every few blocks until I was a half mile from the rented apartment. Ducking into an alley, I removed the SIM card and tossed it into the bushes. Just to be sure, I ground the phone to pieces beneath my heel and dropped the mangled bits into a trash can.

To return to the brownstone, I slipped into the shadow dimension and waited outside the building until someone exited so I could enter while still in the shadows.

My apartment was the only one on the third floor. I dropped back into the physical world to unlock the door. The effort had drained me and left me a little dizzy—a side effect of spending too long in the shadow world, especially with my magic at a low level.

I bent over, sucking breaths, until my head cleared, then moved cautiously through the apartment. Everything was as I'd left it—the blinds closed, nothing out of place. If someone had entered while I was out, they were damn good.

I tossed the garment bag and shoes in a closet and grabbed my laptop. Even using a special password and Krals-only backdoor that Father had had the techs build into the Syndicate's programs, it took me a good two hours to hack into our files, taking care to conceal any identifier that could be traced back to me.

It took another few hours to be completely sure, but I confirmed that Zaq was still missing, and my father in Paris, searching for him.

Goddamn it to Hades. Someone was trying to get me back to New York, or away from Zoe—or both.

It had to be the mole. If only I knew who—and why.

I closed the files and ran a program scrubbing any indication I'd accessed them.

It was after midnight. I grabbed a cold burger from the fridge and ate one-handed while I dug out a new phone, inserted a SIM card, and texted Gabriel, careful to attach my personal code.

Dad's right. We have a mole. Trust no one.

Gabriel replied almost immediately.

Got it. How are things on your end?

I rubbed my eyes. I'd give anything to talk this out with my oldest brother, but until we knew who the mole was, I was afraid to tell even him too much.

Not because I didn't trust him. He'd go to the wall for me, and vice versa.

But someone close to us was a traitor. Even communicating by text was risky. I'd have to wait until we could hash this out in person.

My return message was short and bland.

I have the situation in hand. Will be in touch.

I turned off the phone and stared into the darkness. Picturing Zaq in the photo that had been sent to Father with the message, "*One down.*"

Zaq's wrists had been cuffed with silver and attached to a concrete block wall. He'd stared proudly into the camera, his T-shirt ripped, his lower face covered by a dark scruff.

The scruff couldn't hide the feverish sheen to his eyes—or the puncture wounds on his bruised throat. A vampire had drunk from my brother without permission. The bastards hadn't just kidnapped him, they'd made him into a fucking blood slave.

Thinking about it made me a little crazy. My fangs extended. My vampire-half wanted to rip a hole in the very fabric of the universe, if that's what it took to get Zaq away from those monsters.

He and Gabriel weren't just my brothers, they were my best friends. We'd been a trio from the day I'd first been able to toddle after them.

The pureblood vampire spawn had never understood what it was like for me and my brothers, because they were only children. Pick on one Kral, and you picked on all of us—and together, we could make those faster, stronger young vampires eat dirt.

As the youngest and smallest brother—at least, until my late teens when I'd shot up to my full height—I'd taken more than my share of abuse, and my pretty-boy looks hadn't helped. High cheekbones and long lashes aren't an asset when you're a twelve-year-old boy.

But my big brothers had always had my back.

Which is why I'd do anything I had to do to save Zaq. Anything at all.

✿ 3 ✿

ZOE

"There." Lainey Q, stylist to the stars, finished my makeup and spun my stool so I faced my vanity mirror. She picked up a brush and drew it through my straight, shoulder-length black hair.

"And I think some choppy edges..." She brandished a razor blade.

"No." I held up a hand. "I like it how it is."

"No?" The stylist's dark brows climbed into her carefully mussed silver bob. Lainey Q was an Instagram influencer with over five million fashionistas following her every pronouncement. You didn't tell her *no*.

Even if my mother was paying her double her usual fee to make me over for the Crimson Ball.

I met her eyes in the mirror. "No."

"But it's *the* Crimson Ball, and you're *the* Tremblay Princess."

That's how Lainey talked—in captions. I could almost see the hashtags: *#tremblayprincess #crimsonball #styleinfluencer*

"Everybody will be waiting to see what style you're rocking this year. I won't have them saying you look like last year's—" she crinkled her nose—"leftovers."

Last year's leftovers?

27

I eyed my plain, easy-to-care-for hair. "Looks fine to me," I muttered.

"How about some bangs?"

I shrugged. She was the expert, after all. "Fine—but only the bangs."

Lainey whipped out a towel and draped it around my shoulders. She turned the vanity stool so I faced her and slashed at the front quarter of my hair. Ragged black tufts rained down around me.

"There." She removed the towel and spun me back to face the mirror. "Chic but edgy."

"Not bad," I admitted.

"It's perfect. You're all eyes and cheekbones now. Trés badass, like an assassin working undercover as a model. It's that mix of Russian and French."

I eyed my reflection. I *did* look kind of badass, which was preferable to my usual Ice-Princess look. Cool, untouchable, virginal —with an emphasis on the *virginal*. Which was just sad for a woman about to turn twenty-seven.

"You're right. Thank you."

"Told you." Lainey's bubblegum-pink lips formed a smug smile.

The razor blade moved toward my hair again. I shot out my hand, stopping her. "That's enough."

A sigh. "Zoe."

"No. We're done here." I dug my fingers into her wrist. The razor clattered to the marble floor.

Lainey hesitated. We both knew she answered to my mother, not me. It was Victorine who'd decided my image needed an upgrade, just like she'd picked out my dress for the ball.

"You may leave now," I said in my best vampire-princess voice.

"No problem." Her look was sympathetic. She picked up the razor and set it on the vanity. "But Prima Tremblay wants to see you in the dress."

It was my turn to sigh. For the first couple of days, having Lainey around giving me a makeover had been fun. But it had quickly gotten old.

I knew as well as Lainey that Victorine had demanded to see the entire outfit—a trial run for the masquerade ball Thursday, when everything had to be perfect or she'd be in a cold rage for days afterward.

"Let's get this over with," I told Lainey, who retrieved the dress from the walk-in closet. I slipped out of my tank top and yoga pants and she dropped the silky white thing over my head.

"There. *Très chic*." The stylist was from Korea by way of Los Angeles, but in the two weeks since she'd come to Montreal, she'd begun littering her conversation with French phrases.

I examined my outfit in the full-length, antique silver mirror to the right of the vanity. The dress was beautiful, and so was my new hairdo. I hardly recognized myself. Which was the problem.

"Well?" Lainey asked.

I ran a hand down the short skirt and managed a small smile. I had very few friends, and besides, I liked Lainey. It wasn't her fault my mother had control issues.

"It's great. You're a genius."

She pursed her lips. "Something simple for jewelry. A thin gold necklace with a few strands. Maybe a gold armband?"

"I'll let you decide."

"Awesome." She gave an excited clap as if the jewelry was for her. "You'll love it, I promise."

"I'm sure I will. And pick up something for yourself, too—as a thank you."

"Seriously?"

I nodded, and her face lit up. She danced out of the room, still thanking me.

I heaved a breath. Alone. For a few minutes, anyway.

I went to a casement window. The sun was setting over the river. Farther off, the Montreal skyline was a vibrant smudge against the dusky sky, and in the grounds below, the vampire's night garden designed by my father was in full bloom. Lush white flowers—lilies, hydrangeas, roses—glimmered in the twilight.

The garden's centerpiece was a large bronze fountain guarded by a trio of snarling bears, their backs forming the base. Victorine had erected the fountain as a memorial to her Russian mate, Mikhail

Romanov, the final casualty in the Tremblay/Kral blood feud—and the reason that for her, my assignation with Rafe Kral had been a double betrayal.

Because Rafe wasn't just any dhampir. He was the son of Karoly Kral, the vampire who'd staked my father—and her mate.

In the window's specially darkened glass, the white dress made me appear almost ghostlike against the garden below. The woman everybody saw, but nobody really knew.

Behind me, my bedroom seemed even colder than usual, the black-and-white theme sucking at my soul. Victorine's taste, not mine.

White walls, black trim, white curtains. My bed was a heavy black wood that I hated, the coverings black silk with embroidered white diamonds. Even the pictures on the wall were black and white.

The rest of the suite was the same, with white leather couches and inlaid ebony tables and chairs in the living room.

As a child, I'd longed for color, warmth. My face raised to the summer sun.

But I was that rare being, a vampire born to two vampires. I hadn't been able to tolerate more than a few minutes of sunlight until I'd reached my teens.

I blinked, moved closer to the glass.

A man stood in the woods. I unhooked the casement window's lock and pushed it open.

Rafe?

My cheeks heated. My heart banged against my ribcage. I set my palms on the windowsill, staring hard at the deepening shadows.

But it was only a guard. He moved out of the trees flanked by the pack of wolfdogs that helped patrol the island.

Disappointment whooshed through me. I shook my head at myself. It was only in children's books that the prince rescued the princess.

A rustle in the bedroom doorway made me spin around.

Victorine—I hadn't called her "Mother" since I was a tiny girl— stepped out of the shadow dimension, her slim form sheathed in a chic red dress, accompanied by the spicy orange-and-clove of Opium, her favorite scent.

The door to my suite was still shut. She must have slipped inside when Lainey had left. She'd been here all this time, watching me.

My jaw tightened. I *hated* being watched when I didn't know it.

"Victorine," I said stiffly.

"You and Lainey have chosen your outfit?" She spoke in clipped Parisian French.

"*Oui*. Although we had a difference of opinion on my hair."

She took in the bangs and shrugged a shoulder. "No matter. The dress, *c'est parfait*, though."

The fine hairs on my nape lifted. I fingered the barely-there skirt. "Why am I wearing white?"

Last summer, I'd been commanded to wear red; and the year before, a dramatic black-and-white, shoulder-baring confection. I hadn't worn all white to the Crimson Ball since the year I'd turned twenty-one.

"You look young, very innocent. The men, they will eat you up."

Something was definitely up.

"Victorine," I said between clenched teeth. "What. Have. You. Done?"

She looked at me down her straight nose. No one could do haughty like Prima Tremblay. She was the real thing, an aristocrat who would've died during the French Revolution if not for the vampire who'd rescued and turned her. She'd lived with him in Paris until World War I, when she'd been sent to Montreal by the Paris Primus to found our syndicate.

"I've assured your future. You should be thanking me."

"My future?" My stomach jittered. "Is it Étan?"

The lieutenant had had his eye on me since I was a teenager. Victorine said I should be flattered. The man was gorgeous even for a vampire, with pale blond hair and the face of a storybook hero.

Too bad he made my skin crawl.

My fingernails dug into my palms. "Tell me you haven't made an arrangement with that *tarbanak*."

Victorine's full red mouth turned down. A Tremblay didn't

swear, especially in Quebecois. A Tremblay spoke only perfect Parisian French.

"Only if you agree," she said.

I eyed her. What was the catch? Because with Victorine, there was always a catch.

"Then we don't have a problem," I said. "Tell him I don't agree."

Her nostrils flared. "Do it yourself."

"I can turn him down?"

A slight hesitation. "*Oui*, although I don't advise it. But Zoe?" Her voice chilled. "You will choose a mate. By the end of the Crimson Ball."

"But...that's two nights from now." Fury and a sick panic churned in me. "For the Lady's sake, I'm only twenty-six. You didn't take a mate until you were well into your second century."

"You'll be twenty-seven on your birthday. And I was more stable. You've shown a regrettable tendency to listen to your heart over your head. You do want to replace Étan as my lieutenant, *n'est-ce pas?*"

"Of course." How could she even ask? In the past year since she'd tapped me as her lieutenant-in-training, I'd worked my ass off for her and the syndicate.

"Then prove it."

"I have proved it. I've done everything you asked and more. You know I'd make a better lieutenant than Étan."

"But his loyalty isn't in question."

"What—?" My mouth dropped open. "This is about Rafe Kral, isn't it? It's over. Finished. I haven't seen the man in two years."

And I missed him. My chest squeezed.

Even though I'd pushed him away myself, I missed him. Étan and Victorine had even showed me proof that Rafe had been using me, and even through my humiliation, I'd tried to make excuses for him.

Not even dozens of social media posts of Rafe with beautiful women—on a yacht off the Greek islands, partying at Mardi Gras, clubbing in Manhattan—had cured me of wondering *What if?...*

"And yet, in those two years you've refused every man I sent your way. No, you're still pining for that boy. That *dhampir*." Victorine's mouth pinched like she'd tasted something bad. "I know what happened last year in New York. How you slipped away from your guards and tried to contact him. The son of our enemy. I won't have it, Zoe. Do you hear me?" Hard, cold words that battered me like stones. "I won't have it."

"I hear you." I'd wanted to ask Rafe straight to his face if everything between us had been a lie.

At least, that's what I'd told myself.

Victorine wasn't finished. "Karoly Kral staked your father. Remember that when you yearn for his so-charming spawn. The Krals stole my mate and deprived you of your father. I only made peace with Karoly to save you—he would have come for you next. I will *not* lose my only daughter to the blood feud."

Her face had gone dead-white, her dark irises edged with the unnerving blue of her vampire. "And I will *not* lose you to his half-breed son."

I stared back, throat tight. I knew all this, of course. I'd grown up with stories of the evil Kral Primus. Karoly Kral had been the monster in my closet.

"Don't worry. You're not going to lose me to Rafe Kral. He'd never have me now, anyway. You made sure of that."

"It was for your own good. He was only using you. The man's a liar and a cheat, just like his father. Have you forgotten those texts?"

"No," I said woodenly. "I know he only pretended to be interested in me so the Krals would have an edge in the negotiations."

I'd seen the proof myself on the phone Étan had taken from Rafe. Texts from Rafe to his father, where he'd boasted that I was falling for him: *I've got her so hot for me, she can't think straight.*

To have Étan see the texts had been the final humiliation. I'd wondered if Victorine had done that deliberately, to grind the broken glass of Rafe's deception deeper into my heart.

"See that you remember that," Victorine said. "And Zoe?" Cool fingers touched my cheek. "Choose a mate, *ma fille*. Or I will choose him for you."

She glided from the suite as noiselessly as she'd entered.

$\maltese$ 4 $\maltese$

RAFE

On Tuesday I moved out of my apartment as soon as the sun was high enough to send all but the most powerful vampires to their day sleep. This time, I chose a place thirty minutes north of the city.

I pulled my motorcycle into the driveway, killed the engine—and threw back my head and laughed aloud. My new digs were like something out of a 1950s sitcom: a small red brick house with green shutters and a white picket fence. Pink geraniums sprang from big copper pots on the stoop.

The last place anyone would look for Rafe Kral.

Even better, I was only five miles from Midnight Island.

I unstrapped my luggage from the back of the bike and carried it inside before heading out to the nearest Walmart, where I paid cash for groceries and a half-dozen new SIM cards. Back at the house, I switched out the card in my phone with a new card, disabled the GPS tracking, and used an alias to sign up for a new number. A Canadian number.

Now I'd be damn near untraceable by anyone in the Kral Syndicate, even the inner circle. The flipside was no one—not even my brothers—would be able to contact me.

But Gabriel would guess why I'd gone dark, and if necessary, pass it along to Father and Tomas. And Zaq wouldn't be contacting anyone.

My hand fisted around the phone.

It should be me in that Paris cell.

Zaq was the good brother, big-hearted, laid-back. The Kral who'd emptied his trust fund to aid homeless humans and who volunteered in war zones helping refugees from the humans' endless conflicts.

The only glimmer of hope was that he hadn't been staked right off. They wanted him alive for something—to extort a huge ransom from my father, or perhaps as bait, because Father had flown to Paris to rescue him. Whatever the reason, it bought him some time.

I passed a hand over my face. I'd been up for close to twenty-four hours, and I was exhausted, and hungrier than ever. A bloody steak helped take the edge off, but I needed to feed, and soon.

I crawled into bed and sprawled on my stomach.

Two more days until the Crimson Ball.

I rolled onto my side. The hours were going to crawl by.

Tomas's words niggled at me. *"You must work twice as hard if you are to be worthy of your father."*

Me and my brothers had spent hours each day in physical training, and the vampire spawn had still beat on us at coven gatherings until we'd gotten big and crafty enough to fight them off. Still, Gabriel and Zaq couldn't be everywhere.

Eventually, I'd stumbled on a strategy that worked: Always do the unexpected.

If another spawn came at me with fists, I kicked him in the balls. If he looked for me on the ground, I dropped onto him from the roof. If he tried to make me cry, I laughed in his face.

My scrappiness had earned me a grudging respect, and eventually, the abuse had stopped. But you don't forget something like that.

I hadn't trusted another young vampire until Zoe—and look where that had gotten me.

My mouth twisted. I flopped onto my back and stilled.

Why wait until Thursday?

Maybe most people couldn't get on Midnight Island without the Tremblays' permission.

But I wasn't most people.

⚜

Shortly before dusk, I rode the Honda up the road that intersected the causeway. I pulled a glamour over myself and drove slowly past the entrance, studying it from the corner of my eye.

A solid, silver-reinforced wood gate topped with razor-sharp spikes kept out intruders. A sign warned that the gate was electrified to a voltage that would knock out even a dhampir.

Behind the gate was a second electrified gate, and beyond that a guardhouse with at least one guard. Security cams bristled from tall poles on either side of the guardhouse.

They wouldn't pick me up in the shadows; vampires still hadn't figured out how to detect movement in the other dimension. But on the other hand, while I was in the shadows, I couldn't pass through a solid object like a wooden gate.

I circled back and parked the bike a half-mile down the road, then slipped into the shadows and jogged back to the causeway. On either side was a sheer drop to the river with more silver laced into the concrete supports. A small, dimly lit yacht motored beneath, heading home for the night.

I hunkered down near the outer gate, considering my options. The only way inside was to wait for the gates to open and enter through the shadows. But remaining in the shadows too long exacted its own cost—I was burning through my magic at a rapid rate. Plus, stay in this dimension too long, and I'd become disoriented and pass out—and return to the physical world.

Even as I thought it, a wave of dizziness rolled over me.

Think.

With this level of security, they wouldn't expect an intruder to come through the front gate. That was a weakness I could exploit —but how?

A black SUV exited the island and headed down the causeway.

My heart kicked into gear. I watched intently as the inner gate slid open. The SUV drove through and paused between the two gates while the first gate closed.

Smart. Anyone attempting to slip through while a vehicle entered or exited would be trapped between the gates.

The outer gate opened. The SUV crawled forward.

And I saw my chance.

I shot through the outer gate, leapt onto the SUV's roof, and used my momentum to catapult myself over the inner gate. I came within a hair of touching the top and frying myself, but I twisted my body in time to clear it and landed on the other side. I took off up the causeway.

On the other side of the river was a narrow gravel road that disappeared into the island's thick, old-growth forest. A half mile away, the chateau's rooftop was visible through the treetops.

First things first. I had to get out of the shadow dimension for a few minutes at least.

I raced up the gravel road until I was deep in the forest, then swerved into the trees—and back into the physical world. The forest swooped dizzily around me. I took a few deep breaths, waiting for my head to clear before threading my way through the towering maples and oaks.

A quarter mile in, I came upon a path of black pebbles that led up to the chateau.

My skin tingled. I was one of the Syndicate's best trackers, even if my father seemed to think all I had going for me was charm and a pretty face.

Sometimes I just knew something, and right now I *knew* Zoe was nearby.

The trees thinned. Another few yards and I stood at the edge of a large night garden. Creamy flowers glowed in the gathering dusk. The sweet smell of honeysuckle and roses mixed with the forest's earthy scent.

Crouched on a small hill above the garden was the Tremblay Chateau, a gray gargoyle of a building with thick medieval walls and narrow window slits. A three-story turret with a clock tower at its apex marked the entrance, with a matching turret at the back. On the black slate roof, a flock of turkey vultures perched, backs hunched, like beady-eyed familiars.

On the third floor of the back turret, a woman appeared in the center window. I hurriedly backpedaled into the trees.

Zoe Tremblay, in a dress as pale as the garden's flowers.

I knew even before the setting sun touched her face with gold.

She opened the casement window a crack, and my heart lurched and skidded in my chest like an out-of-control car. Two years since I'd seen her, and she could still make me want.

Gods, I was pathetic.

Zoe turned from the window and spoke to someone.

A low growl made me whip around. A pack of wolfdogs raced out of the woods followed by a vampire in a Tremblay uniform. I re-entered the shadows and darted into the garden.

They halted at the spot where I'd stood and sniffed the ground, whining and snarling. The vampire scrutinized the area, eyes narrowed.

On the chateau's opposite side, an engine purred to life. I glanced back at Zoe's window. She was no longer visible, but somehow I knew she was still in the tower.

So who was leaving? I slipped around the front in time to see Victorine herself exit through the medieval wooden door.

Hate flamed in my chest. I fingered my switchblade.

After Zoe had left that night, Victorine had watched, expressionless as a rattlesnake, while her men beat me.

They started with my face, then moved down my body, concentrating on pressure points.

Throat. Groin. Kidneys.

When I lay broken and bleeding on the floor, the silver cuffs burning into my wrists, Victorine had leaned forward and hissed, "Tell your father the joint venture is off. And if you ever touch the princess again—" she ground a pointy heel into my solar plexus—"I will consider the truce broken. I won't rest until I've sent you and your brothers to the final death."

Now I watched as Victorine descended the chateau steps trailed by two hard-bodied blond vampires. I clutched the switchblade's stainless steel handle.

So. Damn. Tempted.

I'd have signed over my entire trust fund to be able to drop out of the shadows and stab the long silver blade into her heart. But I'd be captured, recognized—and the blood feud would be back on.

I might as well sign Zaq's death warrant myself.

I gritted my teeth and let her pass.

But her exit had given me the perfect opportunity to investigate further. When the heavy door started to close, I went with impulse and shot up the steps and into the chateau. The door thudded shut behind me and I grimaced. I wouldn't be able to leave again without exiting the shadows.

I was in a huge Goth-style foyer. The thick walls and narrow window slits made it feel like I was underground. A typical vampire's lair, although the Tremblays probably had rooms in the basement.

An over-the-top crystal chandelier presided over miles of creamy Italian marble. The window slits were draped in red velvet curtains dotted with tiny black vultures, the Tremblay mascot. Scattered around the foyer were heavy Gothic couches and chairs covered in more vulture-dotted red velvet.

Preparations for the ball were underway. Crates of glassware, plates and other party paraphernalia lined the walls, and black tables and chairs were stacked near the open double doors leading to the ballroom.

Other than the two humans I heard chatting in the rooms off the kitchen, the upper chateau seemed empty except for Zoe. I remained in the shadows anyway, certain that somewhere, a guard was watching through the cams trained on the foyer.

I closed the switchblade, shoved it into my back pocket and went exploring. At the back of the chateau, I came to a parlor filled with more dark Gothic furniture—the real kind, antiques from hundreds of years ago.

At the rear of the parlor, the door to the back turret stood ajar.

A wrought iron staircase spiraled up the center. Worked into the rails were whimsical bats—bats on the wing, bats mating, bats feeding, bats caring for their young. There were even bats hanging upside down from the metal curlicues, asleep.

I jogged upstairs. After the main floor's heavy Goth theme, the second floor was a surprise—an airy conservatory crammed full of plants and flowers. Ivy cascaded down a cast iron gazebo that looked like a giant white birdcage, and more iron benches and chairs were set among the ferns and palms. The windows were of smoked glass that would protect a vampire from the sun's rays.

I was in Zoe's private retreat.

Something moved in my chest. *This* was the Zoe I'd glimpsed two years ago. The warm, fascinating woman behind the princess mask.

The single door on the top floor was open. But Jean-Michel stood in the doorway between me and my goal. I froze. He couldn't see me, but some vampires can sense you in the shadows, especially if they brush against your skin.

I peered around him. Zoe was curled up on a black-and-white couch, reading a book. She'd exchanged the white dress for a flimsy camisole and tap pants that showed off her long legs. The dim lighting emphasized her high, slanting cheekbones and dark, definite brows. Her hair fell, sleek as ebony, over one shoulder.

She turned a page in her book. She looked so young. Sweet, almost.

I stared at her, heart pounding. Wanting her and hating her at the same time.

She could've followed me to New York. She must've known I couldn't come back to Montreal, but she could've tried to come to me. Instead, she'd chosen to remain with her mother.

Maybe she'd even believed that "hype" crap she'd thrown at me.

"If you need me," Jean-Michel said, "I'll be in the ops room."

"All right," Zoe said without looking up from her book.

Jean-Michel started to shut the door. I shot, cat-quiet, past him into the living room, and halted, my back to the wall.

I stared at Zoe. A heartbeat passed, then another.

Her brow crinkled. "Who's there?" she said and rose to her feet.

Bad idea, coming this close. She clearly sensed someone else was in the room.

My hands clenched and unclenched. My head said *hell, no*, but the rest of me wanted to touch her so bad I could almost feel her soft skin beneath my fingertips.

But to do that, I'd have to leave the shadows, and she'd have Jean-Michel on my ass in five seconds flat. Even if she didn't, the cams would detect me.

Another wave of dizziness struck me. I had to get out of the chateau, ASAP.

Reluctantly, I decided to stick to my original plan. I'd attend the Crimson Ball under cover of my glamour and explain the situation to her. Ask for her help.

And if that didn't work, I'd *make* her help me.

At the front of the chateau, I heard the tower clock strike ten. Someone knocked on Zoe's door.

I ran into the bedroom, sprang onto a stone windowsill and took a flying leap through the casement window into the garden.

"Zoe?" came a voice from above me. "I found the cutest armband on Insta…"

※ 5 ※

ZOE

The sounds of the Crimson Ball drifted up to my bedroom. Steamy jazz from 1920s Paris mixed with the clink of glasses and the low laughter of vampires on the hunt for sex and blood.

I grimaced. Happy birthday to me.

I contemplated myself in the mirror. Lainey had outdone herself. I looked stunning, all long legs and mysterious hazel eyes beneath the black fringe, my only jewelry a gold arm band and the necklace Lainey had had shipped from Manhattan.

Stunning...and untouchable in the white gown. The Ice Princess in all her glory.

Rafe had teased me about the nickname.

I touched up my lipstick, stepped into my high heels. Settled my mask over my upper face and gave myself a bitter smile. Zoe Tremblay was going to snag herself a mate.

Why not? The only man I wanted would never have me.

Not that I wanted him anyway.

Okay, that was a lie. I did want Rafe.

I might not trust him, but I wanted him. For those two weeks, he'd brought color and excitement to my boxed-in existence.

Victorine's ultimatum had forced me to take a hard look at

myself. I'd been in a holding pattern for two years. Trying to find a way around the obstacles.

Trying to find a way to Rafe.

But it wasn't going to happen. It was time to accept that this Romeo-and-Juliet romance wasn't going to end any more happily than the first.

I lifted my chin. "You're a princess," I told myself. "Act like one."

In the hall, Jean-Michel waited to escort me downstairs. At my appearance, he gave a small smile. "*Très belle.*"

I shot him a startled look and murmured a thank you. It had been a long time since he'd said anything personal to me. Two years, to be exact.

Our friendship had been another casualty of my "little rebellion," as Victorine called it. Jean-Michel had barely escaped being staked. Instead, my mother had ordered me to snap silver manacles around his wrists and chain him to the basement wall outside my rooms in the Old Town Mansion. She'd kept him there for a month, slowly starving, where I saw him whenever I entered or left my rooms.

Near the end of the thirty days, Jean-Michel had appeared more animal than human. Body hollowed out by hunger. Face a flesh-covered skull topped by matted brown hair. Irises rimmed a brilliant, mad blue. Lips drawn back to show sharp fangs.

He didn't speak the entire time. No recriminations. But no forgiveness, either.

He simply watched me pass by.

Victorine couldn't have punished me more if she'd chained me to the wall instead of him.

"You are ready?" At my nod, Jean-Michel donned a mask and headed down the spiral staircase before me.

The ballroom was nearly full. Candles were everywhere, hundreds of them, a Crimson Ball tradition. They flickered in the chandeliers, in votives on the black-clothed tables, in the opulent flower arrangements. The dim light softened the vampires' cold eyes, gave their smiles a deceptive warmth.

The thralls certainly seemed taken in by it. They clung to the vampires, starry-eyed through their masks. Rubies and emeralds and diamonds glittered—on the women's throats and wrists, and in the males' earlobes. The blood-bonded thralls wore a gold chain around their wrists.

Nearby, Lainey flirted with Olivier, a high-ranking soldier. She'd negotiated attendance at the ball as part of her contract before heading home tomorrow. I suspected her next post would be *#hotsexwithavampire*.

The band swung into a tango. The males pulled their partners close, steering them through the sensual moves, dipping them backward over one arm and nuzzling their necks in an intimate, wolfish dance that was as close to intercourse as you could get with your clothes on.

I'd never met a vampire who didn't love to tango, me included.

Étan appeared, blond and beautiful in a tux and a black half-mask. The vulture tattoo of a Tremblay enforcer peaked out of the collar of his starched white tuxedo shirt.

He jerked his chin at Jean-Michel, and the guard fell back a few steps.

"Zoe." Étan took in my skimpy dress with a possessiveness that made my stomach hollow out. "May I be the first to wish you a very happy birthday?"

Play the game.

I was so close to being appointed Victorine's lieutenant. The youngest syndicate lieutenant in the world. I'd have real power, not just power in name only.

If mating with Étan was part of the deal, would it be so bad?

I plastered on a smile and prepared to make my mother happy.

✾ 6 ✾

RAFE

The Tremblay Chateau loomed above me, ribbons of mist slithering around its thick greystone walls. Candles flickered in its narrow medieval windows. Music and laughter spilled into the night. In the garden, thralls in bronze cages danced half-naked for the vampire guests' pleasure.

I smoothed down my tux, adjusted my bowtie. A black velvet half-mask covered my features.

A whole week I'd been close to Zoe Tremblay without being able to touch her. Tonight, that would change. My mouth curved in a sharp-toothed smile.

As I moved forward, my glamour wavered. I pumped more magic into it.

I should've been afraid. I was nearly out of energy now. If the glamour slipped, the mask wouldn't hide me—too many people here knew my face. The Tremblay enforcers would be on me like dogs on raw meat.

But instead, the danger had me revved.

I adjusted my mask and jogged up the mist-enshrouded steps into the heart of the Tremblay Coven.

The first floor had been transformed into a vampire's lush, opulent speakeasy. Candles burned in the foyer's crystal chandelier.

45

Towering black vases of narrow red tulips rose like blood-tipped spears from the marble floor.

The ballroom's double doors stood open. More candles flickered on the tables and in wall sconces. Vampires danced cheek-to-cheek with thralls—the males in tuxes, the females in tight, barely-there red dresses. The scent of all that warm human flesh kicked my blood hunger into high gear.

My stomach contracted. My fangs pricked against my gums.

"Your invitation, M'sieur?" A hard-faced Tremblay soldier in a black uniform held out a hand.

I swallowed and retracted my fangs under cover of removing the invitation from my breast pocket. The soldier examined the engraved card, then compared it to the list on his phone as his assistant patted me down for weapons.

"He's clear," said the assistant.

The soldier frowned at his phone and glanced again at me.

The seconds ticked by. I waited, outwardly at ease, even a little bored, but ready to run like hell.

If only I had a switchblade... But they would've just taken it from me anyway.

The soldier spoke. "*Qui n'avance pas...*" He stopped, cocked a brow.

Both men looked at me.

My heart thumped. My mouth dried.

It had to be a code. The final test.

I should've guessed the invitation alone wouldn't be enough to get me in. I thought I knew the correct response, but I'd have only one chance to get it right.

"*Recule,*" I returned calmly, as if I had every right to be there.

"*Qui n'avance pas, recule.*" It was an old French proverb: *Who does not move forward, recedes.*

A curt nod. "*Entrez.*" The soldier waved a hand at the double doors.

I released a slow breath. *Thank you, Mom.*

By some strange coincidence, my New Orleans born-and-bred mother had loved that particular proverb. Her French grandmother had cross-stitched it on white linen, and my mother had had it framed and hung in our parlor. It meant something like: *If you don't keep trying new things, you'll go backward instead.*

Behind me, the soldier tested a new arrival with a different proverb, one I'd never heard in my life.

I smothered a smirk. *Up yours, Victorine. I'm here, and the fun is about to begin.*

In the ballroom, my gaze zeroed in on the Tremblay Prima, holding court in a blood-red dress, her hair coiled into a sleek black twist. Diamonds the size of a thumbnail glittered against the smooth white skin of her throat.

The devil in me wanted to saunter closer and do something outrageous, like ask her to dance. If it hadn't been for Zaq, I might've.

Instead, I turned and lost myself in the crowd.

A server in a lacy red mask appeared with a tray of blood-wine. "Something to drink, m'sieur?" she asked in French.

The ruby-colored liquid shimmered darkly in the dim light. I took a glass and gulped it down. The fresh blood mixed into the wine hit my stomach like a contained explosion. Warmth spread through my veins, soaking into my parched cells, feeding my magic.

"More?" the server asked.

I nodded and accepted a second glass. This time, I forced myself to take measured sips as I scanned the crowd from behind my mask. Searching for my prey.

I scented Zoe before I saw her, a springlike green spice that made my lungs squeeze and my stomach lurch.

Unlike the guests, Zoe had made little effort to conceal her identity. Her mask was a strip of black that barely covered her eyes, and the silky white slip-thingy she wore showed all but a few crucial inches of her smooth golden limbs.

Virginal white. The color of innocence and ice.

My mouth curled. The woman sure could rock that touch-me-not look.

I knew different. I'd seen her mouth kiss-swollen, hair mussed from my fingers, creamy breasts bared as I'd tugged her dress down to her waist...

In the candlelit ballroom, the seductive sheen of her vampire skin was more noticeable. Beneath the thin strip of her mask, her hazel eyes were long lidded, inscrutable, her mouth a shiny apple-red. Her blue-black hair fell in a glistening wave around her shoulders and she wore a simple gold band high on her left arm. More gold was draped in sexy strands around her throat.

My groin tightened. Gods, I wanted her...almost as much as I hated her.

She seemed unaware of the bodyguard hovering nearby. Jean-Michel, the dark-haired Frenchman who was the closest thing she had to a father-figure.

No, her smile was for the lean blond asshat looking down the front of her white slip-thingy. Étan, Victorine's current lieutenant and former lover. He'd taken a special pleasure in working me over.

He angled his body closer to Zoe's and fingered a lock of her hair.

A possessive fury surged up my spine, spearing into my brain.

No man but me could stand that close to Zoe. Touch her. Have her.

Jean-Michel's head swung toward me. A vampire couldn't read my emotions like they could a human's, but my muscles had tightened, my stance shifting to the balls of my feet as I prepared to launch myself at the blond douchebag.

Zoe's mouth hardened into a thin-lipped facsimile of a real smile. She pulled away from Étan, forcing him to release her and saving me from myself.

Rein it in, you ass. Or you'll blow your cover.

I tore my gaze away, forced my shoulders to ease.

"Will that be all, M'sieur?" The server in the short skirt again. She'd set down her tray on a nearby table. She moved closer and trailed a finger down my lapel.

Definitely a thrall.

Hunger's bony fingers clutched my belly. I eyed the woman's

throat. It was long and soft and tanned, with two healed-over puncture wounds.

She tilted her head to one side, indicating her willingness to be fed from. The hot tangle of emotions emanating from her—attraction, lust, excitement—said she'd be agreeable to sex as well.

Hunger thrummed in my veins. The two blood-wines had helped, but it was like eating a handful of nuts when your starving body cried out for a full meal.

I *needed* blood. Especially fresh human blood.

Feed. Feed. Feed.

My fangs elongated. The effort of powering my glamour had taken its toll. My control was in tatters.

I glanced at Zoe and retracted my fangs. Somehow, I couldn't bring myself to feed from another woman when she was this close.

"Some other time," I muttered and turned away.

Jean-Michel was still eyeing me. The music changed to a foxtrot.

I caught the thrall's hand. "Dance with me."

❧

The thralls at vampire balls traditionally took anonymous names so they could pretend to hide behind their masks. Of course, any but a newly made vampire recognized their thralls by a combination of scent and emotion.

"Call me Silver Rose," said the thrall dancing with me.

I learned she was from Quebec City, but she'd moved to Montreal for the clubs.

"And the vampires," she added with a suggestive rub of her breasts against my tux.

I smiled down at her, only half-listening. Zoe was dancing now, too, this time with a dark-haired vampire.

Silver Rose caught the direction of my glance. "I heard the princess is choosing a mate tonight."

My grip tightened on her. "Princess Zoe?"

The thrall's throat worked. She tried to pull back, but I kept her close.

"Answer me."

A quick, nervous nod. "You didn't know? Everybody's talking about it."

I forced my fingers to loosen. "I heard something," I lied. "I didn't know it was set for tonight."

"That's what I heard."

A black fury blanked out my vision. Zoe was taking a mate? Over my dead body.

I gave myself a shake, reminding myself why I was here—to find out what the Tremblays knew about Zaq's kidnapping. Not for a do-over with Zoe.

Around me, the crowd had grown larger, louder. The air conditioning pumped out icy air, but it struggled with the heat of so many human bodies. The emotions of a hundred horny thralls scraped at my skin.

Silver Rose pressed her lips to my jaw. "You seem on edge. I could help you with that."

I focused on the thrall. Maybe she was right. I wasn't doing Zaquiel any good in this state. Hell, I could barely form a coherent thought beneath the steady drum of the blood hunger.

Feed. Feed. Feed.

My nape tingled. My head swung around.

Zoe was dancing with Étan now. She stared at me over his shoulder, forehead puckered.

Like she could see through my glamour.

☙ 7 ❧
ZOE

Rafe Kral was here. In the chateau.

My slow-beating heart jolted into a faster, almost-human rhythm.

I dragged my gaze away from him and forced myself to focus on Étan.

It couldn't be. I must be imagining it.

I chanced another look.

He'd made an attempt at a glamour. His hair was longer and streaked blond, and his face different enough—shorter nose, weaker chin, thinner lips—that your gaze slid past him. But it was him all right.

How in the Lady's name had he gotten through security? Even if he'd somehow forged an invitation and managed to finesse the password, the men at the door should've seen through the glamour. It was like a gauzy veil laid over his sculpted, Greek-god features.

Yet no one but me seemed to see through it. Victorine was cheek-to-cheek with her current favorite thrall. Lainey was being fed chocolate-covered strawberries by Olivier, unaware that #dark-angel was dancing a few yards away from her.

And Étan's attention was on me.

He smoothed a hand down the back of my dress. "You look beautiful tonight. White suits you."

"Mm." I stole another hungry look at Rafe.

The glamour only changed his face. His body was exactly as I remembered: lean, hard, powerful. In his black evening clothes, he appeared sleek and a little dangerous, like the Crimson Ball was a stop on the way to a rendezvous with an enemy spy.

The cute little thrall in the postage-stamp skirt was certainly interested. She gazed at him like he was a treat she wanted to gobble up.

My mouth turned down.

Étan lifted a brow. "Is something wrong?"

I forced the corners back up. "No, no. You were saying?"

I zeroed in on Rafe's bowtie. Blinked, looked again. From far away, it appeared to be red-and-black polka dots, but the black dots were actually snarling wolves, the Kral mascot.

Trust Rafe to flaunt his syndicate affiliation in our face. This was the Tremblay Syndicate's biggest event. The entire inner circle was present except for those handling security.

Étan spoke again. "...that dress for me?"

I widened my party smile. "I beg your pardon?"

He tightened his grip on my back, pulling me closer so that the tips of my breasts brushed his tux. His sharp male scent invaded my space. "Did you wear that dress for me?"

My smile froze.

Étan was a good match. Smart, capable, good-looking, and like me, he wanted to take the Tremblay Syndicate to the next level.

The perfect mate for Princess Zoe.

But there was a Zoe inside the princess, and she had other ideas. She knew Étan could never be my true mate, the one with whom I could form a mate bond, a unique, soul-to-soul connection.

I pulled back so we weren't touching.

His blue eyes sharpened. He swung me in a circle, dipped me over his arm.

"I *will* have you," he said, his face an inch from mine.

Play along. Keep your options open. Nothing's been decided.

"Will you?" I gave him a small smile, aware of my mother's all-seeing gaze, and spun away.

Victorine had promised the choice was mine. My mother could be cold and controlling, but she didn't lie.

That didn't mean I could drop my guard. She was also capable of setting a snare for me to walk into, unsuspecting, and before I knew it, I'd be mated to Étan.

I might even convince myself it was what I'd wanted all along.

"Oh, yes." Étan drew me closer again. This time, I allowed it. It made it easier to peer over his shoulder, searching for the cocky dhampir who'd crashed our most exclusive party.

Rafe had disappeared into the crowd, but I knew he was still in the ballroom. My skin was electrified, my heart still beating fast and hard.

What did he want?

Étan spoke. "You're a beautiful woman, Zoe. I've watched you grow up. Waited for you."

Whoa. I stopped searching for Rafe and gave Étan my full attention.

"I've always thought of you as a friend...an older friend, like an uncle." I emphasized the word *uncle*. "That means a lot to me."

An indulgent smile. "With your father gone to his final grave, I was happy to fill that role. But you're an adult now, *chérie*. And my regard for you has only grown."

Deflect. Deflect.

I forgot all about playing along with Étan. I stared up at him—and swung my head left. "Is that Marie-Pierre? I haven't seen her for years."

A quick, irritated frown. "She was on an assignment in Bordeaux, overseeing the vineyards."

"I've never been to Bordeaux. That's where you were turned, wasn't it? Victorine found you working at the Chateau de Peyron." It was one of the Syndicate's largest vineyards.

His eyes hooded. "Is that a reminder that I'm not a blue blood like your mother and father?"

I felt a flicker of shame, because I knew it was a sore point with him, although I'd only said it out of desperation. Étan had been picking grapes when Victorine had seen him and taken him as a thrall. Eventually, he'd convinced her to turn him.

"Of course not," I said. "You've earned your position in the Syndicate. Victorine thinks very highly of you. We all do."

A cold nod. But he fell silent.

The song ended. "Thanks for the dance," I said and tried to move away.

Étan tightened his grip, keeping me where I was.

I stiffened. Everyone was looking at us, including Victorine. Especially Victorine.

He traced a fingertip over my jaw and down the center of my throat. Toyed with the strands of the gold necklace.

You didn't touch a vampire's throat without permission. He might as well have announced to everyone present that I was his.

I swallowed something acrid, not quite daring to slap his hand away. He'd be humiliated, and I wasn't sure what he'd do if I pushed him too far.

Étan moved his hand to my shoulder. His fingers dug into the soft flesh. "We'll speak later," he promised—or maybe it was a warning.

I dredged up my Ice Princess glare. "As you wish. Now, if you don't mind..." I glanced pointedly at the hand on my shoulder.

He waited three long beats before releasing me.

An enforcer stepped up—Louis, another vampire I'd known since I was a toddler. "May I have this dance?"

"*Bien sûr.*" I moved into his arms without another look at Étan.

He watched me, though. His stare burned into the vulnerable spot between my shoulder blades.

Louis complimented me on my dress, then got right to the point. "I'd be honored to take you as a mate."

My step hitched. I was still back there with Étan, furious and a little afraid. That snare was looking harder and harder to avoid.

Louis smoothly righted me and kept dancing. With an effort, I brought my attention to him.

"Word's gotten around," I said. Louis didn't even belong to my mother's coven, but to one based in Quebec City.

A small shrug. "You know how it is."

My mouth twitched wryly. "I do."

Vampires liked their gossip as much as humans, and my mating was valuable intel if you wanted to move up in the Tremblay Syndicate hierarchy. By now every syndicate in North America would've heard, and probably the ones in Europe as well.

"And?" Louis prompted.

I cast a surreptitious look around the room. Where was Rafe? But there was no help from that quarter—and really, why would there be?

I met Louis's eyes. He was powerful, yet easy in his skin, with a native Quebecois's dark good looks.

And I felt...nothing. No spark. No heat. Not even a hint of the belly-deep excitement simply being in the same room as Rafe ignited.

"I'll consider it," I said.

He inclined his head. "Thank you."

We moved onto small talk. The weather and how the vineyards were having a good year. The human economy and how it affected the Syndicate's interests in Quebec.

With each second, my body wound itself tighter and tighter, until it took all my self-control to keep myself from doing something very un-Zoe-like, like throwing back my head and laughing hysterically.

Rafe was *here*. A Kral, in the chateau. At the freaking Crimson Ball.

I should report him. It was my duty to report him.

Simply remaining silent made me complicit in whatever he meant to do.

And yet I couldn't. Not until I knew why he was here.

By the time the song ended, I desperately needed a drink. I thanked Louis for the dance and headed for the crystal fountain spouting arcs of blood-wine—and almost ploughed into Rafe and the thrall plastered to him like a starfish.

The near collision lashed me like a jolt of electricity. I went stick-still, aftershocks reverberating in my chest, my stomach, even my fingers and toes.

Rafe's mouth curled in his trademark lopsided grin. Without taking his gaze from mine, he set the thrall away from him.

"Some other time," he told her in an American accent no glamour could camouflage.

"But—" She placed a hand on his arm.

"Later," he said in a soft voice that somehow sliced like a knife. She jerked her hand away and slunk off.

Rafe's dark eyes remained trained on me. Daring me to out him. "*Bonsoir*, Princess."

Around us, couples danced and talked, but they seemed somehow far away. The music had grown softer, the lights dimmer, like we were alone in the ballroom.

I swallowed, unable to find the words to respond. Half-convinced I was dreaming and if I moved, I'd wake up and everything would be ruined.

Someone jostled me and I came back to myself. I'd taken too long to answer. People were shooting curious looks in our direction.

And no, this wasn't a dream.

"Good evening." I inclined my head and continued toward the fountain. A server handed me a glass of wine. I sipped it and waited through another song, smiling and nodding as people wished me happy birthday.

The aftershocks hadn't settled. Instead, they'd generated new tingles. Excitement mixed with uncertainty mixed with flat-out suspicion.

I tracked Rafe from the corner of my eye as he moved to the edge of the ballroom and slouched against the wall like he had every right to be there.

What did he want?

And did I care? Because he was here, and that was almost enough.

But we couldn't talk here. When the song ended, I set down the glass and left the ballroom.

Rafe would follow. Of that, I was certain.

Upstairs, I almost stopped in the conservatory. It was my baby, my happy place, an indoor garden with a fake sun to mimic the one I could only observe from behind smoked glass. The place where I felt most able to meet Rafe on equal ground.

But the cams would pick him up, and security would wonder why I was meeting privately with an unknown vampire.

So instead, I continued up another floor to my suite. Rafe would find me; beneath that suave, who-gives-a-hell veneer was a smart man. I left the door ajar, because to follow me undetected, he'd have to enter the shadow dimension, and while we're in the shadows, we can only interact with the physical to a point. We can walk up steps or ride in a car, but we can't open doors or pick up objects.

I went directly to the bathroom, the one place free of cameras. A few taps on my phone, and a blank feed of my rooms was fed to the cams. To security, it would appear I was still in the bathroom.

Back in the living room, I left the lights off; I didn't want to chance being seen from the gardens. I lit a couple of black pillar candles and went into the bedroom. I dropped my mask on the vanity, then checked my hair and touched up my makeup.

The way a woman did when a man mattered.

Because Rafe mattered. I might not want him to, but he did.

The turret had air conditioning, but I rarely used it. Like a cat, my cooler-than-human body craved heat. Instead, I'd left the casement windows open.

I should've guessed Rafe would come in through a window—the man never did the expected—but instead, I was watching the front door.

Which is why I gave an embarrassing squeak when warm lips touched my spine above my dress.

8

RAFE

From the garden below, the turret had been silent, the third floor dark, but my gut said Zoe would want to confront me in her lair. The first floor of the chateau was filled with Tremblay vampires, so I'd joined a few other guests strolling the grounds. I'd wandered to the garden's edge, ducked into the trees and faded into the shadow dimension.

A running jump took me halfway up the tower. I continued up, scaling the rough greystone to the open casement windows on the third floor in time to see Zoe walk into her bedroom.

I crouched on the wide stone windowsill, watching from the shadows as she brushed her hair and rubbed a tube of something glossy and red over her lips. She set the tube down on the vanity and turned away, a slim white silhouette in the candlelight.

The back of her dress dipped in a deep V, exposing her shoulder blades and upper spine. The bare, fragile vertebrae made my breath snag in my lungs.

There you are, said something deep inside...something vulnerable, needy, primal.

At last.

It drew me closer, too powerful to resist...even if I'd wanted to.

I dropped out of the shadows and pressed a kiss to her moon-soft skin. Her scent curled around me, new green grass after a rain.

Zoe's muscles locked. She swallowed but didn't speak or turn her head. Instead, she moved unhurriedly out of the bedroom, heels tapping on the marble tiles. I stayed near the window, glamour still in place, waiting to see what she'd do.

She shut the door to the stairs and touched a keypad, locking us inside the suite. Only then did she turn to face me.

"Hello, Rafe," she said in her best Ice Princess voice.

So we were private. That's all I needed to know. I dropped the glamour, dragged off my mask.

"Hello." The ragged edge in my tone shocked me.

That flash of vulnerability—of *need*—had left me shaken.

I took a breath, prepared to turn on the charm. It was what I was known for, after all. The likeable, media-savvy prince whose primary job was to put a human—well, half-human—face on the Kral Syndicate. It didn't even matter if now and then the façade slipped. Humans love a badass.

Zoe studied me from across the living room, her long-lidded eyes glimmering gold in the candlelight.

"Explain to me," she said in tones that had dropped another ten degrees from ice to arctic permafrost, "why I shouldn't call security on you."

I shoved the mask into my pocket and closed the distance between us. "Because you missed me."

Her lip curled. "Try again."

"Because you don't want to see me held down and beaten to a pulp by your mother's enforcers." I halted a few feet away from her —and decided the hell with being charming. "Oh, wait. You already did that. If you didn't want to fuck, Princess, you should've told me straight out."

Something flitted across her face. Remorse? Sorrow?

"I shouldn't have let things get that far."

"You think? They beat me, Zoe. Your mother threatened to stake me if I ever came back. And she said she wouldn't stop with me, either—she'd go after my brothers, too."

Her face shuttered; whatever I'd thought I'd seen replaced by a frosty stare. "I didn't know."

"And that's supposed to make it all right?"

"No, but—"

"You left me to take the fall—for something you set up. Because the way I remember it, *you* came on to *me*."

Her chin came up. "I thought it was mutual, but blame me if you want."

My fingers clenched, unclenched. "Oh, I do blame you. For coming to my room that night. For making sure I sent my bodyguard away so that I had no warning when your mother showed up. Alone, both of us—that was the agreement. And yet, Jean-Michel was with you, wasn't he?" My mouth twisted. "I guess I should be grateful for that. Hell, if he hadn't warned us, Victorine would've found me balls-deep inside you. Or maybe that was the plan? Get me naked and weaponless so your men could take me without even having to break a sweat."

Zoe went rigid. "You think I set it up? I was as surprised as you when she showed up."

"Yeah? You're the one who arranged the time and place. You're the one who came to my hotel—alone. And yet somehow your mom turned up just in time to save you from the Big Bad Kral."

I prowled around her, aware I'd gone way past charming to flat-out offensive. But now that I'd started, I couldn't stop.

I *wanted* to hurt her. I'd trusted the woman. I'd even let myself fall a little in love.

And she'd stabbed a knife in my chest, then stomped on the twitching corpse.

"I wanted to see if you lived up to the hype."

Maybe Zoe couldn't have prevented the beating, but she'd humiliated me in front of Victorine and her thugs. She might as well have kicked me in the nuts and been done with it.

"You didn't think I was serious, did you?"

"You let me suck your tits." I was behind her now. The high heels gave her an extra few inches, but she was still three inches shorter than me. I leaned down, put my mouth next to her ear. "Stick my fingers up your cunt. Your hot, wet, needy cunt."

A tremor went up that fragile, delicate spine, and the gods help me, I felt a dark thrill. I backed up, not sure who I was more disgusted with, me or her.

"You're wrong." Zoe turned to face me. "I didn't want my mother to catch us, and Jean-Michel was supposed to wait in the lobby. Think about it. I had more to lose than you."

"Yeah." I sneered. "Guess you didn't want to be caught with a Kral, *Princess*. And a dhampir on top of that."

Her mouth compressed, but she didn't deny it. And why that hurt after all this time, I don't know.

"You didn't come all this way to pick a fight," she said. "I want to know why you're here—now—or I *will* call security."

"Stop pretending you're going to call security on me. We both know you won't. Because you still want me. You've wondered what it would've been like if we'd finished things that night."

Her mouth opened, then shut. Then she swallowed.

So I was right. She did still want me.

My dick stirred, all that anger needing an outlet—or at least, that's what I told myself. Because I was damned if I'd admit even in my own head that I'd wondered myself what it would have been like.

"Try me." She folded her arms over her chest, causing the tiny white handkerchief of a dress to ride up and show even more of her long, toned legs.

My dick got harder. Two years, and I still wanted her. Two years to replay that scene in the hotel room over and over in my mind. Two years to absorb how Zoe had played me for a fool. Two years to promise myself I'd never get caught like that again.

Two damn years, and I still wanted the woman—and gods, I hated her for it.

I moved closer, toyed with a lock of her hair, deliberately imitating Étan.

She brought her arms back to her sides and stilled, her face an expressionless mask that I longed to rip off just to see if there was still a real woman beneath.

"Étan put his hand on you. Here." I touched the hollow of her throat. "He was *claiming* you. He might as well have put a blood-bond bracelet on you."

I'd wanted to break every finger in the lieutenant's hand. Slowly. Painfully.

"And I know you didn't want him touching you," I added, "which makes me wonder why the hell you let him."

Zoe's mask broke. She hissed and showed her fangs.

I was making her edgy.

Good. Anything was better than that expressionless façade.

"Tell me you're not going to mate with that asshole. The man treats you like you're a brainless doll."

During the negotiations for the joint venture, Zoe had represented the Tremblays, but Étan had come to every meeting and proceeded to interrupt her and correct her statements until I hadn't known who was really in charge.

"Get. Away. From. Me." She shoved me back a step. "I don't have to explain myself to you."

I raised my hands, palms out. "Okay, okay."

Focus, Rafe. You're not here to sex Zoe's brains out—or even to rescue her from Étan and her viper of a mother. You're here for Zaq.

Zoe's irises were rimmed vampire blue. At her sides, her fingers curved into claws. "My mating has nothing to do with you. *Nothing,* do you hear?"

And that was the problem, wasn't it? Her mating had nothing to do with me.

I dragged a hand down my face. "You're right, it doesn't."

"Now for the last time," she said between her teeth, "why are you here?"

Charm her, you ass.

But instead, I found myself speaking the simple truth. "I need your help."

Zoe shook her head and started to turn away.

"Not for me," I hurried to add. "For my brother—Zaquiel."

"I see." Her shoulders slumped, as if I'd disappointed her somehow.

"He's been kidnapped by the slayers."

"Which doesn't explain what you want from me."

"Hear me out. Last we knew, Zaq was in Paris. We think he was captured and held there by the slayers. You know Moreau." Philippe Moreau was a high-level Paris enforcer, but more importantly, he was Victorine's sire and sometime lover. "There's no way in hell he wouldn't know if a cell of slayers was operating in his city."

She moved a shoulder in a shrug. "So ask Philippe, not me. Or take it up with Slayers, Inc. Sounds like a rogue—let them handle it. Or your father for that matter. You're not telling me Karoly Kral can't take out a rogue slayer?"

"*Listen to me, damn it*." I took a breath, then continued more calmly, "It's not just the slayers. Zaq's neck showed bite marks. A vampire's been feeding on him—maybe more than one."

Zoe made a shocked sound. "You're sure?"

Only another vampire could understand the shame of being fed from against your will. It wasn't simply the loss of blood, it was the humiliation of someone taking it without permission, of a vampire touching that no-go zone. To us, it was a form of rape.

"Yes," I said grimly.

"But why do you think SI is involved? That's not their style. They don't take prisoners. When they target you, you don't end up in a cell. You end up with a stake through your heart."

"Exactly. Which is why we think a vampire is involved—like Moreau."

She pursed her lips. "I don't know. It doesn't sound like Philippe, either."

"Look." I jerked a phone from my tux jacket, downloaded the photo of Zaq from a secret, triple-protected cloud server, and thrust it at her. "See for yourself."

She took the phone. Swallowed. She was silent for a few seconds, then she handed the phone back to me.

"That's not proof Philippe's involved. It's not even proof your brother was kidnapped. It could be photoshopped, a story you made up to cover why you're really here."

My hand tightened on the plastic case. What had I done to make Zoe so suspicious of me? She was the one who'd come to *my* hotel room, allowing me to do everything but fuck her, and then left.

While I'd stayed to face down Victorine, Étan, and two enforcers bent on breaking every major bone in my body.

"It's the truth, damn it. Zaq disappeared in Paris and no one's heard from him since. Hell, look at his fucking neck." I jabbed a finger at the screen. "A vampire fed on him. They chained my brother with silver and let a vampire drink his blood."

"All right," she said. "Say it's true and your brother's been kidnapped by Philippe or the slayers or both. Why come to me? Why not take this up with the Paris Primus?"

"Leo? Moreau is one of his top enforcers. You really think he's going to admit Moreau has Karoly Kral's son? They'd stake Zaq for sure."

"But what can I do?"

She was going to make me say it.

I shoved the phone back into my pocket. I'd had days to decide what to tell her, but this was still hard. I had some trust issues of my own.

Still, one of us had to give, and from Zoe's stony expression, it would have to be me. It was time to lay it all out there.

"We believe Victorine's behind it. That Philippe Moreau is the front. He's involved—he has to be—but he's doing it for her. Or maybe they're in it together. And they're both hiding behind Slayers, Inc."

Her definite black brows snapped down. "So that's why you're here? To accuse my mother of kidnapping your brother?"

"You can't tell me she wouldn't like to send me and my brothers to the final grave—especially me. Hell, she told me so herself."

Her eyes narrowed. "You're saying my mother broke the treaty?"

"Not exactly," I said carefully. "But she could be honoring the letter of the treaty, not its spirit."

It was genius, actually—and very Victorine. Get Slayers, Inc. to eliminate me, Zaq and Gabriel, and Zoe's mother would have her revenge on my father without having to dirty her own hands.

"No." Zoe set her jaw. "She signed that treaty in good faith."

I spread my hands. "Think about it. Take out me and my brothers, and my father loses his heirs. The succession would be in doubt. A power vacuum would open up, and while my father regrouped, Victorine could make her move, claim our territory for your syndicate."

And no one in the vampire world would stop her. That's how things worked. Either a primus or prima was strong enough to hold their territory, or they lost it.

"You're wrong," Zoe said. "My mother wants peace as much as your father does."

"I'm not so sure of that."

"Well, I am—and I would know. Victorine's training me to become her lieutenant. I've been shadowing her for the last year. I've been at all the important meetings."

"Maybe she doesn't want you to know. Because of us."

"There is no 'us,' and she knows that."

"Please, Zoe. I'm just asking you to look into it for me."

"No. I'm sorry about your brother, but I can't help you." Zoe's mask was firmly in place again. "You're asking too much. Even if I believed my mother was involved, I wouldn't help you. You'd just take anything I told you back to your father."

I stared at her. "You saw that photo of Zaq and you can still ask why you should help?"

Her throat worked. But she shook her head.

I shoved my hands into my pockets, mind churning. Desperately searching for the right words, the ones that would convince her to help me.

"What if I swear that any information you give me, I'll follow it up myself? That no one but us two will know you helped me?"

"There's no information to find," she said between gritted teeth. "Your father's wrong. Go back to New York and tell him that Victorine's not the one behind your brother's kidnapping."

"Okay." I switched gears. "Say you're right, and Victorine's hands are clean. What about Étan? Maybe he's doing this to suck up to your mother." Or to seal the deal for Zoe, but I didn't say that aloud.

"Étan doesn't need to suck up," Zoe said flatly. "She already treats him like a son."

The son she'd never have, because a vampire-vampire mating produced just one spawn. Zoe was it for Victorine.

An unwelcome sympathy for Zoe twisted through me. My brothers and I might be the half-bloods, the dhampirs whose father had had to fight to have accepted as his heirs, but being Victorine's only spawn had to be worse. Karoly Kral might be a ruthless S.O.B., but I'd always known he'd loved me.

"Suppose it was Étan?" I asked. "How would you go about finding out?"

She moved a shoulder. "He's smart—he'd cover his tracks. The best way would be to fly to Paris and see for myself what's up."

"You'd do that?"

She held up a hand. "Hold it right there. That was a hypothetical answer to a hypothetical question. I am *not* going to Paris."

I fisted my hands in my pockets. Out of arguments, but unable to make myself leave.

I'd learned enough in the past week to believe Father might be right. Something about Zaq's abduction smelled fishy, including the fake messages to me.

Zoe was my only way in. Victorine trusted her. No one else close to the Tremblay Prima would help me, that was for damn sure.

"Please," I said. "We both know what your mother is capable of. She was forced to sign that treaty. My father gave your mother an ultimatum. Either she signed the treaty, or he'd keep coming after you."

Her mouth turned down. "Sounds like Karoly."

I set my teeth. "It goes both ways. Victorine sent assassins after me and my brothers, too—multiple times. But that's not the point. The point is, forming an alliance with Slayers, Inc. would be the perfect way for Victorine to eliminate me and my brothers without appearing to break the treaty."

Zoe blew out a breath. "Rafe. I can't."

"Can't? Or won't?"

"Can't and won't. I'm a Tremblay, Rafe. And you're a Kral. In the end, that's all that matters."

We stared at each other. She looked away first.

Disappointment hollowed out my chest. This was it, my last chance to find out something that could help Zaq. I'd have to return to New York emptyhanded.

Like hell.

I moved closer. Words hadn't worked. I might as well try seduction. What did I have to lose?

"Are you sure?" I wrapped my hand around her nape and brushed my lips over hers.

It was manipulative as fuck. But my cock still stirred and began to harden.

A tremor went over her. Her mouth softened, clung to mine.

Triumph shafted through me. "You still want me."

Her throat worked. "Yes. No."

I kissed her again, hot and slow. "Which is it?"

Her chest heaved. She set a hand on my tux and pulled back to meet my eyes. "So that's the deal? I help you, and in return, I get your gorgeous body?" She tried to sneer but couldn't quite pull it off.

"Is it working?"

"No." But her hand stayed on my chest.

I nibbled her earlobe. "I'm only asking you to do a little investigating. Zaq might not have much time left."

She shook her head and tried to push away, but I tightened my grip. "Please, Zoe."

"Let me go," she said wearily.

I growled and lifted my head. My hunger was rising again, and my edginess had returned in full force.

"You owe me," I gritted. "I trusted you, and you left me to get worked over by those bastards."

Her mask cracked. "The hell I do. What about you? I know why you pretended to be so interested in me. Karoly sent you instead of your brother Gabriel for a reason. Get Zoe hot and bothered so you could stick it to us in the negotiations."

I reared back. "What the fuck are you talking about? I was interested in you because you're *you*."

"I saw the texts, Rafe. The one you sent Karoly. *I've got her so hot for me, she can't think straight.*" Her voice faltered. "Victorine said you were going to blackmail her into sweetening the deal."

"What texts?"

"The ones you sent your father—on your own phone."

"Who showed you, Étan? The prick took my phone before they worked me over. He could've had a tech hack into it and add whatever he wanted.."

Her neck muscles tensed beneath my hand.

I swore. "It *was* him, wasn't it?"

"Yes."

"And you believed it." I shook my head and moved away. "I didn't tell my father a fucking thing about us. You think I wanted him to know? That casino was my chance to prove myself. I knew damn well I was risking the joint venture by meeting you in secret like that."

"Maybe you thought having sex with me would make things easier for you."

"Like hell. You sure didn't seem like a woman who'd let sex get between her and business. And I definitely wasn't planning on blackmailing you—or Victorine, for that matter."

"Why should I believe you?"

"*Because I didn't send those texts.* Is it so hard to believe I wanted you for yourself?"

"But Victorine said—"

I growled. "I know she's your mom, but this is Victorine, right? The woman who made sure you were never alone with me, because the gods forbid a dhampir touch her precious pureblood daughter? Whatever she told you about me was a lie. What happened between you and me had nothing to do with the joint venture—that was business. What happened between us was personal."

Zoe's brows scrunched together. Vampires can't read each other's emotions like we can a human's. She had no way to tell if I was telling the truth, or vice versa.

Indecision flickered across her face. "But—"

"Wake up, Princess. Your mother didn't just want me gone. She wanted you to hate my guts."

She swallowed and shook her head. "I—just go. I have to get back before they miss me."

"Wait." I grabbed her arm. "Tell me one thing. You owe me that much, at least."

I'd lost. I knew that.

But I was damned if I'd let her go without answering the question that had burned in me for two years.

"Why humiliate me like that? I thought we were friends at least. I understand why you didn't fight your mother. But the rest? I didn't deserve that."

"No." Her gaze slid from mine. "You didn't. But I couldn't stop them from beating you. If I'd tried, it would've only made things worse."

"Damn it, Zoe." Suddenly, I couldn't bear to touch her any longer. I released her and stepped back. "I'm not saying you could've stopped the ass-kicking. Victorine was out for my blood. But you acted like I was nothing to you except the pretty boy you picked to punch your V-card."

"I'm sorry." She heaved a breath. "I—that was wrong. I could tell you I was trying to make it convincing, that they'd have hurt you worse if I'd acted like you mattered. But I did it for me, too. To save face."

I curled my lip. "I hope it worked."

"No," she said flatly. "It just made me feel like crap."

I expelled a breath. "So that's it. You're sorry. And you're not going to help me find Zaq."

"Rafe, I—" She wrapped her arms around herself. It was clear her mind was made up. "I'm sorry," she said again.

So much for my famous charm. I'd have to go back to New York with nothing.

No information that could help Zaq. No closure with Zoe. Hell, I hadn't even gotten to dance with her at her goddamn ball.

"The hell with your apologies," I said, low and bitter. "But you know what? I'm sorry, too—that you're so blinded by your mother's lies that you can't see you're just a pawn to her. She pushes you around like a piece on a chessboard. The woman won't even let you choose your own mate."

I stalked back into the bedroom and leapt onto the windowsill.

"Oh, and by the way"—I arranged my mouth in a mocking smile because that's what Rafe Kral did when things went south—"happy birthday, Princess."

9

ZOE

Rafe crouched on the windowsill, a sleek black wolf in a tux.

Let him go.

I'd *known* he hadn't returned to Montreal to see me. But my heart had hoped I was wrong, that he'd come back for me. That second chances actually existed.

I should've called security on him the moment I found him in my rooms. But I couldn't think straight when he was around.

Let him go.

Rafe Kral was a weakness—a craving—I couldn't afford, especially now.

I was this close to having the one thing I'd always wanted. Power.

Real power.

The kind where no one would ever again brush me or my ideas aside because I was too young and "soft"—or leave me on an island for months at a time with just Jean-Michel, the servants and a couple of thralls to make sure I was fed.

Rafe's body grayed-out, losing color and blurring at the edges as he entered the shadow dimension.

And I couldn't do it. I couldn't let him go.

I'd tried to forget the man for two years, and it hadn't worked. I was damned if he'd crash my party, get me all churned up, and leave.

"Prove it." I shot forward and snagged his wrist, anchoring him in the physical dimension. "You say my mother and Étan lied about those texts? Then prove it."

He twisted his arm, forcing me to release him, and clamped his fingers around my wrist instead. Dark eyes scorched into mine. "How the fuck am I supposed to do that?"

Need licked at me. In the ballroom his glamour had muted his raw sex appeal. Now, it battered me like a hot, wild storm.

The pent-up longing of two years swamped my emotions. My fangs pricked out.

I wanted to bite him and drink deep.

I wanted him to hold me down and bite me back.

I wanted to feel his hard body naked and moving against mine.

"Answer me." He gave my wrist a shake. "How am I supposed to prove I didn't send those texts?"

I snatched my hand back. "I don't know. Why don't you start by telling me why you came on to me in the first place? Why you kept after me until I met you in that pub? Why you asked me for a 'real date'?"

My voice broke on the last two words. I swallowed and prayed he didn't notice.

He took the slow breath of a man grasping for the last, tattered shreds of his patience. "Because I wanted you, damn it. Why does it have to be complicated? I. Wanted. You."

I shook my head. "I don't believe you."

"Think about it," he said. "Your mother had every reason in the world to lie. She wanted me gone, and you so pissed off at me you'd never speak to me again."

I stared at him. Had I been too quick to accept that he'd sent those texts? To believe he couldn't possibly want me for myself?

Because it was true; Victorine would've done anything to split us up. Rafe was the first man I'd ever shown interest in—a Kral. And to put the cherry on the wrong-man sundae, he was a dhampir, too.

My mother wouldn't have been content with simply humiliating me by bursting in on us like that. She would've wanted to make sure I hated Rafe, that I believed everything he'd said or done was a lie.

"It's the truth, damn it." He dropped back to the floor and took me by the arms. When Étan had grabbed me, I'd wanted to shove him away, but with Rafe, my knees went wobbly, which pissed me off almost as much.

"Let me go." I tried to jerk away, but he hung on.

"No. You asked, now listen." His gaze went to my mouth.

My skin tingled, every nerve ending alive. He was going to kiss me. I touched my tongue to my lower lip.

He drew a ragged breath through his teeth. "I should hate you. I *do* hate you."

Hurt slashed me. I jerked in his grip. "Then let me go."

"And if I don't?"

"I'll scream the tower down."

I should've known better than to give Rafe Kral an ultimatum. He leaned closer.

"Go ahead. Scream."

I bared my fangs and hissed at him.

A feral smile. "That's my vampire princess. Gods, you're so fucking hot."

My frustrated growl came from my deepest self. "I'm not your vampire princess. I'm not your *anything*."

"But you want to be." He stroked my upper arms, toyed with the gold arm bracelet.

I glanced down. Confused. Aroused. When had his hard grip changed to caresses?

His body radiated heat. I leaned into him, soaking up the warmth like he was Apollo, and I was some teenage Greek groupie.

"No, I don't," I rasped.

But I was trying to convince myself more than him.

"No?" His mouth curved like he knew I was lying, but he didn't call me on it. He released me and took a step back.

My hands shot out, latching onto the pleats of his tuxedo shirt and dragging him back. He was right there with me, his reflexes as fast as mine. Our mouths met in the middle.

He immediately took control, his body hard against mine, his powerful arms wrapping around me. His tongue licked into my mouth, slow and deep.

Sanity flew out the open windows along with my self-control. My nipples stabbed against the thin white dress. I twined a leg around his and rubbed against his erection.

The kiss didn't end, it flowed into more kisses—on my lips, my chin, my jaw. He nibbled his way to my earlobe and sucked on it, sending a thrill down my spine and straight to my clit.

The groan that escaped my throat was pure, raw need.

"Easy," he soothed—and captured my wrists, anchoring them behind my back with one hand while he stroked the other down my hip to the hem of my dress.

He inched up the hem. "We never finished what we started." His tone was so low and dark, it was almost a threat.

"No." I shivered, a good shiver.

He had a firm grip on my wrists, but I could've escaped if I'd wanted to.

I didn't want to. He was pushing all the right buttons, the ones that opened the door to my secret fantasies.

"I've had two years to think about a do-over," he said against my ear. "Even while I was hating you for setting me up like that, I wanted you. Wondered what it would have been like."

The room was so hot. Too hot. Even my lungs felt on fire.

"Me, too," I admitted.

"So you thought about me?" He toyed with the waistband of my panties.

"You know I did." I dropped my head back, exposing my throat to him.

His breath snagged, and I froze. Baring my throat had been instinctive, a response to his dominance. He didn't take advantage, though, simply pressed a kiss to the hollow of my neck over the gold necklace.

His fingers slid into my panties, stroking, teasing. "You're so wet for me."

I choked back a moan.

His dark eyes glittered in the candlelight like the shadowed heart of a geode. "What do you want? Tell me."

"That. Touch me. Just like that."

Without removing his hand from my panties, he walked me backward until my shoulders hit the wall. He still held my wrists. The position arched my back, lifting my breasts toward him. The top of the dress draped in loose folds over my cleavage. I was pretty sure he could see straight down to where the dress's self-bra barely covered my nipples.

He kissed a line along my collarbone and down to the arm bracelet. "I like this," he said against the wide gold band while his fingers worked their magic in my panties. "You look like an escapee from a harem. A naughty princess. Is that what you want, Zoe? To be bad?"

My inner thighs constricted. *Yes, please.*

I tried to pull my wrists free, to pull his mouth to my breasts, but he tightened his grip.

"You do, don't you?" His voice was a wicked rasp.

"Yes." This time I managed to say it aloud.

"Poor princess. Maybe I can do something about that." He nuzzled my cleavage. His cheeks were sandpaper-rough with black stubble. The prickle against my tender skin sent an answering tingle through my blood, made heat flare deep in my belly.

He kissed the top of my left breast, then nipped the same spot with sharp fangs, and Holy Dark Lady, I liked it.

I gasped and clenched my inner thighs around his fingers. So that's why thralls got addicted to a vampire's bite. Even though he hadn't taken any blood, that hint of pleasure/pain sent a dark thrill shooting through me.

He lifted his head and stared at me unsmiling, his cheekbones flushed with arousal. A hot blue halo encircled the iris, his vampire in control now.

Still holding my wrists, he yanked my panties down my hips and gazed down at where I was bared to him.

A beat passed. Two beats. Three.

I couldn't see myself—not with my back arched—but I felt exposed and even more turned-on. He so clearly liked what he saw.

His gaze came back to my face. A corner of his mouth tipped up. "Breathe, cher."

Shocked, I realized I was holding my breath, that I had been for a while. Even a vampire needs to breathe every twenty seconds or so. Maybe that's why my head was swimming.

But the jagged breath I gulped did nothing to help.

Rafe stroked his free hand down my bare ass, over my hips. "You have the most incredible legs." His gaze followed his hand past the panties bunched up around my upper legs and back up along my inner thighs. "I've spent way too much time thinking about what they'd feel like wrapped around me while I was buried deep inside you. Or how they'd look if I bent you over…maybe over that stool." He nodded at the vanity.

A zing skipped up my spine, like he'd tripped a finger up the vertebrae. I could picture myself bent over the vanity stool, unable to touch him, while he could touch me any way or anywhere he wanted.

"Would you like that?" he said in my ear. "I think you would. Me thrusting into you from behind. I could watch you in the mirror as you come. You could watch yourself…"

"Yes," I breathed.

His fingers were back on my sex again. I instinctively widened my legs as much as the panties would allow. "Yes, what?"

"Yes," I said more loudly. "I'd like that."

Because that picture he'd created in my head? It was the hottest thing.

How did the man read me like that? It was as if he could hear my thoughts, which I knew was impossible. Then I remembered how many women he'd had. If you believed Instagram and the tabloids, the man was as randy as a tomcat.

It's just sex to him, Zoe.

I told myself that was all it was to me, too. Because that was all it could be. A fleeting moment in my life before I was bound to another man forever.

"But you're new at this—maybe I'm going too fast for you. You are new, aren't you?" He toyed with my clit. A sensual smile played on his lips, but his eyes narrowed. "Did you fuck anyone since me?"

"No. Not anyone. Ever," I tacked on as if he couldn't figure that out for himself.

A husky growl. "Ever?"

I shrugged a shoulder. "Haven't been interested."

They weren't you.

"Your first. I shouldn't find that a turn-on, but I do." He did something with his fingertip that made me gasp. "Guess I'm more of a caveman than I realized."

I barely heard, my attention on the erotic sensations his fingers were drawing from me.

In the garden below my window, a woman gave a high, excited laugh. A man's low voice answered her.

It was like being slapped awake from the best dream ever.

I stiffened and recalled the ballroom of people waiting to celebrate my birthday. Any minute, Victorine would send someone to get me, or come herself. The last thing I wanted was a repeat of the scene in the penthouse.

My chest heaved. "Stop."

Rafe stilled. His thick dark lashes came down. "Damn it, Zoe."

"We can't do this." I set my forehead against his. "My mother—"

His jaw worked. "Right." He released my wrists and removed his hand from between my legs. His arms came around me in a loose hold. His fingers constricted on my back, like he didn't want to ever let me go. "Then meet me later. I'll wait for you here."

I was tempted. So tempted.

But I couldn't risk it.

"I can't," I whispered.

His hold didn't loosen. "Please?"

I squeezed my eyes shut, sorrow warring with regret.

"Zoe?"

A bitter taste filled my mouth. I slid from his grasp. Pulled up my panties.

"I have to get back downstairs."

His lips twisted. "So that's it? Goodbye, Rafe, it's been nice seeing you—and by the way, I'm going to choose a mate tonight."

"I can't—" I waved a hand between us. "We can't. I told you. It would never work."

"Because you're a coward."

I took a slow breath, trying not to show how much that hurt. "Because I'm thinking with my brain, not my cock."

His eyes flickered, the only hint I'd scored a hit.

He dragged a hand over his hair. "Fuck. I need a drink." He took a bottle of blood-wine from the small refrigerator built into the living room wall and ripped out the cork with his bare hands.

"Help yourself," I muttered.

Suddenly, I realized something. The signs had been there—the edginess; the feral, angular look of his face; the blue rimming his irises—but I'd read them as lust...sexual lust.

But he was feeling the blood craving, too.

My brow furrowed. "When's the last time you fed?"

He moved a shoulder and took a long drink. My eyes locked on his strong throat. His Adam's apple bobbed, and desire stabbed me.

Desire, and a soul-deep, bittersweet sadness.

I smoothed down my skirt. "Will you be all right?"

"I got in here. I can get out."

That wasn't what I'd meant, but I let it go.

I went to the vanity and picked up a lipstick. He leaned against the bedpost, the wine bottle in his hand, watching with hooded eyes as I repaired my makeup.

"At least give me this much," he said. "Keep your mind open. Nose around a little. You know damn well that if Victorine could take me and my brothers out without it pointing back to her, she'd do it in a heartbeat. Zaq"—his voice cracked—"he may not have much longer."

I briefly closed my eyes. I had to admit that photo had left me shaken. If it wasn't photoshopped, something was seriously wrong. And I couldn't help picturing Rafe chained in that cell instead of Zaquiel.

"All right," I said. "I'll see what I can find out."

Rafe's eyes blazed. "Thank you." He rattled off a phone number. "You can contact me through that number—anytime. Got it?"

I repeated the number back to him. "I'll do what I can, okay? But don't count on me finding anything, because I don't think there's anything to find."

"All I want is the truth. Anything you find, please pass it along—even something small. I'll stay in Canada a couple more days in case you need me. For anything," he added.

I set down the lipstick. "I won't need you."

"No." His mouth curled in another of those mocking smiles I was coming to hate. "I don't suppose you will." He took another long drink. "You'll be sorry if you mate with that prick. You know that, don't you?"

I settled my mask over my eyes without replying.

"Tell me something. Are you mating with him to escape from Victorine? Because if so, you have your head up your ass. Mate with Étan, and you'll have two watchdogs, not just one. He's your mother's man."

I shook my head and turned toward the door.

"Thanks for the wine—and the kiss." He lifted the wine bottle to me in a mocking salute. "You can pretend all you want, Princess. But you want me as much as I want you. You're going to spend the rest of your life wondering what it would've been like."

I swung to face him. "My loyalty is to the Tremblay Syndicate. Yours is to your father's. Which of us would have to give?"

His jaw set. "We could figure it out. If you wanted it enough."

"Goodbye, Rafe."

I felt his gaze on me the whole way across the living room. I stopped, and without turning, said, "Drink another blood-wine if you want. I have the security feed set to look like no one is in here. But don't be here when I come back."

His only response was a grunt.

I let myself out the suite door. Security might wonder why the cams hadn't picked me up walking from the bathroom to the door, but a small glitch like that wouldn't be enough for them to send someone to investigate, especially when they could see me on the cams now.

It wasn't until I'd hit the pad to engage the lock that I realized Jean-Michel was coming up the winding stairs.

Damn, damn, damn.

I stared at him as he ascended the last few steps, his thin, handsome face impassive.

Had he heard me and Rafe? We'd kept our voices low, but he seemed to have a sixth sense about these things.

I squared my shoulders and waited for him to ask who was in my suite.

He tipped his head at the stairs. "Victorine will be wondering where you are."

"Yes."

He knew. He knew there was a man in my suite.

Something in his very stillness gave him away, but for his own reasons, he'd decided to pretend he didn't.

I drew a calming breath and, hoping this wouldn't come back to bite me, started down the spiral staircase. But when I reached the second floor, my feet turned toward the conservatory.

"Zoe?" Jean-Michel asked.

I didn't look at him. "I need a little time. Ten minutes."

A sigh. "As you wish."

The lights in the conservatory glowed at a low level comfortable for vampire eyes. Leaves brushed my arms—ficus, corn plants, palm trees, ferns. I'd deliberately placed the plants close together in an imitation rainforest.

I kept walking until I was out of sight of Jean-Michel and the entrance, then sagged against the gazebo. Ten minutes, that's all I needed.

Ten minutes in this oasis I'd made for myself, enfolded in its moist green air.

Jean-Michel had told me that my father had loved plants, too, that he'd designed the night garden as a gift to Victorine. I'd hugged that information to myself, a connection to the man I barely remembered.

Sometimes I wondered how my life would've been different if Father were still here. I'd been so young when Karoly Kral had sent him to his final grave. I couldn't even picture him clearly—all I had were fragments; images that, like a puzzle with too many missing pieces, I couldn't form into a whole.

Mikhail Romanov.

A Russian prince, and not just in the vampire world. He'd been a distant cousin to the last czar, the one executed by the Bolsheviks after the Russian revolution. My father might have lost his life, too, if he hadn't been a vampire. He'd escaped Russia concealed in the shadow dimension.

Memories flitted through my mind: A darkly handsome man helping Victorine into a little red sportscar.

Tiger-gold eyes that could be hard as metal but that warmed for me.

Strong arms lifting me from my crib when I woke at dusk and carrying me to a window to view the last orange fire of the setting sun.

That Victorine had smiled. Not often, but when she had, it had been genuine, not a cool, calculated curve.

I fingered a palm's broad fronds, thinking about what my mother had said the other day: "I only made peace with Karoly to save you."

Victorine could be ruthless, even brutal, but her word could be trusted. When she signed a treaty, she kept it.

Unless the treaty was with Karoly Kral.

Her hatred for him went bone-deep. She wouldn't break the treaty, but setting the slayers on his sons was exactly the sort of devious thing she might do.

Stop it. I compressed my mouth. *That's Rafe talking, poisoning you against her.*

The ferns rustled, and Victorine appeared as if conjured up by my thoughts. "So, you've made your decision?"

Her pleasant tone made my shoulders tighten. I willed myself to relax.

"Not yet. It's hours until dawn."

"Then why are you here instead of the ballroom? I intend to make the announcement at midnight."

My stomach muscles jittered. I fingered the soft purple petals of a moth orchid.

"I needed some air. And midnight is too soon. I need more time."

"Is that so?"

I turned my head to see her eyes slit with suspicion. I stared back steadily. If she didn't believe me, if she got it into her head to check my suite, Rafe was dead.

"Étan is agreeable," she said at last. "I know he's spoken to you."

"*Oui.*" My fingers constricted, snapping the orchid off its stalk. I stared, horrified, at the crushed petals.

Victorine made an impatient sound. "Look at me, Zoe."

I set the broken flower in the pot and turned to face her like the obedient doll I'd been raised to be.

"He's the best choice. With him as your mate, you'll be accepted immediately as my lieutenant."

"But I'll never bond with him."

"You don't know that. Give it time. The mate bond may come."

"Please don't make me do this." My hands balled into fists. "I want what you had with Father. Is that so much to ask?"

Her expression softened. She took one of my hands, smoothed out the fingers.

"Trust me, *ma chère*. This is the best way. Otherwise, you'll be open to a challenge."

"You think I don't know that?"

I hated that she was right, but she was. I was very young to ascend to lieutenant. Étan would be within his rights to challenge me for the position. It might never come to that, since Victorine would consider a challenge to her only daughter a personal insult, and Étan knew it.

But if Victorine squelched Étan's challenge, I'd appear weak, the woman who'd been appointed lieutenant only because her mother was Prima.

And I was done appearing weak.

I'd worked for this. I deserved it.

Victorine was ignoring one thing: I was the brains behind the Tremblay Syndicate's recent growth. I might be young, but I'd been blessed with a sharp, analytical mind. Backed by her ruthlessness, my strategies had doubled the Tremblay Syndicate's wealth in the seven years.

She'd grown to depend on me.

It was time I reminded her of that.

"I'll choose someone," I said. "Maybe it will be Étan, and maybe it won't. But it will be my decision."

Her face hardened, the brief softness gone as if wiped away by a giant eraser.

"Or?" she returned.

I returned her gaze, letting her *Or* hang there, unanswered.

I would *not* let her back me into a corner. It was enough that we understood each other.

She adjusted the strap of my dress. "Don't let it come to a challenge. Étan won't easily give up his position."

I lifted my chin. "He wouldn't dare."

"Don't be silly, *ma petite*." A sharp scarlet fingernail tapped my cheek. "If it were anyone but you, he'd remain my lieutenant. Of course, he would dare, and if he challenges you publicly, I might not be able to stop it without shaking up the entire hierarchy. And we both know Étan would win."

My chest clenched. *Thanks for the vote of confidence, Mother.*

"Come." She glided out of the conservatory, sure I was right behind her. "Our guests will be wondering where we are."

My jaw tightened, but I followed.

Étan stood at the foot of the stairs. "Where have you been?" he demanded. He didn't wait for an answer, just held out a hand. "People have been asking about you."

My hackles rose. Since when did I answer to him?

But I placed my fingers in his.

Play the game, I told myself. But my inner voice had a desperate edge.

He tucked my hand into his elbow. My mother came up on my other side.

Apprehension squeezed my chest. Only years of practice kept the tension from my face as we returned to the ballroom.

If I mated with Étan, this would be my life. He was a dominant vampire male. He'd expect me to dress to please him. Tell me what to do, what to think.

But as lieutenant, I'd outrank him.

My step checked.

"Are you doing this to escape from Victorine? Because mate with Étan, and you'll have two watchdogs, not just one. He's your mother's man."

Suddenly, Victorine's strategy was clear to me. Take Étan as my mate, and I'd be the Tremblay lieutenant in name only, while he remained her actual lieutenant.

My mother would have us both exactly where she wanted.

And between her and Étan, I'd be ensnared as thoroughly as any blood slave.

❦ I O ❦

RAFE

I stared at the closed door, hand fisted around the neck of the wine bottle.

This isn't over, Princess.

Half of me wanted to dart into the hall, grab Zoe and throw her on the bed so we could finish what we'd started. The other half wanted to spank her for being so damn stubborn.

On the other side of the door, Jean-Michel spoke.

I went ninja-still. Not moving, not breathing. I strained to hear what they were saying, but the thick wood blocked everything but their tone of voice. Zoe's response was calm, though. I relaxed slightly, but didn't move until I heard them descending the winding iron staircase.

Okay, that was close.

I scrubbed a hand down my face and took a hefty swig of wine, then paced her rooms, edgy and wondering what to do now.

A glimpse of myself in Zoe's mirror stopped me cold. I was wrecked—wild-eyed, my fangs glinting in the dim light. I'd burned through the last dregs of my magic to start the fade on the windowsill.

Even if I wanted to leave, I couldn't, unless I was willing to show

85

myself in my own skin. I needed to regroup, replenish my energy—and then I was going to start digging.

Because maybe I didn't need to wait around to see what, if anything, Zoe came up with. Maybe I could find my own answers. I was damned if I was going back to New York empty-handed.

She had to have a laptop around here somewhere, and the ball would last until dawn, time enough for me to crack her password and see if I could hack into the Tremblay system. No one would call me a world-class hacker, but my education had included the basics.

I finished the bottle of blood-wine in my hand and started searching for Zoe's laptop.

Outside, the garden had gotten busier. I heard the low murmur of voices and high-pitched giggling. From somewhere nearby, Étan spoke.

I crossed to a bedroom window and flattened myself against the wall. Night had fallen, turning the garden into something dark, sensuous. Orange and red lights illuminated the fountains, changing them into fantastic liquid bonfires. Old-fashioned metal torches lit the garden paths and cast a flickering light on the thralls gyrating in cages.

A vampire in a slinky red dress had a male thrall pressed up against a honeysuckle-draped gazebo, his eyes glazed with pleasure as she drank from him. Two male vampires, a mated pair from the look of it, were deep in conversation on a nearby bench, shoulders touching, fingers intertwined. A giggling thrall darted around the side of a fountain, her vampire lover prowling behind.

Étan appeared on a path near the tower, a curvy redheaded thrall clinging to his bicep. My hand went to my back pocket. But I'd had to leave my blades at the rented house.

His hand closed on the thrall's breast. He tweaked her nipple and she gave a that-hurts-so-good squeal.

My teeth clenched so hard I was surprised they didn't crack.

How could Zoe even consider mating with that bastard? He couldn't even bother to pretend for one night that she meant anything to him other than a means to an end.

I left the window to prowl around the suite.

I needed blood. Fresh blood. The blood-wine simply wasn't cutting it.

And downstairs were all those willing thralls. Maybe my glamour would last long enough to coax Silver Rose into a shadowed corner?

My ability to disguise my appearance was unique among my brothers. Most dhampirs could only conjure a weak glamour, but I could change myself into almost anyone. If I wanted, for instance, I could look just like Étan. Unfortunately, as soon as I spoke, the game would be up, because although my French was good enough, I could never imitate his working man's accent.

But I was tired, and it wasn't worth the risk. I got another bottle from the refrigerator and continued my search for Zoe's laptop. I opened drawers and rifled through her closet. I even lifted the black-and-white photos in the living room to see if they concealed a safe. But if she'd brought a laptop to Midnight Island, it was either locked away somewhere I hadn't thought of or it wasn't in her suite.

I shrugged out of my jacket and sank onto the couch, staring into the dark red wine as if it held the key to Zaq's disappearance. After a while, I took another sip.

It was a very good wine. I drank some more, gradually slipping lower until my head rested on the couch's arm. I undid my bowtie and tossed it on my jacket. Swung my feet off the floor and onto the couch.

Vampires and dhampirs don't get drunk easily, but I'd had a lot of wine in a short time. I was a little buzzed when I heard someone fumbling with the door to Zoe's suite.

I jolted upright and reached for my switchblade until I remembered the "no weapons" policy.

Hell.

The blood-wine was still working its way through my body to replenish my magic. I felt better, but I didn't dare risk going into the shadows yet.

So I grabbed the empty wine bottle and pressed myself against the wall next to the door.

❧ 11 ❧

ZOE

The Crimson Ball was in full swing, the band playing a hundred-year-old French tune, the singer channeling her inner Edith Piaf. Victorine loved prewar French jazz.

To my nocturnal eyes, the candlelit room was bright and beautiful, even in my shaky emotional state. The lush reds against the black-and-white backdrop. The sensuous music and the warm lighting. The vampires lean and gorgeous, the thralls cover-model material.

Our kind didn't tolerate flaws.

Étan took my hand. "Come. Let's dance."

I danced with him a second time. I even let him pull me close. I couldn't let him see the panic pricking me like a thousand tiny needles.

I can't do this.

Not when my head was full of Rafe. His scent, his touch. That sexy, damn-your-eyes smile.

After Étan, I danced with a steady stream of vampire suitors, enforcers and soldiers who saw me as their ticket up the hierarchy.

Étan left the ballroom for a few minutes, but he soon returned. He lounged against a wall, watching me. Not even pretending to dance.

His *she's-mine* attitude spread through the ballroom until the line of men asking me to dance dwindled to nothing, leaving me standing near the wall by myself.

I snagged a blood-wine and sipped it. Angry and chilled, but not knowing how to stop him.

Fortunately, not even Étan could scare off Prince Brien. His father was Primus of the Maritime Syndicate on Canada's east coast, and his parents were partners with Victorine in a couple of joint ventures, which made him the closest thing to a friend I had.

I'd been wary of Brien when we'd first met as kids. The little Maritime Prince was too good to be true, with perfect manners and a sharp intelligence. The kind of boy your mother urged you to play with, hoping some of his stardust would rub off on you.

What Victorine didn't know was that the perfect prince had a devilish side. I'd been right to be wary of him, but he never turned that sharp wit against me. Instead, I became his partner in the small crimes we managed to get past our parents, like sneaking blood-wine from his father's cellar or slipping away from our bodyguards for an entire half hour.

"Want to dance?" The prince flashed his megawatt smile and held out a hand.

"Brien!" I grabbed onto him like a drowning woman going down for the last time.

The band launched into an energetic salsa. Our feet moved automatically through the steps. Like most vampire spawn, we'd had years of dance lessons.

Brien gazed down at me, a smile playing on his lips. He was stunning, with dark blond hair, smoky green eyes, perfectly symmetrical features (of course), and a cute cleft in his square jaw. I was aware of envious looks from most of the other unmated vampires in the room, female and male.

"Let's get the crap out of the way, okay? I'm not looking for a mate. You're a beautiful woman, but I'm having way too much fun to settle down."

My tension uncoiled a few notches. "No offense, but you're too high maintenance for me."

He gave a shout of laughter. More heads turned in our direction.

I didn't have to look at Étan to know he was frowning.

I raised my chin and moved closer to Brien. "But if you change your mind..." I toyed with the hair on his nape.

His smoky eyes rounded like a deer caught in the headlights. "You're messing with me, right? Because you and me? It would be like doing my own sister."

"Ew." I wrinkled my nose. "Thanks for the visual. But don't worry, I'm messing with Étan, not you."

Brien's brow creased. "He's the frontrunner, then."

"Afraid so."

"What in Hades did Victorine bribe you with to get you to agree?"

I moved a shoulder. "Guess."

"She won't appoint you lieutenant unless you choose someone."

I nodded.

"And you're going to let her get away with it?"

I expelled a breath. "It's complicated."

"With her, it's always complicated." He sucked in a breath and pulled back his shoulders like a man preparing to charge into a burning building. "Forget what I said. Mate with me, Z. We like each other. We'll make it work."

"Damn it, Bri." Hot tears pricked the back of my eyes. I swallowed them down and pressed my lips together to keep myself from accepting. "I appreciate the offer—so much—but I can't do that to you."

He scowled. "Why not? There's no one else, is there?"

I met his eyes without speaking. He hadn't been in Montreal two summers ago, but he knew Rafe, and I'd given him an edited version of what had happened.

"Zoe. Not a dhampir. I mean, I'm not prejudiced, but your mother will go ballistic."

"Not here," I hissed. We'd conducted the entire conversation in low, barely audible voices, but the ballroom was packed.

He shrugged and steered me into a showy turn. For a few minutes, we danced in silence.

"It's not just that," I said after a while. "You deserve to find your true mate. The person who is your other half."

"Or I may never find them." He pressed a kiss to my forehead. "The offer stands. Anytime. Call me, and I'll be here."

This time a tear escaped. I wiped it away with a finger and muttered a gruff thanks.

The band cued up another prewar French song.

Enough. I pulled Brien across the floor toward them. Because it was *my* birthday, and I was tired of Edith Piaf.

I lifted a finger, caught the singer's eye. She nodded and segued into Ariana Grande's "Into You."

The younger thralls perked up. A few of the older vampires stood back and watched with hooded eyes, but most went with the flow. When you'd already lived the equivalent of two or three human lifespans, change was a given.

Brien and I started dancing again, not touching this time, just moving to the music. The singer dropped her voice, and one of those eerie hushes fell on the crowd.

Got everyone watchin' us
So baby, let's keep it secret
A little bit scandalous

She could've been singing about me and Rafe. Yearning curled through me.

Brien's brow creased. "What's wrong?"

"Nothing." I shook my head and kept dancing.

Two servers appeared with a giant gold platter holding my birthday "cake," a tower of chocolate truffles. Three kinds—white, dark and salted caramel—were arranged in spirals and topped with a big red bow.

They set the platter on a small table. Victorine raised her hand and the music stopped.

My stomach clenched.

Brien grinned and urged me forward. "Your birthday chocolate's here."

The servers started lighting the twenty-seven tiny votives encircling the tray.

Victorine smiled at me. A warmer smile than she usually gave me. A real smile.

I can't do this.

She beckoned to Étan, who moved up beside her. The two of them shared a look. Suddenly, I *knew*. They were going to trap me into accepting him as my mate.

Suddenly, the music seemed too loud. I drew a calming breath.

Victorine loved me. I knew that. But her kind of love required me to remain her obedient spawn. Not a person in my own right, a person with my own needs and wants.

She'd made up her mind, and nothing would change it. I was trapped.

I can't do this.

I edged backward toward the door nearest my tower.

"Zoe?" Brien said.

I took his arm. "Cover for me," I whispered. "I need ten minutes. Fifteen minutes, tops. Tell them...my heel broke off." I dragged off my shoe and waved it at my mother. "Be right back," I mouthed.

She frowned and shook her head, but I was already pushing the door open.

Behind me there was a stunned silence. Then Victorine said, "I beg your pardon. My daughter will be right back. But please, enjoy the dancing for another few minutes."

I pulled off the other shoe and, transferring them both to one hand, dashed up the stairs as the tower clock struck midnight.

Please let Rafe still be in the tower.

But if not, I had his number.

I fumbled with the keypad to open the door, getting it wrong the first time. I drew a breath through my teeth, tried again.

The living room was empty. My heart sank. I shut the door—and jolted as Rafe emerged from behind the door, a bottle raised above his head.

"Hey." He lowered it with a sheepish grin.

"We have to leave. Now." I dropped my shoes on the floor and locked the door. In the bedroom, I shoved a few things into a small carry-on suitcase—jeans, T-shirts, underwear, a light jacket.

"You're going to help me?" He appeared at my side.

"Yes." It was perfect, really. It would buy me a few days to figure out how to handle Victorine's ultimatum that I mate.

She'd be furious at me for slipping away from my own ball, and even madder that she didn't get to make her midnight announcement. But I was banking on the fact that she'd forgive me as long as she didn't find out who I'd left with.

Meanwhile, I could prove to Rafe—and to myself—that Victorine wasn't working with Slayers, Inc., because he'd created enough doubt in my mind to make me uneasy. I needed to know, one way or the other, before I made a final decision about Étan and the lieutenancy.

"How did you get here?" I dragged off my dress as Rafe watched, two vertical lines creasing his forehead.

"Tonight? By motorcycle."

"What about to Montreal? Did you fly or drive?" I pulled on skinny jeans and a turtleneck, both gray. For once, I was glad of my monotone wardrobe. Easier to blend into a crowd.

"I took a flight to Toronto and rented a Honda to drive the rest of the way. I figured your mom has people watching the Montreal Airport."

"You're right." I stepped into low black boots and grabbed my laptop and a pair of silver stilettos from a wall safe hidden behind the bedroom mirror. "Can your Honda carry two people?" I sheathed the knives in my boots and tucked the laptop into my suitcase

A nod. "It's a mid-size bike—has a V-twin engine. What's going on, Zoe?"

I gave him a confident grin to cover the slamming of my heart. "We're going to Paris."

His eyes narrowed. "To find Zaq?"

"If he's really there. But you have to get me out of here without anyone knowing. *Now.*"

❧ 1 2 ❧

RAFE

I wasn't sure why Zoe had changed her mind about helping me, but I wasn't going to give her time to rethink it.

"I'll get my bike," I told her. "Can you get out of the tower without the guards knowing?"

Zoe gave me a don't-be-ridiculous look. "Yes. But we have to hurry. They'll come looking for me any second now."

"Meet me on the other side of the gates. I'll wait for you at the bend in the road."

She nodded, picked up her suitcase, and faded into the shadows. I snatched up my bowtie and jacket, leapt onto the windowsill and followed her. I only had enough juice for a few seconds in the shadow dimension, but that didn't matter, because as soon as I landed in the garden, I powered my glamour and came out of the shadows.

My glamour felt solid. Thanks to the blood-wine I'd drunk, I'd be able to power it long enough to get off the island.

I retrieved my bike from the parking lot and rode across the causeway. The guards waved me through the gates. Zoe must have been running alongside me, because when I pulled off the road to wait for her, she was right there.

"Go." She swung onto the bike behind me, a sexy cat burglar in a hoodie and black leather jacket.

We made a quick stop at the rental house for my things. Zoe kept watch in the foyer while I stowed my stuff in the duffel bag and changed into jeans, a T-shirt and a leather jacket. When I came back downstairs, she was peering through a sidelight.

I looked over her shoulder. "Any sign of your mom's men?"

"Not yet." She reached for the door knob. "Ready?"

"Not quite. There's something I haven't told you."

She turned around, eyes wary. "What?"

"Victorine didn't just threaten me and my brothers. She said that if I ever touched you again she'd consider the treaty broken. If she finds out, the blood feud's back on."

"Crap." She blew out a breath. "All right. It's not like I plan to tell her where I went or who I was with."

"She won't hear it from me. You have my word."

"Good. And you have my word, too." She turned back to the door.

"Hang on." I set my hand on the wood. "What about your phone? Can your mother track you?"

"I took out the SIM card while you were upstairs. The GPS in my laptop is already disabled."

"Good."

We hurried down the walk, both of us keeping a wary eye on the shadows. But nobody appeared to stop us. I stowed the duffel bag and we got on the Honda.

By then it was after one a.m. Sunrise was less than five hours away. We'd have to hurry if we were going to make Toronto before dawn.

"It's going to be a hard ride," I warned.

"Just get me out of Montreal." She put her arms around my waist and slipped into the shadows until we'd left the city behind us.

We rode straight to Toronto with only a quick stop for gas, but by the time we reached the outer suburbs, thin fingers of pink and gold had spread over the sky. Behind me, Zoe slipped on sunglasses and pulled her hood over her face.

I frowned at her over my shoulder. She was so young for a vampire. "You can't take even a little sunlight, can you?"

"I'm okay," she muttered, then spoiled it by resting her head against my shoulder. A moment later, her hands slid limply down to my thighs.

I swore and grabbed her wrists, holding them against my waist with one hand while operating the bike with the other.

"Zoe." I elbowed her in the ribcage. "Wake up, damn it. You can't fall asleep—not yet."

She grumbled under her breath in French but woke up enough to grab my hips again. I aimed for the nearest exit and the cheap hotel I'd spotted. I zoomed into the hotel's parking lot and grabbed for my last bit of magic to conjure a glamour. All I could manage was something quick and dirty: lighter hair and a bend in my nose so it looked like it had been broken at some point.

I hustled Zoe into the lobby. "A room." I threw a credit card at the clerk. "Now."

Five minutes later, we were upstairs. I had Zoe wait in the hall while I went into the room and pulled the rubber-backed curtains across the windows to block the sunlight.

When I went to get her, she was wavering on her feet, eyes half-closed. I drew her inside. "I'm okay," she mumbled.

"Yeah, yeah. You're superwoman, right?"

She chuckled.

I helped her out of her jacket and gloves. She stumbled past me and sank onto the mattress. She smoothed a hand over the blue polyester comforter.

"We did it," she said with a crooked smile. "They'll never look for me here."

I grinned back, then leapt to catch her as she slid bonelessly off the bed. "Are you okay? I should have stopped sooner. You should've told me—"

She touched my cheek. "Hey. I'm fine. Just...sleepy." She closed her eyes and went limp in my arms.

I placed her back on the bed, then took off her boots and removed her hoodie, leaving her in a tee and jeans. Her face had a touch of sunburn—her long cheekbones were touched pink, and the tip of her nose was peeling.

I ran a finger down her petal-soft cheek. Not even a flicker of her eyes from behind her closed lids. She was completely out...helpless.

The Tremblay Princess at the mercy of a Kral.

My heart clenched. "You do trust me," I murmured. "A little, anyway."

Two years ago, I'd have done anything to have Zoe under my control, defenseless. I'd pictured how I'd snap cuffs onto her slim wrists, make her beg, maybe even give that pretty ass of hers a few hard smacks.

She could've told her mother the truth—that she'd wanted that little assignation as much as I did. Instead, she'd been deliberately cruel.

But hell, if I'd been raised by Victorine Tremblay, maybe I'd have done the same thing.

I tucked the comforter around her slender form. I was bending forward to brush my mouth over hers when I halted and pulled back.

Nothing had changed. Zoe was still Victorine Tremblay's precious spawn. She'd agreed to help me find Zaq, not run off with me for a hot-and-dirty weekend.

I took off my leather jacket and sat on the edge of the mattress. The adrenaline that had allowed me to push myself and the motorcycle through the night had dissipated. I hadn't had any fresh human blood in more than a week. I was exhausted and lightheaded with hunger. Hell, I'd even found myself staring at the hotel clerk's bearded neck. If I was going to be of any use to Zaq, I needed to feed.

I put on my sunglasses and went back outside. I got lucky almost immediately. Without my glamour, the twenty-something hotel employee arriving for the dayshift recognized me immediately.

"Holy shit." She did a doubletake. "Are you Rafe Kral?"

"Guilty." I gave her the smile that seemed to melt the panties off humans.

"Ohmigod, ohmigod. Don't go anywhere. I—" She fished a phone out of her backpack. "Can I please get a selfie?"

"Sure. If I can feed first." I wrapped an arm around her and before she could aim the phone, sank my fangs into her neck.

"Oh!" Her eyes went wide. She stiffened and tried to struggle free.

I kept her where she was. It wasn't right to feed from a human without their consent. My mom would have my head if she knew. But fuck ethics. Zaq was more important. The clerk would recover, and I'd make sure she didn't remember me.

I pulled her behind a big green dumpster and drank.

Zoe was still out when I returned to our room, sated and sleepy. I took a quick shower and crawled naked under the comforter next to her.

❧

I emerged first from the day sleep. The comforter had slipped beneath Zoe's breasts. She lay flat on her back, her chest rising and falling almost imperceptibly.

I rolled onto my side and propped myself on an elbow. Her straight dark hair was sexily disheveled, and the traces of makeup—mascara smudges beneath under her eyes, a hint of lipstick at the corner of her mouth—made her look so hot, like a starlet who'd collapsed into bed after a night out clubbing.

I'd woken with my dick hard anyway, but having her this close, and looking so available made me want to drop back my head and howl at the rising moon.

The peeling skin on her nose had healed. I trailed a finger down the long, straight bridge, and her nostrils twitched.

"You awake?" I asked.

No response.

I continued down her face, outlining her mouth with my finger, rubbing the pad of my thumb over her full lower lip.

Something—the scent of my blood, or maybe me playing with her mouth—made her fangs extend. One cute tip protruded over her lower lip. I rubbed my thumb over the sharp point and her mouth worked like a baby suckling.

I couldn't resist. I cupped her cheek and leaned over to kiss her awake. Her lips clung to mine. She sighed and muttered something unintelligible. Beneath her lids, her eyes flickered like she was dreaming.

Hell. She probably didn't even know who she was in bed with. I eased back.

She opened her eyes and looked at me drowsily. "Rafe?"

"*Bon soir,* Princess." This close, I could see all the colors that made up the hazel of her irises: green and gold at the outer edges, with a burst of amber-brown radiating from the center.

A sleepy smile. "Good evening."

"Did you sleep well?" I brushed her spiky black bangs back from her forehead. "I like the bangs, by the way."

"Thank you."

"You're welcome." I nuzzled her throat, inhaling her spicy green scent.

Now that I'd fed, the blood-craving wasn't riding me anymore. I could focus on other things like her soft, cool skin and the needy moan she made when I scraped my teeth over the sensitive spot beneath her jaw.

Not yours, I reminded myself. But damn, it felt good having my dick pressed up against her thigh, even if it was through her jeans.

She rubbed her eyes. "We're in Toronto?"

I nodded. "We're at a hotel just outside the city, about twenty minutes from the airport. Which reminds me, I need to book a flight for us."

Because if I didn't, I was going to start something I wasn't sure either of us wanted.

"Wait." She grabbed my arm.

"What is it?"

She propped herself up on her forearms and glanced at my very hard, very ready erection. Her eyes widened. "Oh." It came out somewhere between a sigh and a mewl of appreciation, which my dick loved.

It swelled even more.

I sat up and shrugged. "Hey, I'm a guy."

"I can see that." She sat up as well, her gaze still on my lap. "Zoe?"

"Mm?"

"Is there some reason you don't want me to book a flight?"

She flushed and lifted her eyes to mine. "Victorine will be watching Toronto, too."

"No problem. I fed this morning. I can power a glamour long enough to get us to Paris without being recognized."

"What about me? I can't hold a glamour longer than a few minutes. And what I can do is pretty lame."

"How lame?"

She shrugged, clearly embarrassed. "It's not one of my skills, okay? About all I can do is take the sheen from my skin so I look human instead of vampire."

"I see." I should've asked sooner—the ability to produce a glamour varied greatly among our kind. "But you're a vampire spawn."

Her shoulders hunched. "Yeah, well, I'm a disappointment to my mother, too."

I silently cursed myself for putting her on the defensive. "No offense, but your mom's an idiot."

She shook her head, but an uncertain look flashed across her face, like she was absorbing what I'd said. Turning it around in that smart, strategic brain of hers that was nevertheless blind when it came to her mother.

Victorine had really done a number on her daughter.

"I mean it." I ran my thumb over her cheekbone. "You're a special woman. Intelligent, beautiful, hard-working. If she can't see that, it's her problem, not yours."

Our gazes snagged. My heart thumped, hard and slow.

"We should book a flight." I nibbled her plump lower lip. "Don't worry about your appearance. A blond wig should do it."

"Mm-hm," she said against my mouth. "Which US airport is closest?"

I traced a finger over the delicate wings of her collarbones. First the left side, then the right. "Buffalo, I guess."

"Let's fly out of Buffalo, then. I'm pretty sure Victorine doesn't know you're in Canada, so it won't occur to her that I might be with you. Once she realizes I'm really gone, she'll check the Canadian airports for flights out, but if we cross the border into the United States, she shouldn't be able to trace us. Even if she does, we'll be in Paris by then."

I nodded. Buffalo was in Kral Syndicate territory. "So you want to catch a flight to Paris from Buffalo?"

She nodded. "I can compel the border guard to look the other way so he doesn't remember me."

"Sounds like a plan." I unzipped her hoodie and caressed her breasts through her T-shirt. Her bra was thin as air. I could see the outline of her small, rose-brown nipples, and when they beaded beneath my fingers, I felt every sweet detail.

"Rafe?"

"Five minutes. Just give me five—" I shoved up her T-shirt and bra and latched onto one of the tightly furled points, sucking hard.

Her body arched. She made a low sound of arousal and wrapped her arms around me. Her fingers feathered over the hair at my nape.

Competing needs fought in me. The need to take her. The need to keep her safe. The need to get to Paris and my brother as soon as possible.

I brought my mouth to her other nipple, sucked again. Her hands tangled in my hair, pulling me closer. I was on top of her now, her legs twined around me, my erection cradled in the V of her jeans.

I rocked my hips against hers and we both groaned. I felt her damp heat through the denim. I rotated myself against her, so damn ready I was about to explode.

I dragged in a breath. "We don't have time for this."

She blinked up at me. "No?"

I grimaced. "Afraid not."

A heartbeat passed. Neither of us moved until I gave her a long, we-will-finish-this kiss and reluctantly moved off her.

"Let me clean up, and then I'll call Buffalo and get us on a flight to Paris while you get ready."

She heaved a breath. "Okay."

I was back in five minutes. She rose from the bed and gave a long, catlike stretch. "Give me fifteen minutes."

I watched as she padded to the bathroom. The woman had a truly fine ass, firm and heart-shaped, and the tight jeans showed it off to perfection.

I scrubbed a hand over my face and got dressed before reaching for my phone. I would've preferred to go straight to Paris, but there were no direct flights from Buffalo to France.

I toyed with booking a private jet, but the Paris Syndicate would monitor incoming flights as a matter of course, just as my father's people monitored flights to and from the East Coast. A private jet could trigger attention neither of us wanted. We'd have to fly commercial.

The best I could do was a flight with a two-hour stopover in Newark, New Jersey, and then on to Paris. We'd land in France a little after dawn, but it was either that or wait another night to travel. Zoe wouldn't be able to travel even a mile in the full sunlight, so I booked a room near Charles de Gaulle Airport.

By the time she emerged from the shower wrapped in a fluffy towel, I was packed and ready to go. "We have a flight out of Buffalo in two hours."

"Perfect," she said and dropped the towel on the bed.

My brain fogged. I swallowed hard. I'd never seen her completely naked.

She opened her suitcase and took out a pair of black boyshorts, pulling them up over her toned thighs and ass. Next was a plain black bra.

I watched, my mouth literally watering with the need to taste those dusky-rose nipples again, as she put on the bra and the same clothes from last night.

She sleeked her damp hair back into a ponytail and reached for the suitcase. "Ready."

I moved around the bed and blocked her, so close the toes of my boots touched hers.

Her brows lifted. "Something the matter?"

"No." I wrapped a hand around her ponytail and tugged back her head. "Just a promise."

"And what's that?" Her tone was almost bored, but her pupils were large and dark.

"This." I nibbled my way along her firm little jaw until I reached the soft spot right before her ear. I caught the skin between my teeth, hard enough to make a mark.

She shivered; the kind of shiver that makes a man want to pounce, and dug her fingernails into my arm.

I gave the mark a slow lick and flicked her on the nose. "Let's go."

I tucked our luggage under one arm. With the other, I opened the door for her.

She shrugged into her leather jacket. "Not bad, Kral." She patted my cheek as she passed me. "But can you make good on that promise?"

I stared after her, mouth ajar and so hard I hurt, as she walked, heart-shaped ass swinging, to the elevator.

I hid a smile and pressed the elevator button. I liked teasing Rafe. The man was entirely too sure of himself, although maybe he had a right to that self-confidence. For a guy who was only twenty-five, he sure knew how to push all the right levers on a woman's body.

That sharp little bite had had me creaming my panties, everything female in me crying out. *Yes, please.*

While Rafe checked out of the hotel, I picked up my suitcase and headed outside. The parking lot was empty. A warm drizzle fell from the dark sky, the kind of rain you can walk through for hours. I left my hood down and lifted my face to the misty drops.

Rafe caught me a few feet from the Honda. He looped an arm around my waist, pulling me against his hard body. The suitcase dropped at our feet, forgotten.

"Fair warning," he growled. "This is the last time you're walking away. Next time, I'm not stopping for anything. They can set off a fucking bomb, for all I care. But we *will* finish this."

I turned in his arms. He smelled of leather and hot, aroused male. I pressed a kiss to the underside of his jaw. "I can't wait."

His mouth opened, then shut. I'd surprised him again. This time he saw my smile.

He shoved his duffle bag into the bike's luggage compartment and strapped my suitcase on the back. "Get on the damn bike."

I did, setting my hands on his hips as he accelerated out of the parking lot. My core was liquid, my clit way too aroused to be riding a motorcycle pressed up against the man who'd starred in my every fantasy for the past two years.

We hit a bump. I stifled a moan and tightened my thighs around his hips.

Rafe's tone was raw. "Hell, woman. You're killing me here."

I fingered the ridge tenting his jeans. "I can't wait for 'next time.'"

"You are *so* bad. But if you don't want me to run off the road, you'd better keep your hands to yourself." He moved my hand back to his hip.

"Yes, sir," I said, all fake obedience.

"Very bad. I may just have to spank you."

I chuckled, giddy with arousal and freedom.

Freedom from Victorine. Freedom from the Tremblay Ice Princess and everything that meant. Freedom to be with Rafe.

Just free.

I'd made it out of Montreal—on the back of a motorcycle, yet. And no one in the whole world knew where I was except Rafe.

I knew I didn't have much time. By now, Victorine would have the entire Tremblay Syndicate looking for me. But they'd search Montreal first, then turn to New York and the Kral Syndicate. Victorine wouldn't contact Paris for a while, if only because it would never occur to her that I hadn't been kidnapped, I'd left under my own power.

Meanwhile, I was driving into the night with my own private Dark Angel. My birthday wish come to life.

I laid my cheek against Rafe's leather-clad shoulder—and smiled.

At the Canada/US Border, a bored customs guard glanced at our passports—Rafe's fake, mine real.

I caught his eye. "You didn't see me," I murmured.

His face slackened. "I didn't see you," he repeated—and waved me through.

Our next test came at the Buffalo airport. "Use your glamour," Rafe said as we pulled into the parking lot.

"Got it." I conjured my human-looking glamour, and for good measure put on sunglasses and pulled up the hoodie, hiding my hair and most of my face.

Rafe got our luggage from the back of the bike. "Let's go. If our flight is on time, it's already boarding." We took off at high speed for the terminal, weaving through the cars dropping off passengers. To humans we'd be a blur, and hopefully, there were no vampires at the terminal. Even though we were in Kral territory now, I had the distinct feeling Rafe didn't want to be seen any more than I did.

We slowed to enter the terminal. I shot more power into my weak glamour with an envious glance at Rafe, who had changed everything about himself—hair, face, even his freaking height— except for his dark eyes. He even had a passport to match.

The next hurdle was TSA, but a nudge of compulsion, and the woman on duty ignored the blades we both carried on our bodies. We made it to the gate just before they closed the plane door.

I slid into the window seat. Rafe shoved our luggage into the overhead compartment and dropped onto the seat beside me. "Sorry it's not first-class," he said, "but that's what your mother would expect."

I touched the vinyl-covered armrest. I couldn't remember ever taking a commercial flight before. Victorine kept a Gulfstream jet for our personal use.

"You don't have to apologize. I'm not the princess you think I am." Well, I was—a little, anyway—but I was trying to change that.

He slanted me a look. "You're having fun, aren't you? This is a big adventure."

"So?" My chin jutted. "I'm helping you, aren't I? Nothing says I can't have fun while I do it."

A grin spread across his face. "Well, hello there, Zoe Tremblay."

I narrowed my eyes. "What's that supposed to mean?"

He squeezed my knee. "You'll figure it out."

⁂

In Newark, things went smoothly until Rafe saw a vampire he apparently knew. He muttered a curse and changed his appearance yet again.

"This way." He urged me down another corridor.

So he *was* avoiding his own syndicate. Interesting.

Dropping our luggage, he pressed me to the wall and hovered his mouth over mine. He looked like a California surfer with sunburnt skin and a mane of blond hair, but he smelled and sounded and felt like Rafe, and my body responded.

My heart gave a skip of excitement. I wound my hands around his nape.

"Don't look around," he said against my lips.

"What's the matter?" I whispered back.

"You saw the vampire?"

"Yeah, but he's one of yours, isn't he?"

The vampire hadn't hidden who he was—a high-ranking syndicate man. Dark suit, dark hair, cool dark eyes. The humans had given him a wide berth.

"I don't want to have to explain why I'm with you."

"But you're a Kral prince. You could order him to keep his mouth shut."

"Mm."

I pulled back so I could see his expression. "What's that mean?"

His eyes slid from mine.

My mouth compressed. "So I have to trust you, but you don't trust me?"

"Damn it, I *can't* tell you. My dad would have my head."

Holy bat crap. I dropped my head back against the wall with a thump.

"It's not just Victorine," I breathed. "You suspect someone in your own syndicate."

He released me, picked up our bags. "It's safe now. Let's get to our gate."

"I'm right, then."

"Drop it, Princess."

"D'you think they're working with the slayers, too?"

A hard stare. "I said, *drop it*."

So the Kral Syndicate had a traitor. Someone they suspected was working with Slayers, Inc.

We were almost to the gate when my step faltered.

What if SI didn't stop with Zaquiel? He was the Kral who didn't give a bloody damn about the Syndicates. He did only what his father required of him and spent the rest of his time in war zones and refugee camps, aiding humans.

If you really wanted to hit Karoly Kral where it hurt, you might start with Zaquiel, but you wouldn't stop there. You'd go after his other two sons next.

Which meant Rafe could be heading straight into a trap.

"Zoe?" Rafe frowned at me over his shoulder.

A chill trickled down my spine. *He knows.*

Rafe was too smart not to have realized this could be a trap.

But everyone knew how close the Kral brothers were. I might not know Rafe well, but I knew this much: Nothing would stop him from getting on that jet to Paris and doing whatever it took to rescue Zaquiel.

That was when I knew I was in deep.

Because my whole body clenched up tight at the chance Rafe might end up in a cell next to his brother...if he didn't end up dead.

I blew out a breath and hurried to catch up with him.

RAFE

I stared at the flight announcement board, barely aware of the humans hurrying past.

That had been close. Too close.

My shoulders were still knotted, my heart pumping, my whole body battle-ready.

Jozef was one of the soldiers who'd come from Slovakia with my father to help found the Kral Syndicate. Not part of the inner circle, but close enough. He could be the spy.

Zoe bumped her shoulder against mine. "Maybe we should sit down?"

I took a deep breath, rolled my shoulders and focused on the board. Our flight wasn't due to take off for another hour. "Yeah, sure."

We found an out-of-the-way corner and sat down. My jaw was still clenched. I worked it from side to side.

Jozef hadn't realized it was me or he would've approached us. My glamour was solid, and I'd used a brand-new persona that no one, even my brothers, had seen before. I could've explained my own presence in the airport, but explaining why I was with Zoe would've been a hell of a lot tougher.

Why had the soldier been in Newark, anyway? We were in the

international terminal. It didn't make sense for a Kral to take an international flight from New Jersey—we almost always flew out of JFK Airport in Queens. In fact, I'd chosen Newark because I'd figured we weren't likely to run into anyone I knew.

Maybe I was just paranoid? But this was no longer just about Zaq; Zoe was involved, too. Even if Jozef wasn't the mole, a Kral traveling with the Tremblay Princess would send shock waves through the vampire world. Victorine would hear, and the gods knew what she'd do.

I massaged my nape. Damn, I hated not knowing whom to trust.

"Are you hungry?" Zoe asked.

"Nah. You?"

She shook her head. "I fed right before the ball."

A man in an expensive suit headed toward us. My jaw tightened again. The tension spread to my shoulders and down my back. I slid a hand into the pocket of my jacket over my switchblade.

But he stopped a few yards away, broke into a grin and greeted another human in a Midwestern accent.

I let go of the switchblade and fingered the phone in my other pocket. Desperately wanting to talk this over with someone, but my reasons for going dark still held. I simply couldn't trust anyone except family, and maybe Tomas, my father's lieutenant. The big blond man was more like an uncle than an employee.

Should I call Tomas? Just before Father had gone dark, he'd ordered me to inform Tomas as soon as I made contact with Zoe, but things had happened too fast last night.

Still, I could've phoned him earlier tonight while I waited for Zoe to wake up. I'd decided against it for the same reason Father had gone dark. If no one knew I was in Paris, the information couldn't be leaked.

Now, I was uncomfortably aware that if I didn't call Tomas soon, I'd be disobeying a direct order from my primus. Yeah, it was because I was worried about the mole, but I knew damn well Tomas wasn't a spy. He was my father's oldest friend, the two of them a team since they'd been turned back in a little Slovakian mountain village.

Hell, I might as well admit it. I hadn't contacted Tomas because I'd pictured myself springing Zaq and returning home with him, triumphant. The youngest brother, the lightweight, playboy Kral succeeding where everyone else had failed.

Uneasiness pricked at me. Father was already in Paris, and as far as I knew, he hadn't managed to find Zaq yet. He'd be furious if I appeared out of nowhere and fucked things up.

I slid lower in the cramped plastic chair, stuck out my legs and stared at my boots. Zoe sat primly beside me, legs crossed at the ankles, hands folded on her lap, gazing with interest at the sea of humans.

I came to my feet and excused myself to use the john. On the way back, I ducked into an alcove and called Tomas.

"Where the hell are you?" he demanded in his Slovak-accented English. "Karoly has been asking about you."

That was Tomas, blunt, unpolished. No one would call him a diplomat, but everyone trusted him. No one guarded my father's interests better than Tomas.

"Newark," I said.

"You have left Montreal? Why?"

"First, what about Zaq? Has Father found him?"

"No. He is still missing."

My heart sank. I'd hoped Tomas would have good news for me.

"Okay. I'm on my way to Paris to follow up a lead."

"I see. And what about Princess Zoe? You have seen her?"

I hesitated, suddenly reluctant to tell him Zoe was with me. She'd stuck her neck out for me. The least I could do was keep her presence a secret.

"I spoke to her, yes. She says that Victorine has nothing to do with Zaq's disappearance."

"And you believe her?"

"I believe that *she* believes it."

"So, what is this lead you are following?"

"I'll know more when I get there. I'm sorry, I don't have much time. My flight's about to board. Just let my dad know I'm on my way to Paris, okay?"

"Do not hang up," he barked out. "You have spoken to Gabriel?"

I gritted my teeth, but said, "Not since Monday, and that was just a text."

"Good, good. Do not speak to him. Do not text him, either."

My nape tightened warily. Something seemed off.

But this was Tomas. The man was practically family.

"Why not? What's the matter?"

"He has taken that human woman into his home. Camila."

"She's back?" Camila Vittore had broken Gabriel's heart, not that my big brother would admit it.

"Yes. And your brother, he trusts her immediately." Tomas's tone was thick with disapproval.

"He loves her," I said simply.

"Bah. What is love? You are both too trusting. He does not see this woman for three years and now, she returns—and Zaquiel disappears."

"Yeah?" I thought about it, shook my head. "Mila's good people. She just got scared when things got serious between her and Gabriel. She didn't want to be mated to a Syndicate man, so she ran."

That's what my brother had said, anyway, and he'd know.

"She could be a slayer," Tomas said.

"Mila? A slayer?" From what Gabriel had said, she was just a young, in-over-her-head human who'd freaked when she realized she'd fallen for a syndicate prince. "They were together for two years. If she'd wanted to stake him, why not do it then? Why leave and then come back three years later?"

Tomas grunted. I knew that grunt. It was his I-know-better-than-you grunt. I'd heard it enough times as a kid.

I darted a glance around me. I'd left Zoe alone and unprotected for too long.

"They're calling my flight," I lied.

"I will let Karoly know you are on the way. What day will you arrive?"

"Tomorrow night. Or Sunday at the latest." It was Friday night. We'd land in Paris early Saturday morning, but Zoe would have to sleep until nightfall. "Don't contact me—I'm switching phone numbers when I land in Paris. I'll be in touch if I find anything important."

He started to object, but I pretended I hadn't heard and ended the call.

Zoe didn't appear to have moved since I left except to remove her leather jacket, which she'd folded and set on the suitcase by her legs. Her hood was still pulled around her face, her glamour dimming her allure. She would've looked like just another young human, if not for her straight back and neatly folded hands.

I concealed a grin. We'd have to work on that finishing-school posture of hers.

"Hey, beautiful." I dropped onto the seat next to her.

"Hey." She smiled at me. A shy, happy-to-see-you smile that sent a stab of want straight to my lower belly.

I took a deep breath, reminding myself that to Zoe, this was an adventure, nothing more. A chance to escape her gilded cage for a few days.

The princess might want to fuck me, but that was it. If I tried to make it anything more than that, I'd get my heart stomped, just like last time. She had too much to lose by mating with me.

"Some birthday, huh?" I draped an arm around her shoulders. "You didn't even get to eat your birthday chocolate. When we get to Paris, I'll buy you a big box of salted caramel truffles."

Her shoulders tensed. I started to lift my arm, but she didn't appear upset. More stunned, like nobody had ever put an arm around her. I settled the arm back onto her shoulders.

"Thank you," she told her folded hands. "I love truffles, and salted caramel is my favorite."

"I know." I nudged her chin so that she had to meet my eyes. "I remember."

"Oh." No smile this time. Even her eyes were cool.

But I was starting to see beneath the mask. She was feeling uncertain.

Because I had my arm around her? Or because I'd bothered to notice her favorite candy?

I made a mental note to buy her a big box in Paris and feed them to her, one by one, until she was satiated, those soft, full lips smeared with the sweet confection.

And then I'd paint her body with melted chocolate and take my time licking it off...

I caressed her nape. The tension drained out of her in slow increments. She turned into me, laid her head against my chest. She smelled clean and lemony from her shower earlier.

Her hand fluttered a few inches above my abdomen.

I held my breath, waiting to see what she'd do. The hand came to rest on my stomach. She spread her fingers out, a light, tentative touch that I somehow felt everywhere.

Something in me loosened, softened. The anger and hurt that for two years had fisted my gut every time I thought of her eased.

I placed my hand over hers and pressed a kiss to her shiny black hair.

$$\text{❦} \quad 15 \quad \text{❦}$$

ZOE

We had another two-seat row for the flight to France. Dinner was served soon after lift-off. Rafe ate both meals while I stuck with wine. We hunched down, shoulders touching, drinking cheap red wine from plastic cups and talking, low-voiced. Around us, sleepy-eyed humans watched movies or dozed.

Rafe nuzzled my hair. I turned my face and kissed him.

He'd warmed toward me, become more like the fun-loving, easy-going man I remembered. The kind of man who makes you believe in fairy tales and happily-ever-after.

And I was eating it up, that needy part of me that Victorine said was too human craving his smiles, his kisses, his heat.

I hadn't been forgiven. I didn't expect it. I'd let him take the fall for something we'd both planned, both wanted. Gods, what a coward I'd been.

But maybe he'd decided to put what had happened behind us?

I hoped so. I was pathetically eager for even a few crumbs of affection. To a starving woman, a mouthful can mean as much as a meal.

"Mm," Rafe said against my mouth. He ran a hand up my thigh. "I can't wait until I get you alone."

"Yeah? And what will you do then?"

He still wore a light glamour, but his expressions were all Rafe. His lopsided smile made my inner thighs tighten. "You'll see."

I leaned closer, licked his jaw. Letting myself tease him.

"Show me," I dared.

"So bad," he mouthed against my lips, and slid his fingers between my legs, rubbing the seam of my jeans over my sex.

My breath hitched. I widened my legs.

He rubbed a leisurely circle over the seam, pressing just hard enough that tendrils of sensation teased my clit, heated my belly.

My mouth opened. I gazed at him, heavy-lidded.

His eyes were on my parted lips. "Gods, I want you."

He lowered his head and kissed me. Soft at first, then harder. His tongue pressed into my mouth, slow and deep, as his fingers continued playing with me lower down.

When he removed his hand from between my legs, I whimpered.

"Shh." He stroked the hand up my waist, caressed my breast. "We can't. Not here."

I sucked in my cheeks. "Damn you."

I was wet and so ready I almost didn't care we were surrounded by people. But having sex on a plane—in our seats or in the washroom—was *not* the best way to stay under the radar.

"I can't help myself when I'm around you." His gaze was still on the nipple he'd teased to hardness.

"Yeah?" I must have sounded doubtful, because he met my eyes. "Truth."

I heaved a breath. "You really didn't send those texts, did you?"

"No." Just that one word, but this time, I believed him.

"I'm sorry. But I didn't know you that well, and—"

I'd chosen to believe my mother, because I couldn't believe a man like Rafe would want me for myself.

"Hey." He cupped my cheek with a big palm. "It's done."

"I tried to come and see you last year—to apologize. I had a flight that connected in New York, and I left the airport and took a taxi into Manhattan. But Jean-Michel caught up with me and convinced me it was a bad idea."

"Yeah?" Something flickered across his face. He shrugged. "I probably would've shown you the door."

My heart sank. "That's what I figured."

"And then I would've caught you and dragged you back inside."

"Really?" A smile began deep in my chest.

"Oh, yeah." His lips were against mine now. "I'm not saying I would've been nice, but I would've fucked you, good and hard. Talk about an international incident. I would've tied you to the bed and not let you go for a month."

The smile broke through, happiness mixing with arousal in a dizzying brew. "This isn't helping, Rafe."

It was his turn to heave a breath. He released me and sat back.

"Strategy," he muttered. "You said you have a plan?"

"Okay." I took a sip of wine and gathered my thoughts. "The first step is to go to Philippe's mansion, see what I can find out. He has a lower level where he keeps prisoners. If he has your brother, that's where he'd be."

"At his lair?" Rafe looked skeptical.

"Yeah. Think about it—if his primus isn't involved, Philippe will want to keep your brother close. He can't risk another Paris vampire stumbling across him."

Rafe nodded slowly. "That makes sense. But what if Philippe tells your mother you're in France?"

My mouth edged up. "Maybe Victorine should contact him first."

It took him a few seconds, then he lifted a brow. "You mean, you'll pretend to be her? I like it."

"Good. I'll text Philippe as my mother and tell him that Zoe's in Paris and will be stopping by. He won't question it. I pretend to be her all the time."

"You don't need a reason to visit him?"

"Philippe?" I shook my head. "No. In fact, he'd be pissed off if I don't stop by. Victorine always stays there when she's in Paris."

"They're lovers, right?"

"Sometimes. She trusts him, that's the important thing."

I pressed my lips together. I was telling him too much. There probably wasn't much about me and my mother that the Krals didn't know, but I didn't have to hand it to him on a platter.

I pulled back a few inches. Sipped my wine.

Rafe finished his drink and set the plastic cup on the tray. A flight attendant appeared and whisked it up. "Another, sir?"

"I'm good, thanks." He gave her that sexy, cheek-creasing grin and she practically melted at his feet.

"If you're sure..."

I rolled my eyes. The man was a freaking female-magnet. It didn't matter what camouflage he hid behind. The flight attendant hadn't even glanced over to see if I wanted anything.

I straightened. "That will be all," I said in my best icicle voice. I may have inserted a smidgen of compulsion, too. But hey, I was annoyed.

The flight attendant jolted and glanced at me like she'd forgotten there was anyone else in the row. "Yes, of course. But—" she leaned down so her breasts were practically in Rafe's face—"just press the call button if you need me."

"Will do." He gave her a distracted smile, clearly so used to women coming on to him that he barely noticed the mating dance she was practically performing in the aisle, turned back to me. She hesitated another moment, then left.

"You can't use your phone to contact Philippe," Rafe said. "If they've put a tracker on it, they'll find you the minute you put the SIM card back in."

"Doesn't matter—I know her code. He's used to her messages coming from different phones. I'll buy a new SIM card when we land."

"Works." This time, the sexy smile was turned on me.

My stomach did a funny swooping-thing, but I like to think I hid it better than the flight attendant.

"And you don't have to buy a new SIM card," he added, taking out his wallet. "I have an extra." He handed me a tiny gold wafer.

While I inserted it in my phone, he said, "What if Victorine's already contacted Philippe and told him to watch out for you?"

"I'll have to take the chance. But my guess is that she'll search

Montreal and the surrounding area first, and when she doesn't find me, the next thing she'll do is go after your father. Accuse him of kidnapping me, or worse."

"Hell." Rafe pinched the bridge of his nose. "I wanted to rescue my brother, not create an international incident."

I hesitated, but made myself say it. "I could just tell Victorine I'm on my way to Paris."

"How the hell would you explain skipping out on your birthday ball?"

"I'll say I needed time to think. I'm going to have to talk to her sooner or later anyway."

"No," he said firmly. "Don't contact her. She'll just order you home."

I grimaced. "And if she doesn't, Philippe will make me stay with him."

As Victorine's sire, the enforcer took a proprietary interest in me. Not affection—Philippe wasn't a warm-and-fuzzy kind of guy—but Victorine was the only one of his spawn who'd produced a spawn of her own. To Philippe, that made me his, in the way you own your dog's pups.

"So no contacting your mom. Unless—" his smile was sly—"you send your mom a message from somewhere else. Not France, another country. That would buy us some time."

"You can do that?"

"I can. Even better, it will come from your own laptop. She'll believe it. So. Where would you like to visit?"

I grinned. "I've always wanted to go to Japan."

We landed in Paris a little early, but the sun was up by the time we made it through customs. The familiar heaviness weighed down my lids. I sagged against Rafe, who wasn't at all sleepy. Sometimes I wondered why pureblood vampires like my mother were so contemptuous of dhampirs, because it seemed to me the Kral brothers had the best of both worlds.

"Hang in there." Dropping my sunglasses onto my nose, Rafe propelled me through the airport and stuffed me into a taxi while the driver put our luggage in the trunk.

I hissed as the sunlight hit my skin. The sun was higher than I'd ever seen, and it *hurt*.

Rafe swore and pulled my hoodie tighter around my face. He barked the hotel address at the driver in his American-accented French, adding, "Get us there in under fifteen minutes, and I'll double the fare."

"*Pas de problème*." The driver stomped on the pedal. The taxi lurched into motion, darting in front of a bus. The bus driver responded with an ear-splitting blast of his horn.

I laid my head on Rafe's shoulder. "Now you did it," I mumbled.

He chuckled as our driver charged onto the highway, weaving in rabbit-like bursts through the other vehicles.

"Hang in there, Princess."

I frowned. "Don't call me that."

"Call you what—*Princess?*"

"Yeah. It's not *me*. I'm Zoe. A person." I could barely stay awake, but this was important. "Not a princess."

Warm lips touched my brow. "Got it, beautiful."

The short trip passed in a blur. I must have fallen into the day sleep because the next thing I knew, Rafe was dragging me out of the taxi. My tongue was thick in my mouth, and my skin felt hot, dry. Just being touched sent a jolt of agony clear to my bones.

"We're here. You just have to make it inside."

"I'm...fine," I said through cracked lips, and made the mistake of opening my eyes. The sunlight seared them even through the dark glasses. I cringed and flung up a hand to shade my face.

"Yeah, right," he said.

I closed my eyes and tried not to groan.

Rafe handed the driver a hundred-euro note. He thanked Rafe—twice—and zoomed out of the parking lot.

Our check-in was mercifully quick. Rafe hustled me into the elevator and down the hall to our room. Even a light touch was painful on my burned skin, but as the day sleep took me deeper, I couldn't move on my own. I grit my teeth and bore it.

Rafe had me wait outside while he closed the curtains. By the time he returned, I was sitting on the floor, slumped against the doorjamb. He swung me into his arms and tucked me into bed.

The last thing I remembered was him easing me out of my clothes. He pressed a cool, wet rag to my face and cracked lips.

"Sleep, cher. I've got you safe."

At least, I thought that's what he said. But I might have dreamed it.

When I woke up, Rafe was slouched on the room's only chair in a black T-shirt and boxer briefs. He'd dropped his glamour to be his own dazzling self. His dark curls were damp from a shower, his jaw shadowed with sexy stubble.

And he was frowning over my laptop.

I propped myself up on my elbows. I'd healed during the day, although my eyes still hurt from the burn they'd received, and I needed to feed soon.

"Learn anything?" I asked dryly.

"That your password is too easy to crack." He showed me the screen, which he had open to Finder and my files.

I shrugged. "Those aren't the important ones."

I rose from the bed, stretched. This time he'd stripped me down to my bra and the boyshort panties.

Rafe's gaze snapped to me. His eyes darkened. He shut the laptop, set it aside.

A thrill shot straight to my womb, a thrill of desire mixed with power. That skinny, sheltered Zoe Tremblay could pull that look from gorgeous, bad-boy Rafe Kral.

"C'mere." He crooked a finger.

I crossed to him, and he pulled me between his legs. "Where were we?" He shaped my hips with his hands.

"Hm. Let me think…" I set my hands on his thighs and leaned forward to kiss him. "Here."

Strong fingers cupped my nape, pulling me closer. When we came up for air, he dragged me onto his lap.

"Lift your arms," he told me and pulled off my bra. "Actually, I think we were here."

He leaned me backward over one arm. His mouth latched onto my nipple. He sucked strongly.

"You might be right," I managed to say.

His erection prodded my hip. I squirmed against it. I was so wet, so primed for him, and he'd barely touched me.

"Remember my promise?" he asked, and nipped my nipple.

Anticipation shivered through me. Anticipation, and excitement. "I do."

He rumbled his approval like a big cat. "Good."

After that, things got beautifully hazy. He kissed and suckled my other nipple.

I sat up and pulled off his T-shirt. Ran my hands over his powerful chest and shoulders. Scraped my fingernails through the wiry black hair on his chest. Followed the sexy trail down his taut stomach and into his boxer briefs.

I cupped his cock with one hand. It was hot and heavy.

He gave a growl of pleasure.

I squeezed harder, enjoying how his eyes slit. "You like that."

"Oh, yeah."

He pulled my thighs over his so I straddled him, his cock rubbing against me through the thin barrier of my panties and his boxers. He speared his fingers into my hair, pulling my head back so my neck was exposed to him and kissed his way along my collar bone to the center of my throat.

I surfaced from the haze and froze.

"Shh." He stroked my face with his free hand. "I won't do anything you don't want, cher. You trust me, don't you?"

I nodded.

"Say it. Say I can taste you. I'll just take a little." He ran his fangs over my jaw. So gently. Almost reverently.

I swallowed. I'd never let anyone feed from me. But I'd wondered. I'd seen the blissed-out look on thralls' faces, heard them speak of the blood-high.

And I wanted to please Rafe, wanted the connection that letting him drink my blood would bring.

I'd hesitated too long.

He pressed a kiss to my throat. "Never mind. I shouldn't have asked."

I didn't say anything, because a part of me agreed. The sensible, too-damn-realistic part that knew this thing between us couldn't go anywhere.

He stood up with me still in his arms and placed me on the bed's crumpled white sheets. My panties came off, and his boxer briefs.

He knelt on the mattress, his legs on either side of my hips.

He was so beautiful, a sex god with smooth tan skin, ripped abs and hooded dark eyes—and a black wolf tattooed above his left hip bone.

He'd been made as a Kral enforcer.

My heart dipped. It was like the universe was hammering home how temporary our time together was.

His gaze dared me to say something.

I managed a smile. "Congratulations. When did this happen?"

"Last year."

"Ah." I nodded.

He eyed me oddly. "That's all? Congratulations?"

"What do you want me to say?" I traced the dusting of black hair down his taut stomach to his cock. It was hard and flushed, a dark, suckable red. I ran my fingertip around the cap and down to his root.

His whole body tightened. "Nothing." He kneed my legs apart in a dominant move that made me cream with arousal, and crouched over me. "I don't want you to say anything but *Please, Rafe* and *Make me scream*."

I snorted. "You're so..."

"Cocky?" He hooked his hands around my thighs and hovered his mouth over my sex. "You love it and we both know it."

He gave me a slow lick. My hips bucked.

Oh yeah, I loved it.

"More?" He licked me again.

"Yes," I said in a voice low and raspy with desire.

"Rafe," he prompted.

I shook my head, confused.

"Say, 'More, Rafe.' Tell me what you want, Zoe—and I'll give it to you."

My mouth dried. I moistened my lips. What could be hotter than this strong, beautiful man between my thighs, promising me any sexual pleasure I wanted?

"More," I said huskily. "Rafe."

He licked me again, and then closed his lips on my clit and sucked gently.

"Yes..." I dug my fingers into the mattress. He kept his mouth on me, licking and sucking.

dhampirs have higher metabolisms than vampires. His lips were so hot. So perfect. The sensation increased until I was on fire.

"Too...much." I writhed beneath him, unused to anyone but myself controlling my orgasms, but he was relentless.

"You can take it." He worked a finger into my slick passage. His tongue played. His teeth nipped.

Everything in me clenched and then I came apart in a flash of heat and light.

When I opened my eyes, he was rolling on protection. I came up on my knees and helped him finish. If this was my only night with Rafe, I was going to touch and taste my fill.

Just my fingers on his cock made his eyes slit with pleasure, even through the condom. I squeezed the base, then went lower to massage his balls.

We were on our knees facing each other. I ran my hands up the hard ridges of his abdomen, teased his flat dark nipples with my nails.

He reached out and snagged me by the nape, dragging me up against him. My breasts were pressed to his chest, his erection hard against my belly.

"You're so damn sexy," he said against my mouth. Below, he did something magical with his fingers that had me clenching my thighs together. He bit my lower lip. "Open to me."

"Yes, sir."

His gaze shot to mine. I'd meant it ironically, but somehow it had come out breathy, needy.

And he liked it, I could tell.

He did that magical thing again, and this time, my nerves sparked and exploded. I gasped and arched with the hot, bright pleasure of it.

The world spun and I was on my back, Rafe above me. A powerful thigh moved my legs further apart, and he settled in the space he'd made for himself.

Espresso eyes smoldered at me. "Tell me you're ready."

"Yes." I opened my arms, gathered him close. So, so ready.

He propped himself on his forearms and set his cheek against mine.

I'd wondered what my first time would be like. Awkward? Painful? Maybe even embarrassing?

But it was the most natural thing in the world. He reached down and guided himself into me. I moaned as my body stretched to accommodate him. There was an erotic burn, followed by amped-up pleasure.

He stilled, his back muscles rock-hard. "You all right?" he asked in a strained voice.

"Mm-hm." I kissed his jaw. The stubble was rough beneath my lips. "It feels good."

"It does. So good." He pulled slowly back and thrust again, a little harder. "So. Damn. Good."

The next time he did it, I tightened around him. That felt even better.

I moaned his name.

Rafe lifted up enough to take my hands. He set them on the mattress above my head so I was stretched out beneath him. Below, his hips kept up a slow, steady rhythm.

He'd never retracted his fangs. He looked fierce, animal-like. I felt like I was being taken, conquered, and I loved it.

My own fangs slid out.

The world narrowed to just us.

Rafe.

Me.

The hot slide of flesh against flesh. The mingling of our scents. His lean, hard-muscled body between my thighs.

I hadn't known I could want this bad. Need this bad.

He lowered his head to kiss me. His tongue stroked into my mouth. I sucked it deeper, and he groaned and thrust harder.

"The Lady knows, I want you," he said against my lips. "Too damn much." He rolled his hips in an unexpected move that had me sucking oxygen.

"You like that?" He did it again.

"Yes, yes ..." I was so close. I pushed against him, desperate for more.

"Do you want to come for me?"

Yes.

I didn't say it aloud, but he seemed to hear me anyway. He stroked into me, hard and deep, and at the same time, nipped my lower lip.

Too much sensation.

"That's it. Take it, baby."

My climax exploded through me like a firebomb. I gasped his name and bucked beneath him, my sex clenching around his.

"Gods. I—" He pumped into me. Firm, fast thrusts. Then he stilled, and with a groan, pressed in so deep he touched my womb, and came.

I wrapped myself around him, trying to imprint everything about this on my brain. The earthy smell of sex. His lightly furred chest against my breasts. The slamming of his heart. His forehead touching mine as he hung over me, taking ragged breaths.

A minute passed, maybe longer, before he lifted off me. I wanted to tighten my arms and legs around him, to keep him where he was, but I forced myself to relax my hold and let him go.

He lay on his back beside me. Our hands touched, and he interlaced his fingers in mine.

I stared at the ceiling, my insides still humming. Gradually, my awareness centered on our intertwined hands. A simple, casual touch that Rafe had probably done without thinking about it.

But I couldn't recall the last time anyone had held my hand. I couldn't even remember the last time someone had touched me with affection.

Étan didn't count. When he touched me, it was to control me. And Victorine's caresses seemed calculated, a reminder that I was her subordinate.

Sadness scraped my throat.

Don't start. This can't go anywhere, and you know it.

I swallowed the sorrow and turned my head to smile at Rafe. "I don't know about you, but I'm starving."

❧ 16 ☙

RAFE

Paris after dark is a vampire's paradise, a chic metropolis that's always awake, always on.

We took a taxi to the Left Bank, where I'd booked us into a different hotel. The summer night was hot and humid and crowded with humans. They dined at sidewalk cafés or strolled along the Seine River, its black water shimmering in the moonlight. Amber lights glowed along the tree-lined boulevards, and steamy music spilled from cramped little bars.

Our new hotel was on a narrow street in the Fifth Arrondissement. The clerk handed me a key card to a room on the fourth floor and directed us to a coffin-sized elevator.

I pressed the button. The elevator descended slowly, groaning and grumbling the entire way, before heaving to a stop with a rattle and a thump.

Zoe and I glanced at each other. "Let's take the stairs," we said in unison.

Our room was only big enough for a queen bed, a table and one chair, but the bed had fresh white linens and the tiny bathroom smelled like lavender. The sole window opened onto a courtyard. Four stories below, teenagers played soccer beneath the streetlights, laughing and trash-talking each other.

I stowed our luggage in the closet and gave Zoe an apologetic shrug. "I know it's not what you're used to…"

"No." She'd changed into a white T-shirt and tight black jeans, and twisted her hair into a messy bun. She looked sexy and sophisticated and very French. "But that's the point, right? No one will look for us here."

She sat on the bed and took off her boots. Setting her hands on the mattress, she crossed her legs at the ankles and looked up at me from beneath thick dark lashes.

I swallowed something both sweet and bitter. Those yard-long legs had been wrapped around me a few short hours ago, and already, I wanted more.

I had the sinking sensation I'd always want more, that I'd never get enough of Zoe—her taste, her scent, the feel of that glorious feline body against mine. She was the one woman for me, the woman I'd hungered for ever since she'd strode into the Tremblay boardroom wearing an icy smile, a prim black suit and blood-red heels.

I shook my head. "You don't belong here."

"Rafe." Her pretty mouth turned down. "I want to be here. Stop treating me like some helpless, overindulged *princess*. I can survive a couple of nights in a two-star hotel."

Hell, now I'd insulted her. I knelt down and took her hands.

"Damn it, that's not what I meant. I want to give you beautiful things, wrap you in softness. Feed you chocolate and paint your body in wine. Instead, your first time was in a lumpy bed in a cheap hotel."

Zoe smiled. A slow, frankly sensual smile. If I hadn't already been on my knees, that smile would've brought me down.

"And it was amazing."

"Yeah?" I felt a flush of masculine pride.

And damn the woman for turning me into this needy version of myself, but it was important to me that it had been good for her.

She was important to me.

She slid off the bed so we were both kneeling. "It was perfect."

She framed my face in her hands. "You were perfect. I don't remember the bed. I remember you."

My arms wrapped around her. Want slammed through me, a vicious blow harder than anything her mother's enforcers had hit me with.

Want, and hope.

I concealed both emotions behind a you-ain't-seen-nothing-yet grin. It was too soon to let her see how I felt—we were both still wary of each other.

Better to take things slow, see how they developed.

"Next time," I said, "will be even better."

"Is that a promise?" Her smile was wicked.

"You know it is." I ran my fingers down her silky ponytail. "But you need to feed. We both do. Let's contact Philippe and Victorine, then go out to that club you told me about."

"Le Sang Bleu?" She ran a fingertip over my lower lip. "If that's what you want..."

No, it's not what I want. I want to lock the door, tie you to the bed and never let you go.

But I rose to my feet and reached for my laptop.

Zoe texted Philippe as Victorine, then sat cross-legged on the bed, watching intently as I used my laptop to route the message to her mother through Japan and on to Montreal. I'd bet good money that next time, she'd be able to do it herself.

I shut the laptop. "That should buy us a few days."

"That's all we need," she said.

We took the Metro north to Montmartre. The white domes of Sacré-Coeur Basilica perched above us, its wide steps crammed with tourists enjoying the view of Paris and the informal, never-ending party: a fire-eater swallowing a blazing torch, hawkers selling statuettes of the Eiffel Tower. A busker played a mournful blues on a shiny saxophone.

According to Zoe, Le Sang Bleu was a seedy club for unaffiliated vampires in nearby Pigalle, tolerated by the Paris Syndicate but not under their protection. We had similar clubs in Kral territory for vampires who weren't affiliated with a syndicate. My father couldn't allow them to roam the streets, feeding off nonconsenting humans, but he didn't allow just anyone into our private speakeasies, either.

Zoe's phone buzzed, Philippe responding to her text. She showed me the message, telling her to come by any time after two a.m. "We still have time to feed," she said. "It's not even midnight."

We were in. My pulse sped up.

"I'm going with you."

Her sooty black brows snapped down. "You can't."

I thought uneasily of Tomas's directive not to do anything before hearing from my dad. But Father had raised us to think for ourselves, and this might be my only chance to spring Zaq.

"Not as myself," I said. "But you've seen my glamours. Philippe will never know it's me."

"He won't let me bring in a stranger."

"Then I'll go as someone from your syndicate."

"He'll know it's you the minute you open your mouth." She shook her head. "I'm sorry, but you'll have to let me do this alone."

"Mm," I said, my mind working overtime. Zoe was right...unless I changed my appearance to someone Philippe wouldn't expect to speak.

"Mm?" She slanted me a suspicious look. "What does that mean?"

I gave her a lopsided smile. "It means I'm thinking. I'll let you know what I come up with."

"You're not coming in," she said in that cool, you-must-obey-me voice.

But I wasn't one of her underlings, and frankly, that tone just made me hot.

I curved a hand around her nape and pulled her close for a slow, tongue-tangling kiss. "We'll see."

Her eyes were dark and beautifully hazy from the kiss, but she still managed to roll them. "Are you always this obstinate?"

I grinned. "Yeah."

Pigalle was a hipper, seedier version of Montmartre, with strip clubs and smoky bars squeezed into cramped buildings next to small, family-owned taverns.

As we turned up a narrow, winding street, a skinny female in a short skirt latched onto my bicep. "Lap dances for twenty euros." She urged me in the direction of a sketchy-looking club. "Very good. Professional."

"No, thanks." I shook her off and kept going.

She came at me again, this time clamping onto my arm with both hands. "You are so handsome, m'sieur. It will be a pleasure."

I expelled a breath. That's what I got for using a glamour—the humans thought I was one of them.

Beside me, Zoe had her lips pressed together, trying not to laugh.

"No," I said firmly.

"You will like. Very much." The would-be lap dancer tried to pull me through the club's door.

"Enough." I dropped my glamour long enough to bare my fangs. "I said *no*."

"Pardon. Pardon." She scurried back into the safety of the bar.

Zoe's mouth twitched. "Stop scaring the locals."

"She's just looking for a sucker to scam. That lap dance would've cost me three hundred euros. Not that I wanted it anyway." I scowled. "You could've helped, you know."

"I figured you could handle a hundred-pound human."

She slid an arm around my waist and laughed up at me.

My heart lurched. No one would recognize the Ice Princess right now, and not because she'd dimmed her supernatural allure.

I dropped an arm over her shoulders and pulled her closer.

It wasn't just her relaxed, happy smile or that she'd touched me without thinking, just because she wanted to.

It was that she felt safe enough to show me the real woman.

Mine.

Right there and then, I made up my mind. The hell with taking things slow.

This wasn't going to end after we left Paris. Somehow, we'd work it out. I was damned if I'd let a two-hundred-year-old feud keep us apart.

"Here we are." Zoe nodded at a cobblestone alley.

My nape prickled. I brushed my mouth over her ear. "Someone's watching us," I said in subvocal tones and palmed a switchblade.

"Mm-hm." She bent and pretended to brush something off her boot. When she straightened, she had a long silver knife secreted in her hand.

We turned casually around and scanned the main street. Three women chatting animatedly in French passed by, followed by a pair of men who were clearly more interested in the women than us.

"Maybe someone's watching from the shadows," Zoe murmured.

Which meant either a vampire or a dhampir.

"Yeah," I said grimly. The itchy feeling increased.

No one but Tomas and Philippe—and possibly my father—knew we were in Paris, and none of them knew where in the city we were. Plus, we were still camouflaged, me with a glamour, Zoe dimming her skin and her hair tucked under a Baltimore Orioles cap I'd given her.

So why the fuck were we being followed?

"Le Sang Bleu is right there." Zoe tipped her head at the next building. "I vote we go inside. As long as we close the door behind us, whoever it is won't be able to follow without leaving the shadows."

I glanced at the dark red door. It was unmarked because we supernaturals knew how to find the club, and the only humans allowed inside were thralls hired by the management.

"All right. You go first. I'll block the way and then close the door."

"*Princess Zoe?*" A silver-haired woman in cropped black pants and pink high tops tripped across the street. "Is that you?"

I swore and grabbed her. Her scent was human, but slayers come in all shapes and sizes.

She squeaked. I shoved her further down the alley and slammed her up against a wall, my hand around her throat. Beneath my fingers, her pulse fluttered like a trapped parakeet.

I bared my fangs. "What do you want with the princess?"

"Rafe, no." Zoe laid a hand on my back. "I know her."

The woman grabbed my wrist and nodded vigorously. "I'm her...sty—"

"Shut up." I tightened my grip on her throat.

The woman's heavily mascaraed eyes bulged. Despite the silver hair, she was young, still in her twenties. She nodded without speaking.

"Who is she?" I asked Zoe without taking my gaze from her.

"Lainey Q. My stylist for the ball."

I glanced at Zoe. "So what's she doing in Paris?"

"I don't know." Zoe turned a glacial look on the stylist. "Spying on us?"

A chill crawled up my spine. Had Victorine already traced us to Paris?

"Talk." I squeezed the woman's throat. "And it had better be good. Because there's no way this is a coincidence."

"But—" Lainey Q gasped for breath and tried to pry my fingers loose. She was turning blue at the lips.

I eased up the pressure. "Go ahead."

Her chest heaved. She inhaled noisily.

"It *is* a coincidence," she said in a scratchy voice. "I swear it." She looked at Zoe. "I'm not spying on you. I didn't even know you were in Paris."

"Let me." Zoe angled forward, staring into the woman's frightened eyes.

I nodded and shifted sideways without releasing my grip.

"You're going to tell me exactly what I want." Zoe's voice took on a seductive cadence. "Aren't you, Lainey Q?"

The young woman's throat worked. "Stop it," she rasped.

Zoe repeated the same words, weaving a compulsion.

Lainey resisted. She had a stronger will than you'd expect, looking at her.

Zoe kept up the pressure. "Look at me, Lainey."

Lainey's gaze darted from side to side, then back to Zoe. Her face slackened. This time, she didn't look away.

"That's good," said Zoe. "Now, talk. Why are you in Paris? I thought you were going home to L.A."

"I changed my mind," she said in an expressionless voice. "The prima gave me a bonus and I decided to come to Paris."

"Why?"

"To shop."

I opened my mouth to ask what else, but Zoe beat me to it. The easiest way to fight compulsion is to give truthful answers, just not the whole truth. Most humans didn't have the strength to fight us even that much, but slayers are trained to resist compulsion.

"Lainey?" Zoe prodded. "Why else did you come to Paris? Did Victorine send you?"

Her gaze swung to me. "Can't...breathe," she said.

I released my grip on her. She sucked in oxygen and tried to sidle away. I blocked her, but it was clear the compulsion Zoe had set on her had been broken.

I waited until she was breathing normally, then fingered her throat.

"We're hungry." I let my vampire into my eyes. "I wouldn't fuck with us. It makes us edgy."

"Fine." She expelled a breath. "Not that it's any of your business, but Olivier invited me to Paris. We left before the ball was over—I swear, I didn't even know you were missing." Lainey looked at Zoe. "But by the time we got here, everyone was looking for you. He patted me on the ass and told me to go home." She pouted. "We didn't even have a night out together. And he promised he'd take me to the Talon Haut Rouge."

The Talon Haut Rouge was an exclusive speakeasy for vampires and their thralls, and those they were grooming to be thralls. I mentally shook my head. Olivier had been trying to entice Lainey into becoming his thrall, and she didn't even seem to realize it.

"So why are you here?" Zoe asked. "On this street?"

"I heard Pigalle is cool, that's all. The hot new Paris neighborhood. Then I saw you. That's the truth, I swear it."

I narrowed my eyes. "How did you know it's the princess? She's using a glamour. You shouldn't have recognized her."

Lainey moved a shoulder. "I just did, is all. There's something about how she moves—like a cat. You know what I mean?"

Actually, I did.

Zoe studied her, then gave a short nod. "I believe you."

She blinked. "You do? I mean, good, because it's the truth."

"But I can't let you tell anyone you saw me," Zoe added.

"I won't. I promise. I—"

"You didn't see me." Zoe's voice was calm, controlled and so compelling she almost had me nodding my head. "Say it."

Lainey's lids lowered to half-mast. "I didn't see you," she murmured.

"You'll return to your hotel and stay in the rest of the night. In the morning, you'll remember none of this."

"I'll return to my hotel and stay in the rest of the night. In the morning, I'll remember none of this."

Zoe stepped back. "Go, Lainey. Go back to your hotel."

She obediently turned and headed back to the main street.

"We'd better follow her," Zoe muttered. "She's a sitting duck in this state."

I nodded, and we trailed the human at a distance until she got into a taxi.

Back at the Le Sang Bleu, Zoe rapped on the red door. There was a pause, and then a pasty-faced vampire in a fifty-year-old suit poked his head out.

He squinted at us, so old even the streetlights bothered his eyes. "Vampire?" He pronounced it the French way, *vom-peer*.

"*Oui*," said Zoe.

The doorman waved a pale, long-fingered hand at the stairs. "*Entrez, s'il vous plaît.*"

I waited until Zoe was inside before following and pulling the door shut behind me. I no longer had that itchy feeling of being watched, but I wasn't taking any chances that someone besides Lainey Q had seen us.

The doorman shrank into a shadowy corner until all we could see were the tip of his nose and the shining blue rim of his irises. "We don't want any trouble."

"That's what I'm making sure of." I stationed myself in front of the door, switchblade ready.

Zoe positioned herself sideways so she could see me, the doorman and the stairs. The princess had good instincts; it was what I'd have done if the situation was reversed. She was right, I had to stop treating her like she was helpless. She'd hadn't had the extensive training in fighting I'd had, but she'd clearly been taught the basics.

Two minutes ticked by without anyone else entering.

I rubbed my nape. "Guess I'm a little edgy."

"Maybe." Zoe sheathed her knife in her boot. "Shall we go into the club?"

I nodded and handed the old vampire a hundred-euro bill. "Don't let anyone else in for the next ten minutes."

He drew himself up. "The boss won't like me turning away paying customers."

"Then stall them." I handed him another hundred euros. "We only need enough time to choose two thralls and take them into a private room."

"Very good, m'sieur." The money disappeared into his jacket.

Zoe led the way downstairs to the club. The walls were cracked, and the concrete stairs stained and crumbling.

I kept my switchblade open, but out of sight between my hand and my thigh. "They don't waste any cash on upkeep, do they?"

She sent me an amused look over her shoulder. "Not what you're used to, *Prince*?"

"Like you are, *Princess*. I'm surprised you even know about this place."

"First time I've been here."

"Figures. Tell me we're not about to get staked."

She turned and continued walking down the stairs backward. "Can I say I'm almost sure we won't be?"

"Now she tells me." I reached around her to open the door with my free hand.

An unshaven human in a gray T-shirt sat on a high leather stool. "*Soixante euros*," he said around a hand-rolled cigarette.

I passed over sixty euros and he looked us over, bored. "You know the rules? Cash money to the servers, no rough stuff."

Zoe nodded. "*Oui.*"

He waved us in. "*Entrez, donc.*"

The club had been chiseled out of the Paris bedrock. The walls were a dirty limestone, the only lighting from squat black candles. Humans in short dresses with deep Vs to show off their throats sat at the small tables or lounged at the curved red plastic bar. A few of them swayed to the slow, sexy music emanating from a pair of speakers behind the bar.

The vampires in the club eyed us expressionlessly. Probably calculating how easy we'd be to take.

I bared my fangs and made sure they saw the switchblade, and those cold, calculating gazes turned elsewhere.

Zoe selected a male "server" in a businesslike way. I chose a female, and we took them into a private room. The sturdy wood door was reinforced by bands of silver, but I tipped another server —a burly Tunisian—to keep watch in the hall.

"Knock—three short raps—if anyone seems too interested in us."

"Yes, m'sieur."

Zoe dropped the baseball cap on a coffee table, and the four of us shared the only couch, her on one end, me on the other.

There was something so intimate in drinking together like this. Zoe's lids lowered partway, her expression absorbed—like earlier, just before she came.

The slow, sexy beat of the music playing in the main room filtered through the walls. Her eyes opened, met mine.

A jolt went through me. My body hardened. The blood craving is just another kind of lust, and now it homed in on my dick like a heat-seeking missile.

I shifted the woman on my lap to the couch so she wouldn't feel my erection. In the past—hell, even two weeks ago—I'd have been happy to fuck the thrall while I drank, but not tonight with Zoe so close, teasing my senses.

From the opposite side of the couch, my sexy princess lowered a lid in a wink. We held each other's gazes as we continued to feed.

When we'd both drunk our fill, I paid the thralls and added a generous tip.

"Lock the door after you," I told them.

The man slanted Zoe a hungry-male look.

Her fangs were still extended, her cheeks a soft rose. Her skin glowed with the impossible allure of a pureblood vampire.

She was mesmerizing, seductive. A beautiful, dangerous predator.

My beautiful, dangerous predator.

"I can give you my number," he told her.

"*Allez*," I growled. "Go. *Now*."

He went.

I reached for Zoe and sank back onto the couch, pulling her astride me.

She toyed with my hair. "Maybe I wanted his number."

I traced a finger along her collarbone. "I'd slit his throat first," I said pleasantly.

Her eyes glittered. "No one but you, *n'est-ce pas?*" She scraped her fangs down my throat.

Pleasure shivered through me. "That's right." I pulled the elastic band from her hair and brushed the shiny black strands back from her face. "D'you have a problem with that?"

A tiny hesitation. "No."

"Good." I sank my fingers into her hair, dragged her head back. Punishing her a little for that hesitation.

This one night, I wanted to pretend that she was mine completely. No conditions or limits.

Her mouth softened, opened. Inviting my kiss, but I didn't give it to her. Not yet.

"We have time before you have to be at Philippe's."

Her breath hitched. "Here?"

"Here," I said against her lips. "Now."

I kissed her long and slow. Her body melted against mine. Her sex pressed against my erection, a wet heat I felt even through our jeans.

Gods, I loved how she reacted to me. So willing, so ready.

When I lifted my head, her eyes were closed. I pressed my lips to each soft lid and released her hair to push up her T-shirt. She rose up on her knees to drag it off, then sank back onto my thighs.

Her bra was a sugary confection of white satin and lace that dipped low over her cleavage. I filled my hands with her breasts, rubbing my thumbs over the hard points of her nipples.

The woman was a feast, one I was torn between devouring—or savoring.

Glossy midnight hair. Warm satin skin. Plush red mouth. Brilliant gold-and-green-touched eyes.

Her mouth made an *Oh* of pleasure. "That feels so good." She set her hands on my thighs and arched her body to me.

I wrapped an arm around her waist and brought her closer, sucking each nipple in turn through the silky bra. Her needy moan vibrated straight to my balls.

With my free hand, I unfastened the clasp and tossed the bra on the couch. Now I could see her. Nibble her. Feast on her.

And I did, until she was moaning and begging me to stop teasing her.

I lifted her off my lap. "Take off your jeans."

She obeyed, removing her panties as well. I shoved off my jeans and boxer briefs, then sat back, caressing my dick. Zoe knelt on the couch, gaze locked on my lap like she was memorizing my movements, reminding me how new this was for her.

She leaned forward, long and golden-skinned, and took me into her mouth. My muscles clamped.

She lifted her head. "No?"

"Yes." I cupped her face, guided her back down. "Holy Dark Lady, yes."

She wrapped her hand around the base and gave me a few tentative licks. Was this another new experience for her?

Whatever. I couldn't think, not with her tongue exploring my most sensitive skin. She probed the crown with the tip, swiped it over the slit. Then, thanks be to the sex gods, she sucked the whole thing into her mouth.

I groaned.

She gave a hum of pleasure and sucked harder. I stood her uncertain exploration as long as I could, then speared my fingers into her silky hair.

"Deeper," I said in a harsh voice.

Her eyes met mine. Even with her mouth full with me, I sensed her enjoyment. In all our previous sexual encounters, I'd been the one in control, but now, she was the one with the power.

And she liked it.

I'd created a monster. But who cared when the monster had such a hot, wet, talented mouth?

She set a hand on my leg and took me so deep I touched the back of her throat.

"That's it." I waited, stomach muscles tensed, to see if she'd do it again.

She tightened her grip on my thigh and bobbed her head again. Taking even more of me, slow and deep, her gaze locked on mine.

I kept my hands in her hair, guiding her head but letting her set the pace. "That feels so fucking amazing. I'm this close to losing control."

She lifted her head, but didn't stop stroking me. "Maybe I want you to lose control." She squeezed harder.

Yeah, I'd definitely created a monster.

"Not without you." With a truly heroic effort, I lifted her up and set her on my thighs. I hated to put on protection, but I did, grabbing a condom from my wallet and rolling it on.

Zoe raised up enough to allow me room, then settled back onto me, her nipples tight and wet from my kisses, her thighs open and on either side of mine. Her pussy was slick, swollen.

She rubbed herself against me in time to the music, a slow, erotic-as-hell dance.

I groaned deep in my throat, and she slanted me a look from beneath her bangs. The look of a woman coming into her power, thrilled and knowing.

My heart punched in my chest.

Mine.

I gripped her hips. "Ride me."

She lifted up, took me in her hand. Our gazes met, clung. She lowered herself in an agonizing slide that seemed to last forever.

Then I was seated deep inside her.

Blood roared in my ears.

I rocked my hips, needing to go deeper still. We started to move together in a perfect rhythm. I brought my hands to her breasts, pinching and teasing.

She made a sexy little sound of pleasure and let her head drop back, her dark hair spilling around her shoulders.

Time slowed. I stared up at her, drinking in her absorbed expression. She'd given herself up to passion—to me—and I couldn't look away.

She was fucking gorgeous, my Zoe, and she didn't even seem know it.

She sensed my intensity. She lowered her head to stare into my eyes. Sensation crackled through me. All over my body, tiny hairs lifted like lightning was about to strike.

I pumped harder into her. Caught by whatever was brewing between us.

She caught her lower lip between her teeth and circled on me. Her pupils were enlarged. A faint flush touched her high cheekbones. She was close, I could tell.

I slowed my strokes and slid my hand between us, circling the pad of my thumb around her clit. Trying to hold out, to ride the sensations, the sense of *oneness* for as long as I could.

Then her orgasm hit her. She tightened around me and said my name. Just once, the sound so raw and needy, it pulled me over with her.

I thrust into her, hard and fast, and followed her helplessly into oblivion.

17

ZOE

Philippe's lair was beneath a mansion on a quiet, very exclusive street off the Boulevard Saint-Germain. Like him, the mansion was constructed on lean, classic lines. The formal garden had precisely clipped bushes and symmetrical flower beds. Old-fashioned streetlights gilded the mansion's limestone blocks a muted gold; and a pair of bronze griffins, the Paris Syndicate's emblem, flanked the tall blue door.

My steps slowed as I approached the wrought iron gate. Doubts crowded in.

Leaving Montreal had been for me.

Coming to Paris with Rafe had been for us both.

But this was the point of no return, the point where I committed myself to helping Rafe and the Krals. The point where my loyalty to the Tremblay Syndicate was at war with my desire to uncover the truth.

My stomach balled up tight. I came to a halt.

What if Rafe was right? What if my mother *had* broken the truce and was working with Slayers, Inc. to bring down Karoly Kral?

Behind me, Rafe had stopped, too. Energy emanated from him. He was pumped up, ready to rescue his brother.

"You okay?"

"Yeah," I said without looking at him.

"I'll be right there with you. Any problems, and Philippe is going down."

That made me turn my head.

"*No.* You promised. We're going in there to search for Zaquiel—that's it. If we don't find him, we leave. If we do find him, you help him escape. Nobody gets hurt. Nobody even knows it's you with me."

Rafe looked back at me with Jean-Michel's face, right down to the old vampire's world-weary expression. It was the perfect disguise—no one would question my longtime bodyguard's silent presence. He'd even made himself appear shorter, a slim sword of a man in the Tremblay uniform.

But something in me recognized him. Heart to heart, soul to soul.

Realization slammed me in the chest. I'd fallen in love with him. A Kral.

I was so fucked.

It was bad enough I was helping Rafe. But falling in love with him? Victorine would disown me.

"Karoly Kral staked your father. Remember that when you yearn for his so-charming spawn."

Rafe scowled. "What about your mother? We don't know for sure she hasn't contacted him. What if Philippe tries to keep you here? I'm not going to stand by and let him take you prisoner."

"Yes, you are. That's between me and Victorine. I can handle her."

I hoped.

The iron gate swung open. "No interference," I hissed. "If you can't promise that, then tell me now. Or I'll leave you out here."

A muscle in his jaw worked, but he gave a curt nod. "You have my promise. I'm just here for my brother."

"If he's here," I muttered.

"He is. Or he was." Rafe eyed the three-story mansion. "I can feel it."

My heart sank. "You can't know that."

He shrugged.

I took a deep breath. "Okay." I turned up the brick walk.

Rafe touched my lower back, quick and light. "You've got this."

And I tumbled a little deeper.

Because he was doing this *with* me.

Because he trusted my judgment, had worked with me to hash out a plan, and then agreed I should take the lead because it made more sense.

And because he'd somehow seen beneath my emotionless exterior to the real woman, the one who needed warm touches, encouragement. Love.

Philippe's dhampir butler opened the blue door. "Mademoiselle Zoe." Aubin inclined his head stiffly as if he hadn't known me since I was in diapers. "It's good to see you. And you, Jean-Michel."

Rafe nodded without speaking.

I smiled at the butler. Beneath the formal manners, he had a soft spot for me. "*Comment ça va?*"

Aubin unbent enough to give me a small smile in return. "I'm well, thank you," he replied in French. "And you?"

"Good, thanks."

"Come in. M'sieur is expecting you."

"*Merci.*"

We followed him into the foyer and down the stairs. The mansion's three aboveground floors were for human business and Philippe's famous parties. His private quarters were safely underground; he was old enough to recall when humans had hunted vampires with fire and stakes.

The first level held Philippe's apartment, the one below that was for Syndicate business, and the lowest held five cells, which I only knew about because as a ghoulish ten-year-old, I'd begged Aubin to show them to me.

If Zaquiel Kral was here, he'd be on the lowest level.

Aubin stopped on the first level and ushered me through tall doors into the salon.

Rafe remained in the hall. A bodyguard wouldn't be invited into Philippe's inner sanctum.

The salon could've been lifted straight out of an 1800s French chateau. The walls were papered in dark red silk dotted with gold fleurs-de-lis, and the polished oak floor was covered by a hand-knotted Persian rug. The furniture was early nineteenth-century antiques that Philippe had probably bought new—curved settees, gilded wood chairs, a carved buffet and matching side tables.

"Would you like a drink?" Aubin crossed to the buffet, where an open bottle of my favorite blood-wine waited.

"*S'il vous plaît*," I said, and the butler handed me a glass and faded back against the wall.

On the opposite side of the salon, Philippe appeared in the doorway, dressed for the evening in an elegant suit. His jet hair was touched with silver at the temples and a narrow mustache adorned his upper lip. If you ignored his cold brown eyes, you might mistake him for the maître d' at a posh Saint Germain café instead of one of Paris's top enforcers—which was exactly how he wanted it.

"Zoe." He came toward me, hands outstretched. "How lovely to see you."

I set down the wineglass to take his hands. We air-kissed each other's cheeks, European-style.

"Happy birthday, my dear." He pressed my fingers and released them.

"Thank you."

"My felicitations. I hear you're taking a mate."

My nape tightened. "Nothing's been decided."

"No? But Victorine said you and Étan are—"

"Did she? Perhaps she misunderstood. As I said, nothing's been decided."

"Ah."

I formed my mouth into a flirtatious smile. "You're not mated, are you?"

He didn't want me in that way and we both knew it, but it was never a bad idea to stroke Philippe's ego.

He chuckled. "You tempt me." He glanced at Aubin. "Leave us."

The butler nodded and left, closing the door behind him. I

winced inwardly. Rafe wasn't going to be happy about being left on the other side of the door.

Philippe drew me to a silk brocade sofa and sat down nearby. "Is Victorine pressuring you? I can speak to her for you."

"No, no." The last thing I wanted was for Philippe to contact Victorine. "Everything's fine."

He nodded and laid an arm along the sofa back. "So, what brings you to Paris? You must have boarded a plane the moment the ball ended."

"Not really. I arrived last night."

"You came alone?"

I darted a look at him. Why all the questions?

But he gave me a relaxed, just-making-conversation smile.

"Yes," I said.

"Except for Jean-Michel, of course."

"Of course." A wary tingle touched my spine, like an unseen trap was closing around me. I got to my feet and retrieved my blood-wine.

Philippe crossed one leg over the other and watched me, still relaxed. But it was starting to feel like the stillness of a tiger about to pounce.

I sipped my wine and told myself not to be so jumpy. "No party tonight?"

"I have a few people coming in. You'll stay?"

"I'd love to. But—" I indicated my T-shirt and jeans—"I'm not dressed for a party."

"I'm sure Aubin can find you something in your size."

That's what I'd hoped he'd say. It would give me a chance to sneak into the lowest level.

"Then, of course. Anyone I know?"

"A young pianist, very talented. Five or six others. They should be here in a few minutes. I wanted some time alone with you first."

"Oh?" My uneasiness increased. The high ceilings felt like they were lowering.

I crossed to the buffet to top off my glass, then stopped to study a painting. Over the years, Philippe had amassed an impressive collection of art he'd commissioned from artists ranging from Michelangelo to Warhol, all of which showed vampires with humans.

Vampires hunting humans. Vampires drinking. Vampires making love.

Instead of returning to the couch, I strolled from painting to painting until I was a few feet from the exit. I could almost feel Rafe listening on the other side.

I took another sip of wine, wondering if I dared leave.

Knowing I couldn't.

I paused in front of a Degas. "I always liked this painting."

Philippe came across the salon to stand by my side. "Ah, yes. The little dancer is so young and sweet, *n'est-ce pas?*"

"She is."

The dancer was all soft and creamy-skinned in her pink tutu. She sat on a stage a little apart from the other dancers, tying the ribbons of her ballet shoes. A shadowy man watched from back-stage—a vampire, hunting.

"She was a favorite of mine," Philippe said. "It's a shame that they leave us so soon."

"That's you?" I looked closer.

"*Oui.* I commissioned it myself from Degas."

"It's beautiful."

"Mm. Sometimes," he said, his gaze still on the dancer, "I forget how young you are. You still think in terms of a human lifespan, don't you?"

I jerked a shoulder. "I suppose."

"You're good for us. For me, for your mother."

"I am?" I turned my head to see if he was serious.

I'd only ever felt inferior around them both. I was too naïve, too unseasoned, too emotional. My sole purpose was as clay to be molded into the perfect successor to Victorine, and to one day produce another spawn to carry on the Tremblay line.

Philippe nodded. "Oh, yes. You remind us of what it is to be young, to feel strongly. But Zoe?" Dark eyes bored into mine. "A vampire isn't a human. We live a long, long time. Love is for humans or the weak. In the end, power is the only thing worth having. The only thing that lasts."

The trapped sensation had become almost unbearable.

What had Victorine told him? Did he know I'd left Montreal without her permission?

And why was he talking about love?

I licked my lips. "That's what my mother says."

"Ah."

A *tap-tap* on the salon door made my nerves jangle. I tightened my fingers on the wineglass, certain it was Victorine.

"*Entrez*," said Philippe.

I squared my shoulders and forced myself to face the door, but it was only Aubin.

"The pianist, m'sieur." He gave her name, and she entered, a petite American in a blue evening gown.

Philippe introduced us and we chatted for a few minutes. The pianist was followed by a thrall in a flirty pink dress, who made a beeline for Philippe. He set a possessive hand on her ass and she smiled up at him.

A couple of men from the Paris Syndicate arrived soon after, along with two more thralls. I nodded to the vampires, both of whom I knew slightly, and tried not to watch the door.

"Princess Zoe," the larger man said. "A pleasure to see you again."

I smiled and fished his name from my brain. "And you, Samir."

I exchanged air-kisses with him and the other man, keeping a wary eye on the door. When my mother still didn't appear, I released a slow breath.

"You are traveling by yourself?" Samir asked. Something about the way he looked me up and down made me believe that news of my supposed mating with Étan had reached him as well.

Anger pushed through my uneasiness. Victorine had promised the choice was mine. If this subtle pressure was her way of making me accept Étan, she was going to be disappointed.

"Shopping," I returned coolly. "Paris has the best selection, *n'est-ce pas?*"

"But of course."

The pianist seated herself at the grand piano. I excused myself to Samir and moved to where Aubin was pouring drinks.

I waved a hand at my jeans and T-shirt. "Is the magic closet still where it used to be?"

"It is. If you'll wait a moment, I'll escort you."

"Thanks, but I know where it is." I escaped into the hall.

Rafe waited, hands behind his back, the perfect bodyguard. But his eyes were alive with excitement, his body practically vibrating with tension.

I blew out a breath. A cowardly part of me wanted to call everything off and get the hell out of the mansion, but I was committed now. I wasn't leaving until I knew one way or the other.

I *needed* to know the truth.

"Philippe has invited me to stay," I said, "but I need a dress."

I headed down the hall. Rafe would understand.

So far, things had gone as planned. To get to the lower levels, I had to evade security, and the only way to do that was in the shadow dimension. But security couldn't see me disappear.

The plan depended on me entering the shadows undetected in a room with no cams, such as a dressing room. Then I'd leave through the open door, leaving Rafe standing guard. To anyone monitoring the security cameras, it would appear I was still in the dressing room.

Most visitors couldn't have gotten away with it; someone would've been assigned to accompany them everywhere in the mansion. But I was Zoe Tremblay. Philippe's people would never suspect me of evading security.

The "magic closet" wasn't actually a closet. It was more like an exclusive boutique with clothes for both men and women in a rainbow of colors and sizes.

More importantly, it had two dressing rooms.

I selected a couple of short black dresses in my size and took them into the nearest dressing room, leaving the door ajar. I knew I didn't have much time. I hung the dresses on a hook, faded into the shadows, and sprang into action, darting through the open door past Rafe and down the hall to the staircase.

I made it down the two sets of stairs to the lowest level in under three seconds. The door at the bottom was closed, but I'd expected that.

I flicked out of the shadows and slapped my hand on the door, tripping the sensor. A fraction of a second later, I was back in the shadows.

A uniformed guard appeared, a gold griffin embroidered over his heart. I plastered myself to the wall, praying he wouldn't sense me.

The guard glanced around, eyes narrowed. I dug my fingers into my palms, willing him to open the door.

"Nobody's here," he said into his earpiece.

"Better check anyway," came the reply.

I watched over his shoulder as he keyed in a five-digit code. The door swung open and he entered, me on his heels.

The five cells were in a row. Four of the doors were ajar, the cells empty except for a toilet and sink partially concealed behind a concrete-block wall.

The guard unlocked the closed door. A feral hiss emanated from the darkness.

I steeled myself to look, but it wasn't Zaquiel. It wasn't even a man, but a beautiful woman with soulless eyes, a vampire who'd lost herself to the blood craving and had been confined for her own good. It wasn't easy to see, but it wasn't uncommon. Philippe must have held a special affection for the woman. Otherwise, he would've just staked her.

I continued to the middle cell, and froze. A pair of silver cuffs dangled from the concrete block wall. In my mind's eye, I superimposed the photo of Zaquiel against the wall.

It fit. Perfectly.

Right down to the bloodstain on the concrete blocks about where his throat would've been.

No.

The hallway swooped around me. I took a step inside the cell and stared at the silver cuffs. My heart gave a single hard, disbelieving beat.

Rafe was right. Philippe was behind his brother's abduction. He'd kept Zaquiel Kral in this cell, and either fed from him or allowed his people to.

I pressed a hand to my stomach. A syndicate prince, and they'd treated Zaquiel like a blood slave. They hadn't just kidnapped him, they'd set out to humiliate him.

I shook my head slowly from side to side. Arguing with myself.

This wasn't proof Victorine was behind Zaquiel's kidnapping. Maybe Philippe had seized him for his primus.

But the Paris Syndicate wasn't at war with the Krals. In fact, the Paris Primus had pushed for the truce.

I backed out of the cell, gaze still locked on the silver cuffs.

The guard came out of the cell next door. I jolted and forced myself to move before I got trapped on this level.

Three minutes had passed by the time I returned to the dressing room. Three minutes that felt like a lifetime.

I dragged off my jeans and T-shirt and chose the first dress I set my hand on. Dropped it over my head, zipped it up.

Deep down, I hadn't believed Rafe. Not really. Even knowing what my mother was capable of, I hadn't believed she'd sink this low.

I'd figured I'd do this one thing for Rafe and it would wipe out that night two years ago. Or if not wipe it out, at least balance the scales.

But it hadn't balanced the scales. What I'd discovered had made things even worse, and I didn't know what I was going to do about it. Because when push came to shove, my loyalty was to my mother —wasn't it?

Zaquiel's image swam before my eyes. That feverish, strained look on the face that looked so much like Rafe's. His bruised, wounded throat.

She wouldn't. She signed a treaty.

But she would, if she could get away with it.

I dragged a hand down my face. *Don't think about it. Just get through the rest of the evening.*

Then I'd figure out what to do about my mother.

I pulled on my boots, shoved my phone into the top of the right one, and left the dressing room.

Rafe's eyes blazed with questions, but he fell in behind me, maintaining his bodyguard persona.

"Well?" he asked in an undertone.

"Not here," I said out of the side of my mouth.

"Answer me. Is he here or not?"

We were almost to the salon. I turned and nodded as if directing him to wait in the hall.

"No. There's no one down there but an old, blood-crazed vampire—a woman."

Rafe's eyes narrowed. Like he wasn't sure whether to believe me.

My chest squeezed, but how could I blame him? I had every reason to lie.

I licked my lips, and added, "But he was here."

Rafe deserved to know, even if it implicated my mother and Philippe. If that made me a traitor, then so be it.

I think I already knew I'd never be my mother's lieutenant.

His heartbeat kicked up. He leaned in. "You're sure?

"Yeah. I saw the cell—the one in the photo. The concrete had the same blood stain."

He stepped back and lowered his gaze. "Leave as soon as you can," he told the floor. "I have a bad feeling about this. We need to get the fuck out of here."

I gave a helpless shake of my head. "I can't. I have to stay for at least a couple of hours."

"Damn it, Zoe."

"I'll do my best."

In the salon, the pianist was playing a moody piece by Rachmaninoff. The vampires had their eyes half-closed, entranced by the dark, erotic melody, their thralls snuggled up to their sides.

I fought the music's pull on my senses, afraid that if I gave into any emotion, even the soothing darkness, I'd crack wide open.

Philippe nuzzled his thrall's throat, teasing her tender skin with his fangs. He lifted his head and eyed me as I rejoined the group.

I smiled and nodded at him, pretending everything was all right. It wasn't even hard, I was so used to hiding behind my princess mask.

Nobody would guess my chest was a tangled knot of emotions. Guilt that my own mother had probably been behind Zaquiel's abduction. Horror that Rafe had been right; Victorine had broken the truce. And a growing fear for both Rafe and myself.

The music grew darker, more intense.

My gaze was drawn once more to the Degas painting.

The young dancer would've known what Philippe was. Back then, many dancers signed thrall contracts. It was a win-win—in return for blood and sex, the dancer got money and the prestige of being a powerful vampire's thrall.

That was how the world worked. The pretty ballerina had probably done everything she could to attract his attention.

But tonight, it creeped me out. I knew Philippe. I'd bet my favorite orchid that he'd manipulated things so the dancer had no choice if she wanted to eat.

Philippe's hand settled on his thrall's nape. She leaned into him. He kissed her temple and met my eyes.

He knew.

Suddenly, I was certain Victorine had contacted him. That when I'd arrived, he'd already known I'd sneaked out of my own birthday ball and gone missing.

But *what* did he know?

I've never been so thankful that vampires can't read each other's emotions. I gave him a slight smile and focused on the music.

He doesn't know about Rafe. You can still bluff your way out of this.

The music approached its climax. Dramatic, haunting arpeggios that crashed over me like a breaking storm. If I hadn't been so on edge, the loud music might have drowned out the footsteps coming down the hall.

But I did notice. Several people, with the *tap-tap* of high heels ringing out like a warning bell above the others.

My shoulders inched up. The walls and ceiling of the salon closed in on me.

Fear tightened my nape.

I took a step back from the group. Not to run—it was too late for that—but to give myself some space.

The song ended and the room went silent. Philippe released the thrall and took hold of my upper arm.

"Zoe," he said with a sorrowful shake of his head. "I think you've been very bad, *n'est-ce pas?*"

❧ 18 ❧

RAFE

I eyed Philippe's aristocratic profile through the partially open door and fingered my switchblade. The desire for revenge writhed, hot and black, in my gut.

Mess with one Kral, you messed with us all.

Me and my brothers weren't called the Dark Angels simply because we were named Gabriel, Zaquiel and Rafael. That nickname had started in the vampire world. The Kral brothers fought as a unit —and we didn't show mercy.

My fangs pricked my gums. It would be so easy to slip into the salon and stake the Paris enforcer. A quick, surgical strike. I'd never have a better opportunity than now, when he was under the music's dark spell.

But there was that promise I'd made Zoe, and besides, she'd stuck her neck out to sneak me in as her bodyguard. I couldn't repay her by making her an unwitting accomplice to Philippe's assassination.

Footsteps came down the steps. Victorine and Étan, escorted by a member of Philippe's staff. Bringing up the rear was a woman and the real Jean-Michel.

Holy hell.

I instinctively started the fade, but it takes a few seconds. Both Victorine and Étan saw the fake Jean-Michel.

Étan reacted first. His good-looking face twisted. "Thrice-damned Kral bastard."

He leapt forward, but I made it into the shadows just in time. His hands closed on empty air.

I grinned into his furious face. "Missed," I mouthed, even though he couldn't see me.

Victorine raised an imperious hand at a security cam. "Lock down," she ordered.

I took off down the hall. Just as I reached the stairs, a solid steel gate slammed down from the ceiling. I skidded to a stop and shot a glance over my shoulder. The other side of the hall was blocked as well.

Trapped.

"Madame?" The butler appeared in the doorway of the salon. "May I be of assistance?"

"Shut the door," she rapped out. "*Now*."

I was already inside the salon. I raced across the room. Zoe stood alone, shoulders tight, the masklike expression on her face.

Fuck, fuck, fuck.

Behind me, the piano music stopped. There was an excited murmur.

I kept going.

"Victorine?" Philippe cut through the questions. "What's wrong?"

"That man in the hall wasn't Jean-Michel," said Victorine. "We believe it's a Kral."

"*Ah, bon?*" said Philippe in a cold voice. "Well, don't worry, he won't be leaving. All exits have been secured."

I found that out for myself as I dashed through the rest of the apartment. The library flowed into a dining room and then a kitchen. Three bedrooms, including the master bedroom, were down another short corridor. The only other exit had also been blocked by a solid steel gate.

I muttered a curse and returned to the library. Étan, Jean-

Michel, and the two Paris Syndicate men had fanned out to search the other rooms. They couldn't find me while I remained in the shadows, but every moment I spent here drained magical energy.

Worse, I already felt light-headed. It wouldn't be long before I'd pass out and return to the physical world.

Étan reentered the library. His nostrils flared, trying to track me by scent, but my run through the apartment had spread my scent wide enough that he'd have trouble finding me that way, and even if he did, he wouldn't be able to touch me.

Although he could box me into the library by closing both doors.

"Come out, you *connard*." He glared around the room.

"Go to Hades," I mouthed.

Then I went cold all over as I remembered what Étan had spat at me in the hall. *"Thrice-damned Kral bastard."*

How had he known it was me beneath the glamour? And Victorine had said something about me being a Kral, too.

"Talk." Victorine's voice, low and vicious. "Who is he?"

I moved to the salon doorway. Victorine had Zoe by the arm, her pointed red nails digging into her daughter's skin. The pianist and thralls had been herded into a corner of the room by one of the Paris men. They looked everywhere but at the two women.

Zoe's mask was firmly in place. "A friend," she said in a tone as flat as her expression.

Victorine's nails dug deeper. "It was Rafe Kral, wasn't it?"

Tiny beads of blood appeared on Zoe's arm. We all smelled it.

Zoe looked at her arm, raised her gaze to her mother's face. "Let me go," she said coolly. "And then we'll talk."

"You little—" Victorine raised a hand to slap Zoe.

Zoe seemed to pull inside herself, tortoise-like. She still held Victorine's gaze, but it was like she'd pulled her vulnerable parts inside, the things that made her Zoe, leaving nothing but an impassive outer shell.

My muscles bunched.

The hell with my promise. Victorine Tremblay was going down.

I leapt forward, but Philippe reached her first. He grabbed Victorine's arm, stopping her in mid-swing.

"Allow me, cherie."

I halted, stopping myself from leaving the shadows just in time.

Victorine drew a slow breath through her nostrils. "Be my guest," she told Philippe with an icy look at her daughter.

"My dear." Philippe took Zoe's hand. "Tell us what's this about. You're already in trouble. Don't make it worse."

Zoe shook her head but didn't answer.

"Sit, if you please." Philippe guided Zoe to a couch at one end of the salon and sat down beside her.

"Lainey." Zoe eyed the woman who'd come in with Victorine. "I should've guessed you were part of this."

It was Lainey Q, the silver-haired woman from Pigalle. It figured. That story of hers about just happening to stumble upon Zoe had been too pat.

"I didn't really compel you, did I?" Zoe asked. "Are you even human?"

"Oh, yeah." Lainey's smile was smug. "But I'm immune to compulsion. I'm good at faking it, though."

Zoe shook her head, then her eyes widened. She looked a little sick.

"She's with Slayers, Inc., isn't she?" she asked her mother. "He was right. You *are* working with them."

"*Who* was right?" Philippe asked.

Zoe set her mouth stubbornly.

I looked from Philippe to Victorine. Neither seemed surprised at Zoe's statement. They'd all but admitted that Father's suspicions had been correct. Victorine Tremblay had formed an alliance with Slayers, Inc. to take out me and my brothers.

Now I just had to get Zoe and myself out of here in one piece so I could let him know.

Étan had returned to the salon and taken a stance next to Victorine, making it clear whose side he was on. "Rafael Kral," he spat out like I was Public Enemy No. 1. "She left Montreal with him."

"You're wrong," Zoe said. "I haven't seen him in two years."

"Zoe," Philippe said softly. "I have a fondness for you. But if you lie to me, I will be very unhappy."

A tremor went over her.

Étan crouched down and stared into her face. Trying to intimidate her with his larger body.

Zoe lifted her chin and stared back.

Pride surged up in me. That was my vampire princess.

That's it. Don't let them push you around.

"The *petit salopard* is here," said Étan. "We know he's got a gift for glamouring. Man's a fucking chameleon. He pretended to be Jean-Michel so you could sneak him in here."

Zoe's mouth flattened. "If you're so smart, then tell me why I'd bring Rafe Kral to Paris. Why not just run off to New York with him?"

"Because his brother was here," Victorine said.

Victorine had admitted it. And they had to suspect I was listening.

I gripped my switchblade. I had no chance of escape. Better to leave the shadows before I was completely drained of energy. But should I show myself as Rafe Kral or someone else?

"Enough prevarication," Victorine said. "We have intel that you were on your way to Paris with Rafael."

Zoe balled her hands in her lap. "Who told you that?"

"Answer me." Victorine crossed her arms over her skinny chest. "Is he with you or not? I want the truth."

She stared up at her mother. "I feel like I don't know you at all. Any of you." She looked around the room and shook her head.

Philippe expelled a breath. "Zoe," he warned.

"I saw the cell." Her gaze accused him. "The one where you kept Zaquiel Kral. Does your primus know about that?"

What the fuck, Zoe? I grit my teeth. The more she talked, the worse she made things for herself. She must know that.

"Now how would you know it was Zaquiel Kral's cell?" Philippe asked.

Zoe went still as a hunted animal. "I sneaked into the lower level."

"Then you know he isn't here."

"Are you telling me you didn't kidnap him?"

"I'm not telling you anything," Philippe returned, and went in for the kill. "But if you went down to the lower level, then you know Zaquiel's not there. And his father has kept his disappearance quiet. No one outside of the Kral Syndicate knows Zaquiel was kidnapped but the slayers and the people in this room."

"So you're all in on it. Even Étan." She shot the blond vampire a look of loathing.

And suddenly, I understood. Zoe was asking questions because she assumed I was listening. She wanted me to have the truth.

Étan growled. "He got to her. That Kral bastard got to her. It's the only explanation."

"You little fool." Victorine bent down and gripped Zoe's chin. "So you came to Paris willingly. He didn't force you."

I held my breath, waiting for Zoe's answer. She had everything to gain by lying.

"No, he didn't force me." She pushed her mother's hand away. "I came because I wanted to see what was going on for myself."

Victorine's mouth formed a tight, harsh line. "You're helping him. A Kral."

"Tell me he's wrong," Zoe shot back. "Tell me you're not working with Slayers, Inc."

"You ungrateful child, I did it for you. To keep you safe. Do you really think we can trust the Krals to keep the truce?"

"A dhampir." Étan shook his head. "They're weak, all three brothers. It was me who coordinated Zaquiel's kidnapping. It was almost too easy. The man's soft, a pushover for a sob story."

Bastard. My fangs pricked my gums. How dare he mock my brother's big heart?

I'd heard enough. I prepared to leave the shadows. I was damned if I'd let her face them alone.

But when I reappeared, I wanted the maximum element of

surprise. And it wouldn't hurt to keep them guessing as to who I really was.

Always do the unexpected.

They were so sure I was Rafael Kral? Maybe I could shake them up.

I smiled grimly and started to change my appearance.

"I told him you wouldn't break the truce," Zoe said to Victorine. "I came here to prove he was wrong, that you weren't involved in it." She glanced at Étan. "That *we* weren't involved in it."

Étan plucked Zoe off the couch. "You've gone too far." He shook her like she was a child. "You've betrayed your mother and your coven, and embarrassed your syndicate."

A killing rage filled my head. Étan had put his hands on Zoe. Again.

I dropped out of the shadows, switchblade in hand, as he backhanded her across the face so hard her head snapped to the side.

Then he did it a second time.

My vision clouded. A guttural sound ripped from my chest. "You sonofabitch."

All eyes swung to me. My glamour was apparently letter-perfect. Even Philippe did a doubletake.

No one had expected to see my brother Zaq.

Etan shoved Zoe away from him and started to turn toward me.

But I had the element of surprise. It bought me the time I needed to plunge the long silver blade into Étan's chest and up through his heart.

Zaquiel Kral.

His face bloodied, eyes hollow. Silver burns on his wrists and a vampire bite on his neck.

But it couldn't be.

Rafe?

I blinked and shook my head, trying to see past the pain and humiliation of having my face slapped twice in front of Victorine, Philippe, and a roomful of Paris soldiers and thralls.

Rafe lunged at Étan. There was a flash of silver. Étan grunted and lurched into me, and I instinctively caught him. We stared into each other's eyes, then I pushed him away.

Time slowed.

Étan's hand went to the silver handle sticking out of his chest. His face stretched in shock.

My eyes widened, my shock mirroring his.

Étan had been staked. By Rafe.

The blond lieutenant stumbled backward. Reached into a pocket, turned toward his assailant. "You—"

Victorine shrieked, a fierce raptor sound that sent chills up and down my spine.

Étan opened a switchblade and pushed it weakly at the man

with Zaquiel's face, who easily avoided it.

The switchblade fell from Étan's hand. A bubble of blood formed on his lips. He crumpled to the Persian rug at my feet.

"Zoe." He stretched out a blackened, smoking hand to me. "Help...me."

I looked at him, my face still stinging from his blows, then crouched down. The acrid, stomach-turning scent of smoke and burning flesh filled my nostrils. I touched his chest, pretending sorrow for our audience.

Only he heard my muttered words.

"Of course, I helped Rafe. And I fucked him, too. And Étan?" I peeled my lips in a smile only he could see. "It was awesome. The earth freaking moved."

He opened his mouth, but there was nothing but a smoking black hole clear to the back of his skull. Whatever he wanted to say, he never got it out as the final death consumed him like a fast-moving fire.

His eyes glazed over. He jerked and went still. He'd entered the final transition. His blackened skin flaked off onto the rug. Soon he'd be a pile of ashes.

May he rot in a light-filled hell.

I stood back up.

Time returned to normal. Philippe was on his feet, rapping out orders. The two Paris soldiers leapt for the intruder. More vampires poured into the salon.

Rafe's glamour sloughed away like a snake's skin. He dropped into a fighting crouch, lips stretched in a cold grin, a second switchblade in his hand.

My hero. My heart. My destruction.

"Damn it," I rasped. "You promised not to interfere."

Two soldiers came at him from either side with long silver stilettos. He leapt back and nearly crashed into a third man. He spun and slashed out with his blade, catching the man a glancing blow.

"Fuck that." His gaze caught mine for an intense, heart-rending moment. "No one treats you like that. Not when I'm around."

Then the soldiers surrounded him. He drove them off with the switchblade, but he was outnumbered. A blow to the back of his head sent him to the floor.

The soldiers fell on him, slashing at him with knives and daggers.

I drew a jagged breath. "*No.*"

I darted a glance around for help, but Philippe and my mother weren't going to jump in to save him, and Jean-Michel wouldn't dare. The three thralls were huddled in a corner, their pores literally leaking terror. Philippe's female had a fist pressed to her mouth and was making high, keening sounds behind it. The pianist was pounding on the locked salon door, begging someone to let her out, and Lainey leaned against the buffet, arms crossed over her candy-pink T-shirt, her expression unreadable.

"Don't stake him," Philippe ordered. "I need him."

The other vampires growled unhappily. But in his own lair, Philippe's word was law. They sheathed their blades and went at Rafe barehanded.

He fought back, tough and dirty, managing to hold them off until they pinned him to the floor, bleeding from multiple wounds. Two vampires held him down while the others punched and kicked him.

His face. His stomach. His liver.

Each blow he took felt like it landed on my own body.

He grunted, and his pain reverberated in my chest.

My fangs pricked my gums. No more than a minute had passed, maybe two, but I couldn't stand it any longer. I slipped my stilettos from my boots and started forward.

"Zoe." Philippe's hard tones halted me.

I spun to face him. "Then stop them, damn it. He's down. You've won."

Philippe's eyes flashed electric-blue. Belatedly, I remembered whom I was speaking to—my mother's sire, and a vampire with so much power, he could rip my head from my body barehanded.

"He's in my lair," was the icy reply.

My hands clenched on the stilettos' ebony handles. Torn between defending Rafe and obeying Philippe.

Samir kicked Rafe, and his agonized groan vibrated up my spine.

"Please," I said to Philippe. "I'm begging you."

Me, who'd never begged for anything in her life. But for Rafe, I'd swallow my pride.

I wouldn't survive losing him a second time.

"The hell with him," Philippe growled back. "What I'd like to know is why you thought you could sneak him in here. Do you think I'm weak? Too stupid to know when I'm being played?"

Philippe wasn't merely angry, he was furious. All the spit left my mouth.

I'd betrayed his trust. To vampires, loyalty was everything—loyalty to your coven, loyalty to your syndicate—and as Victorine's sire, Philippe was by extension a member of my coven.

I started to apologize, to explain I'd just been trying to discover the truth about Zaquiel Kral's disappearance. But the words died on my lips.

Because I wasn't sorry. Victorine had started this by setting the slayers on the Krals, and Philippe had aided her every step of the way. The way I saw it, that was ten times worse than anything I'd done.

Rafe's eyes were closed. Blood covered his face, seeped through his T-shirt. He'd curled up in a fetal ball, and no longer moved or grunted when they landed a blow. He was either unconscious or so out of it he might as well be.

Something in me broke open. Rafe was hurting.

The hell with begging, or trying to talk my way out of this.

My fangs extended. A livid, animal-like sound erupted from me, torn from a feral part of myself I hadn't even known existed.

I leapt onto the nearest soldier's back and stabbed the stiletto into his arm. When another man tried to pull me off, I jabbed the point into his eye. He swore and fell back, a hand to his bleeding face.

Two more soldiers came at me, a male and a female. At least they'd stopped beating Rafe to fight me. And they were trying to contain me, not take me out, which gave me an advantage.

I dropped into a fighting crouch and backed up they couldn't get behind me—and slammed into rock-solid, living wall.

Philippe.

He grabbed my upper arms. "Drop the knives, Zoe."

"Let me go." I tried to jam an elbow into his ribs, but he easily controlled me.

"Drop the goddamned knives." His grip tightened until I had to bite my lip to keep from crying out in pain. "Now."

"Call your people off." I twisted in his grip. "Rafe's down. He's not a threat to anyone."

"The bastard's really got his hooks into you, doesn't he?" he muttered, but he ordered the men beating Rafe to back off, then gave me a shake. "Now give the knives to Jean-Michel."

I looked down at the stilettos, but I couldn't win against Philippe, Victorine and a roomful of syndicate vampires. I shoved the knives at Jean-Michel.

Victorine hadn't made a sound since that first outraged screech. Now her head swung to me, her eyes rimmed a dangerous blue.

"What. Have. You. Done?"

She didn't wait for an answer. She jerked a stiletto from beneath her skirt and stalked toward Rafe's motionless body.

"*No*." I fought wildly against Philippe's hold. "*Don't*. You have to stop her," I told him. "Please." My voice broke.

"Victorine," he rapped out. "No. We need him alive."

When she didn't seem to hear him, Philippe swore under his breath, shoved me at Jean-Michel with a muttered, "take Zoe," and lunged for her.

The bodyguard grabbed me by the shoulders. "Stop this," he said in his comply-or-else voice, the one I'd been conditioned from childhood to obey.

It halted me long enough to see that Philippe had caught my mother before she'd reached Rafe. I stilled, breath jerking in and out of my lungs.

Philippe snatched the silver blade from Victorine and tossed it to a soldier. "Not in my lair, damn it." He swung her around to face him. "That's not the deal."

She bared long white fangs. "He staked my lieutenant. He dies."

"I don't care what you do to the bastard, but I can't let you send him to the final grave—not here in my own lair. Besides, if his brother fails, we may need him."

On the floor, Rafe groaned. His eyelids fluttered.

Victorine lurched in Philippe's grip, trying to get to him.

"Take him away," her sire snapped at Samir.

"Yes, sir." Samir and two soldiers jerked Rafe to his feet. He swayed, eyes half-closed.

"Release me," Victorine hissed at Philippe. "You have no right to intervene in a blood feud."

"No, cherie." He smoothed a hand down her black chignon. "I'm afraid I can't do that, because if you stake Rafael Kral, his father will come after Zoe. And this time, he might succeed. Is Étan worth that?"

Victorine's chest heaved. Rafe was being dragged, stumbling, toward the door. The look she trained on him should've dropped him where he stood.

"His life is mine."

"Someday," Philippe agreed.

Rafe had recovered enough to dig in his heels. He swung his head around. His gaze locked on mine.

Apology. Sorrow.

And then his cheek creased in a cocky grin. "You're free," he mouthed at me.

Samir kneed Rafe in the balls. "*Enculé.*" Motherfucker.

Rafe grunted and doubled over. Samir and the two soldiers hauled him through the door and down the hall.

The air whooshed out of my lungs.

It was a nightmarish repeat of two years ago, only worse. Rafe was outnumbered, hurting—and I could do nothing to help. And this time, he'd not only been beaten, he'd end up locked in a cell, too.

No.

A silent scream started in my chest and spread to my throat, my head, vibrating in my nerves and pressing against my lungs until I thought I'd suffocate if I didn't release it.

No no nooo...

I bucked in Jean-Michel's grip, desperately trying to get away so I could go to Rafe.

"Calm down," the old soldier gritted.

But I was no longer rational. I slammed my head backward, aiming at his nose, but he managed to jerk back in time so I connected with his chin instead. The shock of the impact exploded through my brain, but I ignored it to keep struggling. He snarled and wrapped me in a bear hug, trapping my arms against my sides. I kicked back, digging my boot heel into his shin.

"Calm yourself, damn it." He dropped his voice to subvocal level. "You're just giving them ammunition."

"Let. Me. Go." I fought harder.

"You want him to suffer? Because if Victorine sees how much you want him—"

That got through to me. I stilled, even though I wanted to go to Rafe so bad I could taste it. But Jean-Michel was right. The more I protested, the more incentive I gave Victorine to hurt him.

Philippe jerked his chin at the remaining soldiers. "Leave. The thralls, too."

They cleared the salon, leaving just me, him, Victorine and Jean-Michel—and Lainey Q.

"That's it," Jean-Michel said. "Compose yourself. You're his only chance," he added under his breath. "Pretend to go along with them. It's the only way you can save him."

I hesitated. Was the bodyguard on our side? Or simply trying to get me under control? But it didn't matter because, once again, he was right. I was Rafe's only chance. I'd already let Victorine see too much.

I couldn't fight all three of them—Philippe, Victorine, Jean-Michel. I needed to calm down, come up with a plan.

"Zoe?" asked Jean-Michel.

I dipped my chin. "I'm okay. You can let me go."

"All right." Jean-Michel released one of my arms but kept a firm grip on the other.

Off to the side, Lainey Q had remained in the salon, watching.

I eyed her. She must have Victorine and Philippe's trust, or else she'd have been removed with the other humans.

A slayer.

I shook my head from side to side.

"Where do you want Zoe?" Jean-Michel asked Philippe.

So I was a prisoner, too. I was still reeling at how fast everything had gone south when Victorine wrenched free of Philippe and grabbed my throat.

"I warned you what would happen if you saw Kral again. I will *not* lose you to a half-breed bastard. And now Étan is in his final grave." She shook me by the throat. "Because of you."

I pressed my lips together. I'd never seen her so angry. My first instinct was to apologize, to make her happy at any cost. Old habits are hard to break.

But that thing inside me that had shattered when they'd beaten Rafe into unconsciousness was still broken and hurting.

And it had had enough.

I'd had enough.

A red-hot fury clouded my vision. Without my volition, my hand shot out, latching onto her wrist.

"Rafe was defending me," I said between clenched teeth. "From *your* lieutenant."

Victorine's jaw dropped. I never talked to her like that. The fingers on my throat loosened.

I shoved her away, and she was stunned enough to allow it.

"Étan *humiliated* me—and you stood by and let him. Your own daughter. You should be thanking Rafe for standing up for me. Neither of you did." I included Philippe in my scornful look. "What I want to know is what in the Dark Lady's name is going on? Because Rafe was right, you broke the truce with the Krals. But why?"

Victorine exchanged a glance with her sire.

My mouth twisted. "Don't hide behind Philippe. Why would he kidnap a Kral if not for you? And why is she here?" I jerked my chin at Lainey. "Rafe said you were working with Slayers, Inc., but I didn't believe that either."

"Zoe," warned Jean-Michel.

At the same time, Philippe snapped, "That's enough, Zoe. *Tais-toi.*"

My fangs pricked out. "I *won't* be quiet," I said, my voice shaking with anger. "I'm through being quiet."

I rounded on my mother. "I defended you. When Rafe told me you might be behind Zaquiel's kidnapping, I was insulted. I told him he was wrong, that you wouldn't have broken the truce. That you wanted peace as much as Karoly. So don't you dare use Étan as an excuse to restart the blood feud. This is on you, not the Krals."

Victorine finally regained her voice. "You ungrateful little viper." She bit out each word separately. "Everything I've done, I've done for you."

"Yeah? That's not how it looks to me. Because when Karoly Kral finds out you're behind Zaquiel's kidnapping, he's going to be out for blood—my blood. All you've done is make me a target. Again."

"Then we'll have to make sure he doesn't find out," Philippe inserted smoothly.

My heart stopped.

I stared at Philippe. It was a threat, pure and simple. Rafe wasn't going to leave that cell alive.

But why had he said they might need Rafe?

Philippe nodded at Jean-Michel. "Take the princess to the yellow guest room."

"Yes, m'sieur." He set a hand on my arm.

I sucked in a breath and made a last-ditch effort to reason with Philippe and Victorine.

"Let Rafe go before it's too late. And if you have his brother Zaquiel, let him go, too. You can't get away with keeping them prisoner. Karoly knows they're in Paris. If you continue with this, he *will* retaliate."

Philippe moved a shoulder in a very French shrug. "I'm counting on it."

I was still trying to figure out what that meant when Jean-Michel hustled me out of the salon.

❦ 20 ❦

RAFE

Philippe's people frog-marched me down two flights of stairs.

I fought to clear my head, but powering a detailed glamour like I had, down to the clothes Zaq had last been seen wearing, was a hell of an energy suck. Suffering a beat down by cold-eyed professionals didn't help.

The adrenaline had worn off, and I was crashing fast.

They shoved me into an small, dank cell. Tiny white lights set in the concrete blocks around the cell's upper edges glowed on. The two men held me against a wall and ordered me to raise my hands. The female clamped silver cuffs around my wrists, securing me to the concrete with my hands on either side of my head.

The burn of the silver shocked me out of my dazed state. The darkness swooped around me. I swallowed queasily.

The three vampires formed a semi-circle around me, their eyes gleaming blue in the dim light. The middle one came at me—a big dude, with cropped dark hair and fists like sledgehammers—and I braced myself for a blow, but all he did was pat me down. He took my phone, which by some miracle was still intact, and the slim silver blade hidden in the sole of my left shoe.

He handed the knife to the female, a curvy blonde with cheekbones that could cut glass, and pressed my thumb to the phone's home button to open it.

He aimed the camera at me. "Smile," he said in French.

I pulled my bloodied mouth into a sneer. "Fuck off."

"Mind your manners." The blond vampire twirled the knife in her fingers. "Or I'll carve my name into your pretty face."

I shook my head in mock-regret. "Sorry, cher, but you're not my type."

She hissed and touched the knife point to my crotch. "Shut. Up."

I froze. The two men chuckled and exchanged a look.

I glared back impotently, but I shut up. Might as well save my strength for whatever was coming.

"That's better." The blond vampire's gaze went to my mouth. Something dark slithered in her eyes. She ran her tongue over her fangs.

I sucked in a breath.

She didn't want to kiss me. She wanted to drink the blood oozing from my split lip.

"Ines," said the man with the phone.

She moved back, her gaze fixed on my mouth.

He raised the phone again. "Smile."

I pasted a fuck-you grin on my face.

He took a couple more pictures before handing the phone to Ines. "Give this to the techs."

She nodded and left.

I swallowed, knowing my family would receive another photo like Zaq's, this time of me. And if Philippe's techs had any brains, they'd change the password so they didn't need my thumbprint and reap any data they could. Fortunately, I hadn't used the phone for anything but to call Tomas.

The shorter vampire had tawny hair and eyes like small brown pebbles. He removed my shoes and tossed them in the hall.

"Not so tough now, are you?" he said in an Italian accent.

I snorted. "Tough enough that it took five of you to bring me down."

He went for me, but the vampire with sledgehammer fists slapped a hand on his chest, stopping him.

"Leave it for now. No need to rush things." The big dude's gaze raked down my torn, bloodied clothes. "It took a week to break your brother." A chilling curve of his lips. "I wonder how long you'll last."

"That's a lie. Zaq escaped because you fucked up." A shot in the dark, but the two exchanged a look. I forced my mouth into another cocky grin. "I'm right, aren't I?"

"Shut it." The big guy slammed a humongous fist into my gut.

My breath whooshed out. I wheezed and pressed back against the wall, silently cursing my smartass tendencies and trying not to pass out.

But I'd confirmed Zaq had escaped.

My assailant regarded me, fingers still curled into a fist. I tensed against another blow, but when I didn't say anything else, he jerked his head at the other guy and they left, leaving me alone in the dark cell.

The tiny lights dimmed.

"It took a week to break your brother."

My bowels iced. Dread licked up my spine.

I set my jaw.

Don't think about it. They're playing head games with you.

I just hoped that Zoe was okay, that they weren't planning to lock her in a cell, too. Even Victorine couldn't be that cold-blooded —could she?

I should probably be ashamed I'd broken my promise to Zoe. She'd sneaked me into Philippe's mansion, and I'd paid her back by staking her mother's lieutenant.

But fuck that. Étan had deserved it. The moment he'd manhandled her, no promise in the world would've stopped me from coming to her defense.

I'd stake that sonofabitch again in a heartbeat.

I rested a cheek against the cool concrete. I could smell the iron-and-salt of my own blood. But something else teased my nostrils, a familiar scent—Zaq's.

The bastards had put me in the same cell.

"It took a week to break your brother."

But he'd escaped. I smiled, even though it hurt. "Hope you took out a few of them on your way out, bro."

My head throbbed, my body ached like a mofo, but I'd already started to heal. Thank the gods I'd fed earlier.

All but my wrists, that is. The silver had already eaten through the top layer of my skin. Soon, the poisonous metal would start to enter my bloodstream...a slow, painful sapping of my strength.

I shifted my position to keep my wrists from pressing too hard against the cuffs, but they were designed to fit snugly.

How in Hades had Zaq busted out of here, anyway? The cell was tightly sealed, with no windows and a fitted door. Unless he'd done a Houdini, someone had helped him.

Maybe the same person would help me, too?

I glanced around as if the walls had answers, but I could barely see my hands on either side of my head. Even a dhampir's eyes require a certain amount of light to see.

I was trapped in a sealed cell, edgy...and getting edgier by the minute. Unable even to pace back and forth to relieve my tension.

Gods, Rafe. You really fucked up this time.

At least I'd taken Étan out before they'd captured me. Zoe could never be forced to mate with that prick.

Too bad I hadn't taken out her mother, too.

I jiggled a knee. Inhaled. Exhaled.

Zaq had survived. I could.

Where was he now? Maybe he was already home. Unless he hadn't escaped, but had been moved to another location.

My lungs constricted.

No. Zaq had escaped. He was safely back in America, being fussed over by Mom. I had to believe that or I'd never survive whatever came next.

I pictured the bite marks on his throat and jiggled my knee harder.

Inhaled. Exhaled.

Peered at the silver cuffs and the bolts securing them to the concrete.

It won't work.

But I had to try.

I took a deep breath and threw my weight into pulling the cuffs from the wall. The poisonous metal ate into my wrists. Agony seared me, followed by the stomach-churning stench of silver and my own burning flesh. I clenched my teeth and tried not to whimper like a baby.

The cuffs didn't budge.

I stopped, regrouped. Eyed the cuffs again.

Could I fade into the shadows to ease the pressure on my wrists, or maybe slip out of the cuffs altogether?

Probably not.

I attempted it anyway, dredging up what little energy I still had to attempt it. But as I'd expected, the silver blocked my magic.

I shifted on my feet and stared into the darkness. Not sure which was harder—waiting for something to happen, or knowing that when it did, it would probably be even worse than this enforced inactivity.

If only I could pace off the tension. I was the kind of guy who was always moving, always doing. Something Zaq and I had in common. As the eldest, Gabriel was the heir-apparent, and Father and Tomas expected more from him. It had made Gabriel a bit of a control freak; he never lost his cool in public, and even in private he was the calm, take-charge brother.

But Zaq and I had more leeway, and we took advantage of it. Zaq might be the big-hearted Kral, but that didn't make him a saint. Whenever he returned from doing his good works, we got together and partied all night, sometimes with Gabriel and sometimes just us two.

I formed my right thumb and index finger into a thumbs-up. "Wherever you are, bro, have a drink for me."

My eyes closed. I slid down the wall, but my weight caused the silver to bite more deeply into my wrists. I groaned and pushed myself back upright.

After that, I drifted in the darkness. Sleep tugged at me, but each time I nodded off, the silver ate into my wrists, forcing me to stand upright. My calves were cramping, and I desperately needed to piss.

The minutes ticked by. Something teased at me. How had Étan known it was a Kral outside Philippe's salon? Jean-Michel had been with them, so Étan had known I was a fake. But he'd said, "Thrice-damned *Kral* bastard."

My eyes popped open.

No one had known I was with Zoe except Tomas and my father. And neither of them would've told the Tremblays I was on my way to Paris with Zoe. It had to be the mole.

Who the hell was it?

Someone high up in the hierarchy, that was for sure. High enough that they'd overheard Tomas saying something, or maybe Tomas had told them himself.

A growl scraped my parched throat. Every single man and woman in the Kral Syndicate had sworn a blood oath of loyalty to my father. The spy had broken a sacred promise.

When my father found out who it was, he or she would be staked. No questions asked, no quarter given.

Unless I found the bastard first, in which case I'd do it myself.

Because I *would* get out of here. And after I'd broken Zoe out, too, I'd damn well find out who'd helped put me here. And then they'd pay.

Night turned into day. Even in the dark, my body sensed the return of the sun.

The cell shouldn't have gotten quieter, but it did. The vampires in the mansion had sought their day sleep.

I licked dry, cracked lips. It was starting to sink in that I was in deep shit. The kind you can't charm or bribe your way out of.

The knife wounds had scabbed over, but they'd been inflicted by silver blades. The healing process had pushed my metabolism into high gear. That feeding at Le Sang Bleu in Pigalle had become a distant memory.

I was so thirsty I'd have drunk from a fucking rat, but Philippe was too clever for that. The cell was clean and completely sealed. Not that I could've caught a rat anyway, restrained as I was.

A glass of blood-wine swam across my vision, joined by a rare steak.

I blinked, and they wavered and disappeared.

Great. Now I was hallucinating.

But that didn't stop my mouth from watering.

I squeezed my eyes shut. When I opened them again, Zoe stood a few feet away, smiling at me.

I smiled back. "You finally stood up to your bitch of a mother. That must've been a helluva shock." I frowned. "But you shouldn't be in my cell. You have to leave before they catch you."

Zoe kept smiling. One of her tentative, I-can't-believe-you-really-want-me smiles.

My chuckle held zero humor. "You're not really here, are you?"

She moved a slim shoulder.

I dragged my gaze from her. When I looked again, she was gone.

I drifted, semi-conscious. Hungering for blood, my mouth so dry it hurt to swallow. Trying to ignore my throbbing wrists, which only made me notice them more.

How long would Philippe leave me here with no food or blood?

Fear clogged my throat.

A dhampir couldn't die from dehydration. But I could go insane.

ZOE

The yellow guest room was across the hall from the library. Jean-Michel didn't release me until I was inside. He closed and locked the door.

Philippe always put me in here. He knew I loved the room's sunny colors and pretty silk bedding. The primrose-sprinkled coverlet was turned down, and the small refrigerator would hold my favorite blood-wines.

I dragged my hands down my face.

How had I not seen that my life was nothing but a series of plush, expensively-decorated prison cells? I might not be bruised and bleeding, but I was as much Victorine's prisoner as Rafe in his concrete-block cell—and had been from birth.

Jean-Michel stood with his back against the thick, silver-reinforced oak door. Not saying anything, just looking at me.

"Go ahead, say it." I lifted my chin. "I'm a traitor. I snuck a Kral into Philippe's lair. If it wasn't for me, Étan would be alive."

The old soldier managed to look both sorrowful and wise at the same time. "Not a traitor. A woman in love."

I made a small, bitter sound. "Tell that to my mother."

He spread his hands. "Victorine is...Victorine. You're not going to change her. But maybe you can find a way to work with her."

"What if I don't want to work with her? What if I want out?"

He pursed his lips. "You don't mean that."

I put a hand to my throat and stared at him. Where had that come from?

For as long as I could remember, my single, all-consuming goal had been to take my place at Victorine's side as her lieutenant. But the past few days had been eye-opening.

I'd felt free. Happy.

Coupled with what I'd found out tonight about my mother and her part in Zaquiel's kidnapping, my entire world had been turned upside down and sideways.

I was no longer sure what I wanted, except that whatever it was, I wanted Rafe to be a part of it. No, I needed Rafe to be a part of it.

"You're free," he'd mouthed.

"Don't I?" I said slowly.

"Stop it." Jean-Michel glanced at the room's single camera.

"They can't hear me. You know this room's not miked."

"Shut up anyhow."

I shrugged and obeyed. I wasn't sure how much Jean-Michel could be trusted anyway.

I sank onto the mattress. Reaction was setting in, and with it the fear that despite what Philippe had said, Rafe wouldn't survive the night.

Because if Victorine had her way, Rafe Kral was dead.

I rubbed my hands up and down my arms, trembling and furious with everyone from my mother on down.

Damn it, Rafe wasn't supposed to get caught. No one was even supposed to know he was in Philippe's lair. We'd planned how this would go down. I'd do the snooping and he'd stay in the background, and we'd leave with no one the wiser.

But Victorine and Étan had known it was Rafe in the hall. I'd heard Étan say his name. Someone had told them he was with me.

I glanced at Jean-Michel. "How did they know it was Rafe there in the hall? His glamour was letter-perfect. Even I thought he looked like you."

His mouth set. For a minute, I thought he wasn't going to tell me, but he must have decided it didn't matter if I knew.

"Someone high up in the Kral Syndicate is working with Victorine."

"Very high up," I muttered.

And very well-informed.

It was as I'd suspected. Holy Dark Lady, this conspiracy had more heads than a hydra. How many people and syndicates were involved? And what else had Victorine not bothered to tell me?

My head spun. I felt unmoored, questioning everything I'd been told about the Krals and the blood feud.

I'd accepted Victorine's story as the truth, but I was an adult now. An adult who, as Victorine's lieutenant-in-training, had seen how far she was willing to go to remain in power.

Looking back, Victorine had never explained *why* Karoly had staked my father. Maybe my father hadn't been the innocent victim Victorine had made him out to be. Maybe he'd attacked Karoly, and Karoly had staked him first.

I massaged my forehead.

One thing was certain. I had to rescue Rafe.

I should be pissed off that he'd jumped in when Étan had started smacking me around. But the woman in me couldn't help swooning a little that he'd risked everything to protect me.

He staked Étan for you. He was defending you.

The hierarchy in a vampire syndicate was clear. Étan was my dominant—no one but Victorine would've stepped in to defend me.

But Rafe had, and I was damned if I'd let him be punished for it. If anyone should be in that cell, it was me.

I pictured Zaq Kral's vampire-marked throat and swallowed sickly.

Jean-Michel was still watching me. I took my hand from my face and rose to my feet, uncomfortable at letting him see my weakness. I'd been trained too well, and I couldn't be sure whose side he was on.

"Excuse me," I said, and went into the bathroom.

The tie holding my ponytail had fallen off, leaving my hair an untidy mass around my face, and the black dress was spattered with blood. My eyes were wide and shocked, and I had fading marks on my cheek where Étan had hit me.

"You're free."

Relief surged up in me, wave upon wave of it. I gripped the edge of the sink, gulping in air.

Thanks to Rafe, Étan was in his final grave. Neither Victorine nor him could force me to accept him as my mate. I told myself I wouldn't have caved to their combined pressure, but I wasn't completely, one-hundred-percent sure.

Rafe had saved me in more ways than one, and I suspected that had been his intention from the moment he'd attacked.

I splashed cold water on my face and glanced at myself a second time. This time, I winced.

You're a princess, Zoe. Act *like one.*

Keeping up my polished image was so ingrained in me that I'd washed my face, brushed my hair, and was reaching for a lipstick when I jerked my hand back like the little metal tube was a live wire.

That was Victorine's voice in my head, telling me I had to be perfect. To always put on my best possible face.

I set my hand on the mirror. The surface was smooth, cold, unforgiving. Like my mother.

I dragged my fingers down the glass, smearing it—and returned to the bedroom without touching up my makeup.

I poured myself a glass of blood-wine and offered the bottle to Jean-Michel, who helped himself to a glass as well. I considered him and decided to take a chance.

"They kidnapped Rafe's brother, you know. You heard Étan. And they were drinking Zaquiel's blood—I saw the photo. Philippe or one of his people. Maybe more than one."

Distaste touched his lean features. "I didn't know."

I stepped closer. "They'll do the same to Rafe if I don't do something. You have to let me out of here."

"I can't. You shouldn't even be asking me."

"Please." My fingers tightened on my glass. "I saw the cell where they held Zaquiel Kral myself."

Jean-Michel blew out a breath. "I'm sorry, Zoe. But I can't."

"Please. You don't have to do anything. Just look the other way."

He set down his glass with a thunk. "I've sworn a blood oath to Victorine. You'd ask me to break it? You think I'm a man of so little honor?"

"No." Appalled, I gaped at him. "I don't think that, not at all. But don't you see? This is bad for everyone in the Tremblay Syndicate. If Victorine's behind Zaquiel's kidnapping, then she broke the truce. Karoly Kral already suspects her. If he can prove it, she'll be in big trouble. And if the other syndicates find out she's working with Slayers, Inc., she could take us all down with her."

It wasn't an exaggeration. The vampire code was simple but harsh. You could lie to another vampire, cheat another syndicate—if you could get away with it—but when it came down to it, you fought your own battles.

You didn't use the slayers to settle scores.

If word got out, Victorine would become a pariah in our world. She'd be seen as weak and lacking in honor. The other syndicates might even band together to take her out.

"Rafael Kral broke into Philippe's lair," Jean-Michel pointed out. "He staked Victorine's lieutenant. Now he has to take the consequences."

"To save his brother," I shot back. "That's the only reason he came to Paris."

"Zoe." Jean-Michel sighed. "Drop it. I can't help you, even if I wanted to. She'd know it was me."

I pulled up short. He was right. Victorine would never buy it. She'd know Jean-Michel had helped me, and this time, his punishment would be even worse.

My stomach sank.

"I'm sorry," I said stiffly. "I shouldn't have asked."

I set down my wine glass and sat on the silk-covered Louis Quinze chair next to the bed, contemplating my little black boots. Jean-Michel stood between me and the door. Even if I somehow sneaked past him, I'd never get to Rafe, even in the shadows. Security would have everything locked down tight.

What had Jean-Michel said about Victorine? That I wasn't going to be able to change my mother, but that maybe I could find a way to work with her.

With Étan in his final grave, the game had changed. Victorine needed me more than ever. I was the only viable candidate for lieutenancy.

Could I pressure her somehow?

I crossed one ankle over another and then froze, staring at my boots. They'd taken my stilettos, *but not my phone.*

The slim rectangle pressed against my inside right ankle.

If only I knew how to get hold of Rafe's father, I could text him. Or I could contact someone I trusted, like Brien, and ask him to pass the message along.

With me vouching that Philippe was holding Rafe Kral prisoner, the Paris Primus would have to get involved.

And Victorine would never trust me again.

My heart thudded in my chest. One slow thump, then another.

How had things come to this?

Dawn was coming. My eyelids closed against my will.

I forced them open. "I'm going to bed," I told Jean-Michel.

He nodded. "Take off your boots, please."

I licked my lips. "Why?"

He crouched and pulled off them off himself. I watched helplessly. It was useless to fight back. He'd call for back-up and the end result would be the same.

"This is why." He palmed my phone and rose to his feet.

My mouth curled. "You call this honor? What they're doing is *wrong.*"

"I'll see you at sunset. I have to lock you in. Philippe's orders."

"You do that," I said bitterly. "I always admired you, you know. After my own father died, I looked up to you. You were about the only person who didn't suck up to me because I was the prima's daughter. I *liked* you. And I respected you because you had integrity."

A muscle worked in his jaw. "Victorine's my prima. I can't serve two mistresses."

Sleep weighted my eyelids. I could no longer resist it.

"Get into bed," Jean-Michel said, not unkindly, and I obeyed because I had no choice.

My last thought was that I'd failed Rafe.

RAFE

Day passed back into night. The door opened and the tiny lights around the cell's perimeter brightened.

My heart bumped against my rib cage. I straightened to my full height.

One man, the Italian guard.

He locked the door behind him.

I waited tensely. My arms might be pinned to the wall, but I still had use of my lower body. He wouldn't take my blood without a fight. He'd win, but at least he'd be hurting.

He stopped a couple feet away. Close enough to knee in the balls.

I showed him my fangs. "Stay the fuck away from me."

He scowled. "You want to use the toilet or not?"

That's why he was here? "Yeah," I said before he could change his mind.

He undid the cuffs and stepped back.

My legs almost gave out beneath me. I stumbled, working out the cramps. But my arms were even worse. They'd gone numb, and moving them was sheer torture. I bit back a groan as I shook them out and brought them to my sides.

"Make it quick." He jerked his head at the cell's tiny bathroom, concealed behind a wall that didn't reach the ceiling.

"Yeah, yeah," I said.

The bathroom was bare bones—a steel sink and a toilet with no lid or seat—but it was a relief being able to move around and take a piss. I washed my face and stuck my head under the faucet to take a drink. The cold water eased my thirst, but somehow made the blood craving even worse.

I gulped down a few mouthfuls anyway, then stuck my wrists under the icy flow, wincing as it hit my raw, reddened skin. But the cold water helped, washing away the silver and easing the burn.

The guard rapped on the chest-high wall between us. "Back against the wall."

I reluctantly obeyed.

As he put the first cuff around my wrist, I attempted a smile. "I don't suppose you have a bloody steak in your back pocket?"

"No." He snapped the other cuff into place.

"How about a glass of blood-wine?"

"No," he said again, and left.

"A man of few words," I muttered at his retreating back.

That was how the next forty-eight hours went. They released me from the cuffs twice a day to use the john and gulp down some water. Other than that, I was left alone in the dark.

I tried not to worry about Zoe. If they hadn't thrown her in a cell, she was probably back in Montreal by now. I only hoped Victorine hadn't banished her to the tower on Midnight Island...or worse.

The silver spread through my bloodstream, seeped into my muscles. I felt hot, then cold. My entire body ached, and my cuts and bruises stopped healing.

Near the dawn of the third day, the door opened, and a male's broad-shouldered silhouette filled the doorway.

A familiar silhouette with short blond hair.

I squinted, trying to make out the man's face. After being in near total darkness for so long, even the hall's low lighting hurt my eyes. Maybe I was hallucinating again.

"Tomas?" My throat was so dry, it came out as a croak. I closed my eyes, looked again.

"Rafael."

A rush of hope surged up in me. I broke into a grin and dropped my voice.

"How the hell—? Never mind. Just get me the fuck out of here."

My eyes had adjusted enough to see details. He wore a T-shirt and rugged tactical pants, both black. With his square face and Slavic cheekbones, he looked like a big blond member of the Russian mafia, the human mafia, that is.

A smile stretched across his face. With Tomas, the wider the smile, the more dangerous he was.

Now it was so wide, I faltered. "Tomas?"

"I am not here to get you out," he said in his precise English.

My spine prickled. "What?"

This was my father's lieutenant. His oldest friend. The man who'd always been there for me and my brothers. Training us. Scolding us. Cheering us on.

I shook my head. He couldn't be an enemy. It wasn't possible.

"Did they capture you, too?" I tried to see past him into the hall.

He held up a blunt-fingered hand. "Wait."

Heels tapped against the concrete floor and Prima Victorine came into sight—and Tomas seemed to be expecting her.

"Ah," he said. "There you are."

The prickle turned to full-blown alarm. All my fine hairs stood on end.

For once, she wasn't wearing a dress. Instead she wore slim black pants, a silky red T-shirt, and short boots with heels so sharp they could've doubled as daggers.

My gaze swung back to Tomas. "What's going on?"

He had that Rafe's-fucked-up-again expression on his face. The one I'd seen more than once as a kid.

"You never could keep the dick in your pants, could you?"

My mouth dropped open. "What the fuck's that have to do with anything?"

"Prima Victorine didn't believe you'd get this far. She thought

Zoe would tell you to go to hell. But I told her that if we give to you enough rope, you will hang yourself. You not only broke into Philippe's lair, you staked the Tremblay lieutenant."

I glanced at Victorine, but I got nothing—her expression was the same cold mask I'd seen more than once on Zoe, although with Victorine, I was pretty sure the ice reached clear to her soul.

I moistened my dry lips. "I don't understand," I said to Tomas. "You're my father's *friend*. Hell, you're practically a member of the family. Why would you help the Tremblays?"

Was Tomas the mole? It seemed inconceivable, but it fit. Étan had not only known that I wasn't Jean-Michel, but that I was a Kral.

And Tomas had known I was in Paris with Zoe. I'd told him myself.

Inside me, a dark fury flamed to life.

Later, I'd come to terms with the fact that the man I considered an honorary uncle had turned against me and my brothers. For now, I was determined to extract as much intel as I could from him.

Because I would escape. And Tomas would pay.

"We have interests in common," Victorine said.

"What interests? What have you done to Zaq?"

"He's in New York," she said.

I was getting more confused by the minute. "But I thought Father's here in Paris."

"He left," said Tomas. "He is supposed to be in New York. Zaq is setting the trap for him."

"What trap? You're planning to stake my father? Your own primus?"

"Not stake him. Save him."

"*Save him?* What the hell are you talking about?"

Tomas had the little smile on his face that was his camouflage. Beneath that smile, he was a cold-hearted S.O.B. But he was supposed to be *our* cold-hearted S.O.B.

My stomach muscles tightened. I felt like I'd taken a gut punch. "You're the mole. The man who's been working with Victorine."

"Yes."

I gaped at him. I'd expected him to deny he was the spy, to tell me I had it wrong. What kind of sick fuck admits to being a traitor? But he seemed proud of it.

"But why?" I asked.

"You make him weak."

"My father? What the hell are you talking about? He's not weak."

"You don't know him like I do. Before you boys, before your mother, Karoly was strong. Ruthless. Now he worries about his family. He makes poor decisions. He makes the syndicate—*our* syndicate—accept his dhampir sons as his heirs."

I stared at him. It was true. My father had named us the Kral heirs despite grumbling from the syndicate's old guard. But that was his right as Kral Primus—which made Tomas a back-stabbing sonofabitch.

He crossed his arms over his broad chest. "He will learn that one by one, you have betrayed him."

"What do you mean?"

"He will turn against Gabriel soon. I've planted information that Karoly will have to believe. And you will disappear after giving the key intel to Prima Victorine."

I glanced at Victorine. "What kind of intel?"

"The location of every Kral coven," she said.

I shook my head. "It won't work. He won't believe I did it."

"No?" said Tomas. "He knows you. That you have the weakness for Princess Zoe. And the women, they are your downfall. He will believe that you were convinced that you had to do it. Perhaps to protect the princess from her mother's anger."

I swallowed, because yeah, my father might believe that I'd done it to protect Zoe, and Tomas was crafty enough to know that and use it against me.

I lifted my chin. "And Zaq?"

"He will set the trap and try to stake your father. He will fail, of course, but Karoly will have to stake him in return. He is Primus. He can't let his own son get away with such an attack."

"That's insane. Why the hell would Zaq stake Father?"

"That is the—how do you say it?—the genius part. Zaquiel

believes Karoly has sicked the slayers on him—and not just him, but you and Gabriel. That's how they broke him. They told him that Karoly has embedded a slayer in Gabriel's staff who will send him soon to his final grave, and that you are next if he doesn't stop your father first. He thinks that slaying Karoly is the only way to save you all."

My stomach lurched. Tomas knew me and my brothers too well. The plan was clever—and convincing. The bastard was using our bond against us.

It felt like the ground I'd trusted, the bedrock that was Tomas, had crumbled beneath my feet and I was in an endless, gut-churning freefall.

"So that was you who texted me in Montreal."

"Yes."

Something occurred to me. "Did you even pass on my message to Father?"

A smirk. "No. And calling him yourself wouldn't have helped. All his calls are being routed to me. He doesn't even know that you're in Paris. I intercepted the photo Philippe's man sent to him."

I jerked at the cuffs, forgetting the silver, forgetting everything but the fury seething in me at his betrayal.

"You thrice-damned son of a serpent." I threw the words at him like the fists I wanted to smash into his lying, grinning face. "Father trusted you. Made you his lieutenant and treated you like family. You swore a fucking oath of loyalty." I sent Victorine a look of loathing. "She must be paying you a helluva lot."

"Victorine pays me nothing." He unfolded his arms and paced closer. "I do not break my oath. But I also do not follow a weak man."

"You won't win. He'll stake you first."

"We shall see. His sons will be dead. He will be strong again. Like a primus should be."

My chest jerked in and out. The depths of Tomas's betrayal was still sinking in, but I turned to Victorine and dredged up a let's-make-a-deal smile. It was the only weapon I had.

"Any chance we can negotiate something here?"

Her upper lip curled. "If it were up to me, I'd have already staked you."

"Yeah, I got that. Loud and clear. But my father's a reasonable man. What do you want in exchange for me? Territory? Gold?"

"Shut up," Tomas snarled.

We both ignored him. Victorine raised a plucked black eyebrow.

"Why would I bargain with Karoly? I hold all the cards."

True—at least, where I was concerned.

I shifted against the wall. "So why are you here?"

And is Zoe all right?

But I didn't ask. Victorine wouldn't tell me anyway, and it would only serve to remind her of Zoe's part in this.

A smile lifted Victorine's lips. The kind of smile that's like an ice pick to the groin. "To remind you of my promise."

Sweat trickled down my spine. For a moment, I was back in the hotel room with Victorine grinding a pointy heel into my solar plexus.

"If you ever touch the princess again, I will consider the truce broken. I won't rest until I've sent you and your brothers to the final death."

"And now you staked my lieutenant." She was a foot away from me now.

She'd regained her composure since the last time I'd seen her. She was pure, ruthless prima. Not a hint of vampire blue tinted her eyes. Instead, they were the unforgiving black of a deep-sea creature.

"I should thank you," she said. "You've given me the perfect excuse to break the truce. We've already leaked the information that a Kral staked the Tremblay lieutenant."

Hell. I suppose I should've seen that coming.

I met her gaze, pretending my insides weren't coated with fear. "To protect your daughter."

Victorine's composure cracked. She hissed. "You have no *right* to protect her, dhampir."

"Go to Hades," I growled back. "We both know you broke the truce first."

"But no one knows that for sure except the people in this lair." She touched a sharp red nail to my carotid.

I locked my knees and glared back, refusing to give an inch.

Victorine let out a slow breath. "We were speaking of my promise. And Rafael? You should know I always keep my promises. But I think"—she pressed the nail a little deeper—"you'll be the last Kral to die. I want you to go to your final grave knowing that your family has been wiped from the face of the earth."

She turned and glided from the cell, the only sound the *tap-tap* of those damn pointy heels.

Tomas shook his head and started to follow her.

I ground my teeth. "You blood-sucking prick. You can try to set us against one another, but you'd better watch your back, because when Father figures out what's going on, he'll hunt you down like a goddamn dog."

Tomas reached out with a big paw to shut the door, closing the two of us in the cell together.

"You're wrong." He prowled back to me. "With you and your brothers dead, Karoly will need me more than ever. I have made sure that the evidence points to Victorine, not me."

A dry laugh scraped my throat. "No, *you're* wrong. You're dead. You're just too stupid not to realize it."

That wiped the smile from his face. His mud-yellow eyes sparked blue. He grabbed my throat with one powerful hand.

"I should break your neck." He stroked my trachea.

My Adam's apple worked.

I was a dhampir—I wouldn't die, but with my human blood I might not heal as cleanly as a vampire, leaving me a quadriplegic. But I knew Tomas. Showing fear could send him over the edge.

"You could." I shrugged like we were discussing the best way to carve a turkey. "But we both know Philippe doesn't want you to kill me yet. He seems to think he might need me."

We stared at each other. His irises were outlined in a bright, neon-blue band now, and his fangs had extended. His fingers tightened on my throat. Then he released me—and smiled.

"You are right. But you are the one who is the prisoner, and no

Kral but me knows you are here. Remember that the next time you call me the stupid one."

He turned and left. The door thumped shut behind him.

I swore and slumped in the cuffs. They seared into my skin, and this time I let them.

❦ 23 ❦

ZOE

The following nights crept by with agonizing slowness. I remained confined to the yellow guest room.

The only person I saw Monday was Jean-Michel, who brought me fresh clothes. When I asked for news of Rafe, all he could say was that he hadn't seen him personally, but that he was still alive and locked in a cell on the lowest level.

After that, Jean-Michel backed out of the room. "I'm sorry, but my orders are to have minimal contact with you."

I spent the rest of the night pacing the damned bedroom until I thought I'd go mad.

Was Rafe all right? Had they drunk from him like they had his brother?

When dawn came, I practically threw myself into the day sleep. Anything to escape from the apprehension churning in me.

Tuesday evening, I came awake to a slow *tap-tap-tap*. Uneasiness trickled through me. My nose twitched at the familiar orange-and-clove scent of Opium.

I clawed myself the rest of the way awake.

Victorine sat on the Louis Quinze chair, tapping a toe of her cherry-red Christian Louboutin booties.

Tap. Tap. Tap. Slow and definite, like a military marching band.

"You're awake." She wore pants, a sign she meant business.

I swiped a groggy hand over my face and pushed myself upright. "How long are you going to keep me in here?"

She swatted the question aside like I was a pesky fly. "I have a task for you."

A jittery ball formed in the pit of my stomach. I swung my legs off the bed. "What do you mean?"

My phone appeared in her hand. "Zaquiel Kral's number has been entered in your phone. I want you to call and tell him we have Rafael. Zaquiel has one week to complete his mission or his brother will be sold to a brothel as blood slave. Zaquiel will believe you. He knows you had a...fling—" her mouth pursed in distaste—"with his brother."

Rafe, a blood slave.

The jittery ball ping-ponged into my chest. All the oxygen seemed to leak out of the room.

"No," I said numbly. "You can't."

"Oh, but I can." She held out the phone.

I pushed it away. "Call him yourself."

She came to her feet. "Don't fight me, Zoe. We both know that won't go well for you. Make the call."

I stood up, too. All I had on was the thin slip I'd worn to bed. It left me at a disadvantage, especially with the high-heeled boots giving Victorine several inches in height.

Work with her.

She held out the phone again. I took it, but made no move to phone Zaquiel.

"You're going about this all wrong," I said. "You've let your hatred of Karoly Kral blind you to everything else. But there are other options."

I took a deep breath—and put it out there. My secret dream. "What if I took Rafe as my mate? His father would have to work with you then. The blood feud would be over for good."

Something dark shadowed her features, but she didn't speak.

I licked my lips and kept going. "Think about it. Imagine how much more power you'd have if we were connected to the Kral Syndicate by a blood tie."

"Mated?" Her mocking chuckle hammered at me and my dream. "With that weak skirt-chaser of a dhampir? You must have oysters for brains if you think I'd agree to that. Now, make the call."

"It could work," I insisted. "It's a strategic mating, one with benefits for both syndicates."

Her eyes narrowed. Her powerful will beat at me. "*Now*, Zoe."

We both knew I'd have to obey in the end—she was my prima, after all, and my dominant—but I dredged up the strength to ask, "And if I refuse?"

"We'll lock you in Rafael's cell. He's shackled to the wall, helpless, and you haven't fed since what—Saturday night? How much longer do you think you'll last before you give in to the craving? A day? A week?" Her smile sent a shudder down my spine. "He might understand, but he'll hate you for it."

No.

My skin went hot and my stomach went cold and my heart forced out blood at a furious rate.

Because she was right. It had been three nights since Rafe and I had fed in Pigalle, and I already craved fresh blood. Blood-wine was a pale substitute for the real thing.

If I was locked in a cell with Rafe, I couldn't be sure my vampire wouldn't capitulate to the blood lust. He might even give me permission to feed from him, but we'd both know it hadn't been a real choice.

I couldn't do that to him.

I fisted my hand on the phone.

"You won't win," I said in a voice as vicious as my mother at her worst. "The Krals are bigger and more powerful than us. This vendetta is going to blow up in your face and you'll take the entire Tremblay Syndicate down with you. When word gets out that you're working with Slayers, Inc., every syndicate in the world will turn against us, but you're too blind to see it."

Her icy reply matched the danger-blue edging her irises. "Make. The. Call."

I obeyed. There was no point in continuing to refuse. If I didn't make the call, she'd have someone else do it, and then throw me in that cell with Rafe.

Forcing me to phone Zaquiel was her way of punishing me.

He answered immediately. A pitch and intonation that was too much like Rafe's, but with an eerie flatness that it hurt to hear.

I explained who I was and why I'd called. Victorine hovered nearby, listening.

"Why are you telling me this?" Zaquiel asked.

My mind blanked. "I—" I glanced at my mother, then lifted my chin. "Because they're forcing me to. But I can tell you that they mean it. If I could help, I would."

Victorine's lip curled.

"Then get him away from them," said Zaquiel.

I swallowed. "I can't," I said lowly.

"I see." His disbelief smeared me from three thousand miles away. "Tell them I'm already in New York," he said, and ended the call.

Victorine thrust out her hand. "The phone."

I handed it over. "Tell me something. Did you ever love me? Or have I always been just another piece on your gameboard?"

Her face tightened. Something moved way back in her eyes. For a moment, I thought I'd gotten through to her, but she stalked out without answering.

"Yeah," I told the closed door. "That's what I thought."

I went to the sideboard and picked up a wineglass. But instead of pouring myself some blood-wine, I stared at the glass. Hearing that voice in my head about what a princess does and doesn't do.

I drew back my arm and hurled the glass at the door.

⁂

It was Thursday evening before I saw my mother again. I'd been awake for over an hour, but I was still in bed staring at the ceiling, thinking.

How could I get Victorine to see that her obsession with the

Krals wasn't just a problem for me, but for the whole Tremblay Syndicate? That if she didn't change course, she was going to take us all down with her?

There was a perfunctory knock on my door, and then Victorine strode inside.

"Get up. We leave for Montreal in a few hours."

"What?" I bolted upright.

"We're leaving," she repeated impatiently.

I brushed my hair back from my face. "Now?"

My mind worked. This might be the chance to escape I'd been waiting for.

She gave a curt nod. "We'll be traveling part of the time during the day, but that can't be helped. I've arranged for a closed box for you to travel in."

Jean-Michel followed Victorine into the room and held the door open. I grabbed a bathrobe from the foot of the bed and shrugged into it as two of Philippe's people carried in a stainless steel box.

I swallowed a spurt of panic.

As usual, my mother had thought of everything. Locked in a box, I'd have absolutely no hope of escape.

And here I'd thought things couldn't get any worse.

The vampires set the steel box down by the wall and left. Jean-Michel followed, leaving me alone in the room with Victorine.

"When we get back to Montreal," she said, "you'll be confined to Isle de Minuit for the next year. If that doesn't cure you of this... attraction, you can stay there for the next decade as far as I'm concerned. With your new mate."

"My new mate?" I repeated.

Étan was dead, and Rafe clearly wasn't an option.

A smug smile. "Several men have expressed interest. You're a prize, cherie."

Dread wrapped itself, serpent-like, around my chest. "What about your promise to let me choose my own mate?"

"You clearly aren't capable of it. So, I'll be interviewing your suitors when we return. They're all strong men who can impregnate you. I don't need you, Zoe. I can take your spawn and raise him or her to be my lieutenant."

I'll kill you first.

I kept my mask firmly in place, but inside, whatever love I'd felt for Victorine shriveled to nothing. She'd finally gone too far.

I would *not* mate with a man I didn't love, and I was *damned* if I'd allow Victorine to raise any spawn of mine.

I had allies in the Tremblay Syndicate, vampires who'd back me when I let the world know what my mother had done. When we got back to Montreal, Victorine would have a civil war on her hands.

But first, I had to get out of Philippe's lair and back to my home territory, even if it meant leaving Rafe behind.

"As you wish," I said expressionlessly.

I waited until Victorine had left. Only then did a few tears trickle down my face.

Because I didn't want to leave Rafe behind. It would take time to organize any kind of resistance against my mother.

Time Rafe didn't have.

I scrubbed the tears away and went into the bathroom to wash my face. I'd learned a long time ago that crying got you nothing but red eyes and a stuffy nose.

After that, I downed two glasses of blood-wine in rapid succession. It wasn't the same as fresh blood, but it was better than nothing.

I needed to be strong, to be the woman Rafe seemed to see in me.

To be the woman I wanted to be.

I took a shower and pulled on some underwear. When I returned to the bedroom, Lainey Q was seated on the Louis Quinze chair filing her nails.

She grinned. "Hello, love."

I expelled a breath. "Go away, Lainey."

"I don't think so." She stowed the nail file in a pink-and-black designer bag. "Get dressed." She lobbed a black dress and a pair of little black socks at me. "We have to talk."

I caught the clothes. "I don't need a stylist," I snarled. "I need a fucking fairy godmother."

"Or a slayer," she said.

I narrowed my eyes. "What's that supposed to mean?"

A shrug. "Get dressed. Then we'll talk."

I got dressed. Lainey watched closely as I sat on the chair to put on my boots.

I stilled. My silver stilettos were back in their sheaths. I glanced at her.

Her mouth curved in a half-smile I couldn't interpret. "Vampire chic." She waved a hand at my outfit. "I like it. The stilettos are a nice touch."

I growled. "Take a picture."

"Maybe I will." Her hand went to her purse.

I eyed the stilettos. Itching to pull one out and slit her silly throat.

"Tonight," I said in a cold voice, "is not a good night to fuck with me."

Lainey stared back, unconcerned. I didn't even sense an increase in her heartbeat. And she seemed different—calmer, less empty-headed, her whole vibe more self-assured.

I straightened in the chair. "Who are you—really?"

"Lainey Q. Stylist to the stars—and a frickin' awesome slayer, if I say so myself."

"Why are you here in a vampire's lair?"

"Not to stake you, if that's what you're thinking."

"I didn't think you were. Unless Karoly sent you."

"Nope."

My lungs compressed. "Rafe," I breathed. "You're here for Rafe."

She looked back without speaking, but I knew I was right. I'd have realized it sooner, if I hadn't been thrown off by the fact that she'd attached herself to me, not him.

My fangs pricked at my gums. I eyed the stilettos again. I was faster and stronger. I could kill Lainey before security had time to react.

But that wouldn't save Rafe. They'd simply assign another slayer to kill him. Once Slayers, Inc. got a contract, they always followed through.

If my mother didn't get him first.

"So you don't work for Victorine."

"No." She stiffened her spine, insulted. "I work for Slayers, Inc."

"But you were in Montreal with Victorine's permission. And now here you are in Philippe's lair." The evidence was piling up. My mother was in this up to her eyeballs. "How did you know Rafe was in Paris?"

She examined her nails. "That would be telling, wouldn't it?"

"You didn't say anything at the Crimson Ball."

"Rafe was at the ball? I figured he never showed up."

I stared at her. "You knew he was in Montreal."

She nodded.

"So a Kral is working with you and my mother. Someone high up." I was curious if she'd verify what Jean-Michel had told me.

A mocking smile. "Very good, Princess."

My jaw tightened. Never had I wanted to use compulsion on a human so bad. Too bad Lainey was immune.

"Tell me one thing. Did Victorine always mean to break the truce?"

She moved a shoulder. "I have no idea what she intended, but I can tell you that she only came to us last year."

A year after that summer in Montreal. By then, it must have been clear to her that I wasn't going to get over Rafe, especially after I'd tried to see him in New York.

"So everything Rafe told me was true. Victorine's working with Slayers, Inc. to take out him and his brothers."

"Did he tell you that? Guess there's some brains to go with that smokin' body."

My hands fisted. "Shut up."

"Or what?" A taunting smile. "You're not in charge anymore, Princess. Now get in the box. Victorine's orders."

I raised my chin. "I want to see Rafe first."

"He's fine. Now get in the goddamned box." She dropped her voice and said without moving her lips, "I'm here to get you out."

My eyes widened.

"Don't act surprised," she warned. "Just nod."

I scrutinized her, but her face gave away nothing.

I obediently dipped my chin. "You want me to get in the box."

"Yes," Lainey replied in a normal tone, then dropped her voice again. "Just long enough for me to freeze the cam for a few seconds. Then I'll let you out of the box. You hide in the bathroom, and I'll restart the cam before I leave. When I open the door to the hall, you can follow in the shadows. I'll leave a side door on the ground floor ajar."

She gave me the door's location.

"What about Rafe?"

"They'll be switching guards on the lower level in exactly six minutes. You can rescue him first, or leave him behind. Your choice."

I met her eyes. "I'll need time to get him free of the cuffs."

She considered that. "A power failure would do it."

"You can do that?"

"Of course. But the mansion's backup power will come on in thirty seconds."

I stared at her. Why would a slayer help us? But I had no choice but to trust her. "Thank you."

"Don't worry. You'll owe me."

"Anything."

A sly, very satisfied smile. "Excellent. I'll be waiting on Pont Notre-Dame with tickets and fake IDs for you both. Now if you'd get inside..." She gestured toward the steel box.

I climbed into it and crouched down. Lainey started to lower the lid.

"Oh, and Zoe?" she said. "Back in Pigalle, thanks for calling Rafe off. He caught me by surprise. You're not as cold as you want people to believe, are you?"

"It would've been too much trouble to dispose of your body."

She laughed and shut the lid.

I had a bad moment when things went dark. If Lainey had lied and engaged the box's lock, I'd be on my way back to Montreal by morning, leaving Rafe to fend for himself.

A heartbeat passed, then another. Four of my heartbeats all together while I listened tensely for the snick of the lock engaging.

I set my hands on the lid, straining to hear what was happening through the half-inch-thick steel. My reflexes were ten times faster than a human's. If Lainey did attempt to lock me in here, I'd have a fraction of a second to react, but that would be enough time enough to shove the lid into her lying face.

The lid lifted. I was never so glad to see someone's face. "You have three seconds to get in the bathroom," she whispered.

I made it in two.

She shut the lid again and opened the door to the hall, and I faded into the shadows and slipped past her.

"See you later," she said to Jean-Michel with a cheery, very-Lainey wave.

I took off without waiting to hear his response.

I raced through Philippe's apartment and down to the lower level. This time I didn't dare create a disturbance to get through the locked door to the cells. I pressed my back to the wall and waited for the change in guards.

Five minutes that felt more like an hour ticked by. At last, a guard appeared and opened the door. I darted into the hall after him.

"Blaise." The guard on duty nodded at his relief.

"Everything all right?" Blaise asked.

"Yeah. He's been quiet."

Blaise grinned and tapped a control, releasing Rafe's door. "Let's see if we can wake him up."

The door swung open. Rafe lifted his head and squinted at them.

My stomach knotted. It was Jean-Michel all over again. The cuts and bruises from the fight had mostly healed, but the silver had eaten away at Rafe, turning him into a gaunt, underweight version of himself.

"Hey, pretty boy," Blaise taunted in English. "How are those wrists?"

Both guards snickered as I ghosted around them into the cell.

"I've got it now," Blaise told the other guard in French. "Have a good evening."

"You, too."

Blaise waited until the main door closed behind the other guard, then reached out a long leg and kicked Rafe in the chin.

The back of Rafe's head banged against the wall. He hung there for a moment, breathing hard.

Blaise sneered. "Not such a smartass now, are you?"

Tarbanak.

Rafe lifted his head. "Go fuck yourself," he said wearily.

I marked the location of the cell's two cameras in my mind and waited for the power to go out.

Five seconds. Four. Three...

The cell's tiny lights went dark. I dropped into the physical world, a stiletto in each hand, and exploded into action.

First the cameras. I shot back and forth in the pitch-black cell, smashing the camera lenses with the hard ebony handle of one of the stilettos. That should buy us a few minutes before security came to investigate.

The snick of a switchblade made me spin around. Blaise was close enough to feel his breath on my face.

I threw myself down and to the left. The lethal silver blade slicked past my right shoulder about where my chest would've been.

I landed in a crouch at his feet. I bounded back up, brushing his abdomen with the back of my left hand to orient myself. I followed that with a sharp thrust of the stiletto in my right hand, shoving it beneath his ribcage and into his heart.

His body jerked. He slashed out with the switchblade. I released the stiletto and jumped back, narrowly avoiding the sharp silver point.

Blaise let out a savage curse in French and crumpled to the floor. The switchblade clattered to the concrete beside him.

Behind me, Rafe snarled. "Who's there? What the fuck's going on?"

I didn't reply. I crouched down and felt for the Bluetooth earbud hooked onto Blaise's ear, smashed it beneath my heel, then jerked my stiletto from his chest and wiped it on his shirt.

"Answer me," he demanded.

"It's me. Zoe." I sheathed the blades in my boots and went to Rafe.

"Zoe?" I felt him reach for me, then hiss. The scent of raw, silver-bitten flesh filled the cell.

The lights came back on.

Thirty seconds down. How much time did we have now?

"Zoe." He closed his eyes. "Crap. I'm dreaming, aren't I?"

I sucked in a breath at the angry wounds the cuffs had burned into his wrists.

"No dream." I touched his face. "It's really me."

His mouth contorted in a heart-breaking imitation of his lopsided smile. "Yeah?"

I wanted—no, needed—to press my body to his, to give him a hard, I-love-you kiss. But the clock was ticking. Now that the power was back on, security would be here any minute to investigate the broken cameras.

Rafe was still staring at me like I was a ghost.

"Hey." I brushed a kiss over his mouth. "I'm really here."

His lips clung to mine. "You're really here," he repeated.

"Yeah." I was growing worried. What had they done to him?

He looked past me at Blaise's disintegrating body. "Nice work, badass."

"Somebody had to save your butt." I wasn't in a joking mood, but it was that or give in to my horror at how bad he looked.

"You're my hero. Tell me you can open these cuffs."

"There's a trick to it." Which I prayed I remembered.

I felt along the silver band on his right wrist, barely registering the burn on my fingertips. Philippe hadn't made it easy for even his own people to release a prisoner. I located the two almost-imperceptible buttons and held them down at the same time.

"There." A metallic click and the cuff released.

Rafe hissed and brought his arm down. I released him from the other cuff and stepped back. He tried to move his arms, winced. He set his mouth and shook them out, then took a stumbling step forward.

I caught him by the shoulders and steadied him.

"Oops." Another crooked grin. Beneath my hands, he was trembling.

I managed to smile back. "Take it easy, hotshot."

He was too weak. He needed fresh blood.

But that wouldn't protect him if we were caught on the way out. The only thing that might save him was for us to mate. Even Victorine would think twice before staking my mate. If Rafe was my true mate—and I was counting on the fact that he was, because I wouldn't know for sure until we swore the blood oath—the bond between us would be unbreakable.

The only way she could break it would be to kill Rafe, and the mate bond was too rare and special for even a prima to reject without a huge blowback. The entire Tremblay Syndicate would rebel if she tried.

To vampires, the oath sworn between true mates was sacred.

Plus, those "strong men" whom she'd lined up as possible mates would probably refuse to take a woman whose mate had been ripped from her that way. For one thing, there was a good chance that if I lost Rafe after we'd bonded, I'd never have spawn.

I rubbed Rafe's shoulders, conscious of the huge step I was about to take.

A Tremblay mating with a Kral would send repercussions across the vampire world. The delicately balanced alliances of the past century would be shaken. But it was the only way forward that I could see.

The only way to save Rafe from my mother's vengeance.

The only way to stop the blood feud once and for all.

The only way I could have Rafe.

"Drink." I pulled down the dress's neck, presenting my throat to him. "Before they come to see why the cameras aren't working."

His gaze went to my throat. "You're offering me your blood?"

"Yes." I moved closer, touched his cheek. "Bond with me. Swear the oath."

"You want me to be your thrall?" With an obvious effort, he tore his gaze from my throat to look at me.

"No, no." I'd done this all wrong. I glanced at the closed door. How much time had passed? I took a steadying breath. "Not my thrall, my mate."

"Your mate." There was a pause that seemed to go on forever, but that was probably just a few seconds. "You're sure?"

His fangs had already extended, and he'd stopped trembling. His gaze locked on my throat again. A flush of arousal touched his cheekbones.

"Yes. Drink, damn you." I wrapped my hand around his nape, dragging him toward me. "Maybe it's not what you want, but it's the only way to stop Victorine from staking you."

"Zoe." His mouth was an inch from my neck, but he lifted his head to meet my eyes. "I do want it."

I swallowed thickly. What was the catch?

But he was sincere. I could see it on his face, hear it in his voice.

A lightness filled my chest.

He cupped my face. "I want you more than I can say. I always did. It was you who didn't want me."

He trailed his lips down my throat and sank his fangs into my carotid. My heart thumped. I'd never had anyone feed from me before. I wasn't prepared for the punch of lust. I was instantly wet and ready.

Rafe gave a sexy growl and shoved me up against the wall without lifting his mouth. His hand squeezed my breast, sending a hot lick of pleasure to my clit. His powerful body pressed me into the concrete, his cock long and hard against my belly.

He could've taken me right there and I'd have let him. It was agony to stop him. But we were almost out of time.

"Rafe." I pushed at his chest, silently wishing my mother to Hades, along with Philippe, Tomas and the entire organization of Slayers, Inc. "The guards will be here any minute. We have to go."

He groaned and thrust his pelvis against mine. A shudder wracked him. But he stopped drinking and lifted his head.

His gorgeous, too-thin face was somber. Midnight eyes burned into mine.

"By the Dark Lady and the moon She rules, I, Rafael Kral, take you, Zoe Tremblay, as my mate. My body is yours. My heart is yours. My soul is yours. I will cherish you forever. This oath I swear on my blood and yours."

He took another long suck.

His words seemed to reverberate in every part of me.

The lightness in my chest expanded. I felt warmth, connection, unconditional acceptance, all wrapped up in the cocky charm that was Rafe Kral.

I wrapped my arms around him, caressing his nape and staring down at his curly dark head.

Loving him with all the strength of my starved and lonely heart.

He licked the small wound, healing it with the special enzymes in his saliva, then spun us around so he was against the wall.

"Now you." He bared his throat to me.

I set my lips to his skin, licked. He tasted of sweat and fear and arousal.

I sank my fangs into his carotid and, mindful of his still-healing body, took just enough to fill my mouth with his blood.

It was rich, salty. Perfect.

I swallowed and gave him my oath. Swearing to cherish him forever.

Offering him my heart and body and soul, although he already owned all three.

The sense of connection between us increased. I could tell he felt it, too.

He curled a hand around my nape. "I love you, Zoe Tremblay."

The lightness spread to my face until I was grinning like a fool. "I love you, too."

And I knew. He was my true mate.

Rafe kissed me. A sweet, knee-weakening kiss that reached

inside me and tore me apart at the same time it healed and reformed me into something new.

A woman who loved and was loved.

When he lifted his head, we stared into each other's eyes. He looked as stunned as me.

"Okay. Yeah." He cleared his throat. "Tell me you have a plan for getting us out of here."

"There's a side door open for us. You have enough strength to enter the shadows?"

"I'll be okay, don't worry."

I bit my lower lip. I didn't like it, but we had no choice but to get the hell out of here.

I gave him the directions to the side door Lainey had promised to leave ajar. "Meet me on Pont Notre-Dame. You know where it is?" It was the bridge nearest the Notre Dame Cathedral, about a half-mile from Philippe's mansion.

"Yep." Rafe snatched up Blaise's switchblade and gestured to the exit. "After you, sweetheart."

Sweetheart. I liked the sound of that.

We peered out the cell door. At the end of the hall, the main door slammed open. A pair of guards rushed toward us.

"Now," I hissed.

We faded into the shadows as they burst into Rafe's cell.

24

RAFE

I reached the Pont Notre-Dame first and dropped out of the shadows near a cast iron lamp post, camouflaged by the weak glamour that was all I could manage. To make it easier, I kept my own T-shirt and jeans, although I had to conceal the tattered, bloodstained material. I also added a pair of fake shoes, since I was in my stocking feet. The pricks had never returned my boots.

Zoe materialized a few yards away and pulled her own human-appearing glamour over herself. But it was still her beautiful face and willowy body in the snug black dress and funky boots.

My chest clenched. *My mate.*

I was still getting used to the idea that this smart, strong, sexy woman wanted me as much as I wanted her. I half-expected to wake up and find I'd hallucinated the whole thing—my rescue, our mating.

But I could still taste the hot spice that was Zoe on my lips, telling me this was real life. In my veins, her blood mingled with mine to heal the silver's damage.

And I *felt* her through the soul-to-soul link that had formed when we'd bonded to each other.

I'd wondered how you'd know when you found your true mate.

But it was obvious, like getting smacked in the heart by a two-by-four.

Zoe immediately zeroed in on me. I had a feeling she'd always be able to find me in a crowd, glamour or no glamour, and vice versa.

Her eyes lit up, but instead of joining me, she tipped her head at a small woman—Lainey Q, looking like just another American tourist from her flowered backpack to the pink high tops.

Right. If you believed that, I was standing on a bridge you might like to buy.

My hand went to Blaise's switchblade, but Zoe gave a little shake of her head. Meanwhile, Lainey started across the bridge toward the Notre Dame Cathedral.

"Follow her," Zoe mouthed and started after her.

I fell in line behind the two women. Apparently, I'd fallen down the rabbit hole and landed in Bizarro World.

The daughter of my father's greatest enemy was my mate.

My father's lieutenant and best friend was the man I was running from.

And the woman helping us was from Slayers, Inc.

Halfway across the bridge, Lainey stopped and rested her forearms on the railing, looking out at the Seine. Zoe stopped a few feet away and gazed out at the river as well. I inserted myself between the two women. Just because Zoe seemed to trust the slayer didn't mean I did.

Behind us, a steady stream of pedestrians, bicyclists and vehicles traveled over the bridge. Music from a Left Bank café wafted across the water, entwined with the low hum of traffic and conversation.

Lainey shrugged out of the backpack and set it on the sidewalk at my feet. She leaned on the railing again, watching as a late-night tour boat passed beneath the bridge, its passengers snapping photos of the scaffolding surrounding Notre Dame's burnt-out shell.

"You'll find passports and tickets to New York," she said in an undertone, her lips barely moving. "The plane leaves a little after midnight. You'll have to hurry."

Before I could answer, someone bumped into me. I whipped my head around, fangs out, but it was just a middle-aged human male.

"Pardon," he muttered without looking at me and kept going.

Zoe set a hand on my forearm, wordlessly cautioning me to relax. I forced my shoulders to ease and retracted my fangs.

"Go," said Lainey. "They probably don't know Zoe is gone yet, but they'll be looking for you, Kral."

"Why should we trust you?" I gazed out at the Seine. "All you have to do is give Victorine or Philippe the info on the tickets, and we'll be picked up at the airport."

She expelled a breath. "Why the fuck would I help you get away from them if I wanted you to be captured?"

"I don't know. Why *did* you help us?"

"Because this vendetta against your family is wrong. It's not what I signed up for. But hey, there's a thousand euros in the pack. Burn the tickets and use the cash to disappear—I don't care."

"Maybe we will."

"Your choice. But I stuck my neck out for you. I'm going to have to start over now with a new cover because Lainey Q is compromised—and I put a hell of an effort into creating her. Those millions of followers on Insta didn't just show up overnight, and I was starting to trend on TikTok." Her voice held a pout.

Was she for real? I eyed her, trying to determine if she was seriously upset about losing her followers. She sure seemed to be. It was insane, but that sulky purse of her bubblegum-pink lips went a long way toward making me trust her. It was so un-slayerlike.

On my other side, Zoe asked, "What do you mean, you didn't sign up for this?"

"SI's mission is to rid the world of the sick vampires, the psychos who are truly evil or are lost to the blood craving. You may not like us, but it's necessary. We keep things in balance. Without us, vampires would've enslaved the humans by now, or been hunted to extinction—and either way, both races lose. But this vendetta against the Krals is effed up." She shook her head. "Rafe's father pushed back against some things that were clearly wrong—and pissed off someone at the top."

She glanced at me. "That's the real reason you and your brothers are being targeted. Victorine just provided the money, and the perfect cover. If something goes wrong, the Board of Directors will pin it on the blood feud."

My lips twisted. "Some mission. You're worse than the syndicates. At least we're honest about what we do."

She moved a shoulder in a small shrug. "Hey, it's not me calling the shots. Like I said, it's not what I signed up for. It doesn't help that you guys are dhampirs."

"So we're not pureblooded enough for Slayers, Inc.?"

"It's...complicated."

"Explain it to me in words of one syllable."

She sighed. "The rank-and-file slayers are cheering you on—half of us are dhampirs, after all. We'd be happy to see you three take over your father's syndicate. It's the vampires who are jealous. You're too famous—the Kral Dark Angels. They hate that the humans love you, that you've connected with them in a way a vampire never could."

My hands tightened on the rail. "Well, fuck them, too."

Like it was fun being targeted from birth for something you had no control over.

"Now, go." Lainey made a shooing motion with her hand. "Or we're all going to end up guests in Philippe's posh little concrete cells."

"Wait," I said as she turned to leave. "What about my brother Zaq? Do you know where he is?"

She shook her head. "He escaped from Philippe somehow. That's all I know."

"That's not what Mraz said. He said Zaq didn't escape, that he was released. That he's in New York to stake my dad."

Beside me, Zoe stiffened. I shot her a glance but she gave a tiny shake of her head.

"Is that so?" Lainey asked. "That's the first I've heard of it. We're only given the details of our own mission."

She was telling the truth. I sensed her sincerity.

"So you don't know if he's been brainwashed into thinking my father is behind the attacks on us?"

She tilted her head like a cute, silver-feathered bird. "Is that what they told you? Clever. But I can tell you this much. The slayers are looking for Zaquiel, too—in the States."

"So he's in America?"

"Last I heard."

So Zaq had gotten back to America. But he hadn't attacked my father yet, or Victorine would've rubbed it in my face. At least, that's what I told myself.

I held out my hand to Lainey. "Thank you. The Krals owe you a blood debt."

She shook it. "I'll hold you to that."

Her grin was all teeth. Suddenly, she didn't appear all that cute. She looked like one of those vicious pint-sized dogs.

I released her hand. "I'll make sure Father knows."

"Karoly Kral in my debt." Lainey chuckled. "My friends at SI won't believe it."

Zoe leaned past me to ask, "What about the contract on Rafe?"

My brows crawled into my hairline. This was the slayer they'd sent to kill me? I didn't know whether to laugh or be insulted.

"The contract's still mine. I'm not leaving SI—I'm part of the resistance. Although you didn't hear that from me. But I need time to establish a new cover, don't I?" A slow smile. "Who knows what will happen between now and then? Ciao, you lovebirds."

She slipped into the crowd and was gone.

I picked up the backpack, but Zoe didn't move. She gazed out at the dark water, jaw set. "There's something I have to tell you. About your brother."

I set the backpack down. "Zaq?"

She dipped her chin. "Two nights ago Victorine came to my room and ordered me to call him. He's okay," she hurried to say. "But she forced me to pass on a message—that he has one week to complete his mission or you'd be sold to a vampire brothel."

I growled under my breath. "So he definitely didn't escape."

"Yeah. They released him. I'm sorry," she added, a miserable look on her face. "I tried to talk her out of it. I even pointed out that it would be to the Tremblay Syndicate's advantage if we mated.

But I didn't have a choice—if I hadn't made the call, someone else would've."

"Hey. It's okay. If I were you, I'd have done the same thing." I tucked a strand of black hair behind her ear. "What did Zaq say, exactly?"

"'Tell them I'm already in New York.'"

I considered that. "All right. That could be good, actually. He's in our home territory—he probably knows the city better than anyone they have monitoring him. He didn't say anything else?"

"Just that if I loved you, I should get you away from them. But I couldn't, Rafe. They had me in a locked room with a twenty-four hour guard. If Lainey hadn't helped me escape, I'd be on my way back to Montreal in a steel box."

"You're fucking kidding me." I hadn't realized how close we'd come to being separated. "Your mom was sending you back to Montreal in a box?"

Her hands fisted at her sides. "Yeah."

Gods. I shook my head. "You'll never have to face her alone again. That's a promise."

In the darkness, Zoe's eyes were pools of dusky gold. "Yeah?"

Reaching for the fist closer to me, I brought it to my mouth and touched my lips to her knuckles. "We're a unit now, sweetheart."

A wondering curve of her lips. "I guess we are."

I couldn't resist that smile. I cupped her nape and pulled her in for a kiss, then asked, "Your mother said Zaq had one week? And that was two nights ago."

"Yeah—Tuesday night."

"And it's Thursday now. That gives us five days to find him—if he hasn't already attacked my father."

"So that's his mission? To stake Karoly?"

I lifted a shoulder, let it drop. "That's what Mraz said."

"Lieutenant Mraz? He's the double agent?"

"Yeah," I said grimly. "He paid me a visit last night, along with your mother."

Zoe's shock was clear. Victorine obviously hadn't kept her in the loop on any of this.

"In Philippe's lair?" she asked. "Your father's lieutenant?"

"Yep." I hefted the pack again. Standing on this busy bridge was making me itchy. "I'll tell you the whole story when we're alone."

I glamoured the brightly flowered backpack so it was a worn, nondescript khaki, and we headed north, putting more space between us and Saint Germain.

That's when I had an idea, a way to buy us a little time to come up with a plan for dealing with Victorine. But we'd have to act fast.

Zoe raised a hand to hail a taxi.

"Hang on." I grabbed her arm. "I may have a way to get your mom off our backs. But we have to find Lainey before she shuts down her social media accounts."

Zoe's brow knit, but she nodded and took off with me. We passed at high speed through the crowd.

For a short woman, Lainey could move fast. By the time we caught up with her, she was almost across the island on which Notre Dame Cathedral was located.

I dropped my glamour and came alongside her.

She glanced at me and did a double take. "What the fuck? Are you trying to get me killed?"

I grabbed her arm and dragged her onto a side street. "You said your Lainey Q cover is blown, right? But before you shut everything down, can you do one last thing? Take some pics of me and Zoe and put them up anywhere you want. Hell, sell them to the goddamn tabloids. If that's okay with Zoe."

I glanced at my new mate. She stared back like I'd suggested stripping down to our underwear and jogging up the Champs-Élysées.

"No, it's not okay. Are you trying to put a target on our backs?"

"It's already there." I raised a hand, palm out. "Hear me out, okay? It's the perfect way to spike your mother's guns. Put the two of us out there everywhere. The Tremblay Ice Princess and a Dark Angel—in love and mate-bonded. The humans will eat it up."

Already, a trio of French teenagers was eyeing me and Zoe. They were too cool to approach us, but one pointed her phone at us.

"Hm," said Lainey. "'Angel Thaws the Ice Princess's Heart.' 'Ice Princess Melts for her Dark Angel Lover.'" She chuckled. "I like it."

Zoe groaned and passed a hand over her face.

"Think about it," I told Zoe. "The whole world will be cheering us on. Victorine has to find out sometime that we've mated. You said yourself it's the only way. This way, she'll be forced to deal with it. There will be no fucking way she can kidnap you, lock you up and pretend it didn't happen."

"Mated?" asked Lainey. "Congrats, you two."

"Thanks," we said without looking at her.

Zoe had paled at the suggestion her mother might kidnap her.

Fury balled in my stomach. For two cents, I'd stake Victorine and rid us both of her for good. Not that I'd ruled that out, by the way. But first, we'd try diplomacy and a little old-fashioned strong-arming.

"It could work," Zoe said. "But Victorine will go ballistic."

"She'll go ballistic no matter what we do. This way the whole world will know we're mates, including both our syndicates."

Zoe nodded. "She'll be furious hearing about this on social media."

I grinned evilly. "Yeah."

"But it *will* make it impossible for her to attack you without repercussions. But what about you, Lainey? What will your bosses say when they realize you were this close to Rafe and didn't stake him?"

"No problem," she answered. "I'll tell them I couldn't risk it, not with you right there. They'll know by then the two of you mated, and they'd know you'd defend him to the death."

"I would." Zoe took my hand in a fierce grip. "Okay, I'm in. Let's do it."

"Awesome." Lainey whipped out her phone and snapped several shots, including one of me deep-kissing Zoe.

Take that, Victorine.

"I'll tag you both," she said as she returned the phone to her pocket.

"Can you wait to post them until tomorrow?" I asked. "Give us some time to get out of Dodge. And make sure you mention that we're mated."

"Oh, I will. I wish I could be a fly on the wall when Victorine hears about this." She grinned. "Don't try and contact me. You won't be able to find me anyway." She walked off, a jaunty swing to her hips.

"I'm thinking we shouldn't use those tickets to New York," said Zoe. "She might believe they're clean, but who knows what her Board of Directors is up to."

"Whatever we do," I said, "I have to get to a phone. There are things my father has to know ASAP."

Like that Tomas was a traitor, Gabriel had a slayer embedded in his staff—and Zaq was trying to kill him.

Zoe went motionless. She nudged me and nodded at the main street.

Jean-Michel eyed us from the corner.

My heart leapt into my throat. "Fuck," I muttered and pulled out my switchblade. My muscles tensed, my whole self readying for a battle.

No one was taking Zoe from me. Not while I had breath in my body.

But Jean-Michel turned his head and kept going.

"What the hell?" I exchanged a glance with Zoe, who looked as puzzled as I was.

"I think," she said slowly, "that was his way of saying he's on our side."

"Yeah? Well, in case you're wrong and he's going for reinforcements, I vote we make tracks."

"Right with you."

We took off at a fast walk in the opposite direction.

"Let's go back to the hotel and see if it's safe to pick up our things," I said. We'd done a good job of hiding our identity up until the moment Zoe had walked into Philippe's lair, and our room was paid up for a week. "I have ID, phones, cash. It would make things a helluvalot easier to get out of France, because I'd rather not use those tickets Lainey gave us."

"Agreed. But I think we should enter the shadows again. Jean-Michel probably isn't the only man out looking for us." Her brows scrunched together. "That is, if you're strong enough?"

I opened my mouth to say *Of course, I'm strong enough*, but that was instinct talking. The instinct to hide any possible weakness from the vampire world.

But Zoe was my mate. If I couldn't trust her, then this was over before it started.

"I think I can just make it."

"Okay." She leaned in to kiss me. "I'll be right beside you. If you need to stop halfway there, that's all right. We can find somewhere to hole up for a while."

I touched her cheek. "Sounds like a plan."

❧

Zoe's blood was apparently powerful, because the small amount I'd drunk kept me going long enough to travel to the hotel in the shadows, then hold a glamour while I grabbed our luggage and left through a side door. Zoe remained in the shadows the entire time. She was too recognizable, even without her vampire glow.

We checked into a large hotel near the train station in Montparnesse where we could be anonymous. My energy was fading fast, and Zoe was getting that tight look around the eyes that meant a vampire was getting edgy from the blood craving.

I was torn between calling my father right away and feeding, but we needed to keep our strength up, so we threw our stuff in the new hotel room, and headed out into the night. We couldn't risk a trip to even a low-rent club like Le Sang Bleu, so we drank a small amount of blood from a couple of healthy-looking joggers and then wiped their memory of us.

Back in the hotel, I grabbed a new phone and inserted a SIM card. "They took a photo of me that first night," I told Zoe as I punched in my dad's number from memory. "To send to Father. But Tomas Mraz said he intercepted it so my father never saw it."

Zoe's breath hitched. Her gaze went to my throat. "Just like your brother."

"Hey." I put down the phone without making the call and pulled her between my legs. "They didn't feed from me. D'you see any bite marks?"

She framed my face with her hands. "I was so worried for you. They had me locked in that damn guest room all that time with no visitors except Victorine and Jean-Michel. Then tonight my mother showed up and said she was taking me back to Montreal. If Lainey hadn't helped us, I'd be back in Canada and you'd still be in that cell."

I stroked my hands up and down her hips. "I would've come for you. Somehow, someway, I would've come for you."

"If I hadn't come for you first."

I searched her face. "So this mating thing—you really wanted to do it?"

"Yes. I think I've wanted to be your mate from that first night we met. It just took a while for me to realize it." Her mouth curved wickedly. "Like Lainey says, you've got a smokin' body."

"So this is all physical?" I nipped her lower lip.

A throaty chuckle. "I'm not going to lie—that gorgeous body is the first thing I noticed about you. But I love your mind, too, and how chill you are. You don't know how good it makes me feel just to be with you. I missed you, Rafe. That time I came to New York, I wanted to see you so bad. After I apologized, I was even going to ask you for a second chance—not that I deserved it."

"Yeah?" The last, residual hurt melted away. In a way, Victorine had done us both a favor. I'm not sure I would've been ready for a mate two years ago. I'd had some growing up to do, and so had Zoe.

I wrapped my fingers around her nape. "Well, you're stuck with me now. Because I'm not leaving. Ever."

We kissed, and then I reluctantly released her and picked up my phone again. "Give me fifteen minutes, and I'm all yours."

"I'll just wait outside."

She backed away, but I caught her and pulled her onto my lap. "Stay. I'm not letting you out of my sight."

"Your father won't mind that I'm listening?"

"If he does, he'll have to deal. We're mates, remember?"

Her face softened in a way that gutted me. Because I saw love there.

Real, forever love.

"Yeah," she said. "We're mates."

It was almost two a.m. in Paris, which made it a little before sunset in New York. I started to enter my father's number again, until I recalled that Tomas had said all calls were being routed through him.

So instead, I phoned my mom. If he wasn't with her, she'd know how to find him.

She answered immediately. "Yes?"

"It's me. Rafe."

"You're all right? Where are you?"

"I'm fine." I broke into a smile. "How are you?"

"I'm good, cher. What have you been up to?"

My smile broadened. It was just so nice to hear her voice. She sounded so normal. Motherly. Asking about my news like I hadn't been imprisoned by a vampire for several days—although of course, she didn't know that, and I wasn't going to tell her.

"I'm in Paris," I said.

"Is that Rafe?" my father asked.

"Father's with you?" Even better.

"We're out on Montauk with Gabriel."

"What are you two doing in Montauk?" My dad wasn't exactly a beach person, and even Gabriel didn't use his beach place very much. He'd built it for Mila Vittore, and then she'd left.

"It's been a busy couple of weeks," my mom said dryly, and brought me up to date on Gabriel and Mila.

It seemed Tomas had told the truth about her coming back. And this time, Gabriel was keeping her.

"Good for Gabriel." I swallowed and wrapped my arm tighter around Zoe. "I have some news, too. I took a mate. Zoe Tremblay. She's with me now."

There was a stunned silence. Mom wasn't easily surprised—she'd raised three dhampir sons, after all—but I'd clearly succeeded.

"*Princess* Zoe? The prima's daughter?"

Zoe had her hand under my T-shirt, stroking my abs like she couldn't get enough of me. Now she stiffened and withdrew her hand.

"It's okay," I mouthed and brought her hand back to my stomach. To my mother, I said, "I'm sorry you couldn't be there, but we had to do it quickly. I'll explain when I get home."

"Well. Bless your heart."

I winced. When a Southern woman says, "Bless your heart," she's really saying something like, *Are you fucking kidding me?*

"Sorry," I said again. "It's been a crazy couple of weeks for me, too."

"Does Victorine know?"

"Not yet. We're working on that. She's my true mate, Mom."

Mom took a deep breath, then said, "Then I'm happy for both of you. Congratulations, cher. Tell the princess I can't wait to meet her."

"I will." I nuzzled Zoe's neck. "And give my congrats to Gabriel and Mila, too. We'll be there as soon as we can."

"I will. Love you."

"Love you, too."

My dad came on the phone.

"You heard what I told Mom?" I asked. "That I've mated with Princess Zoe?"

"Yes," he said, and then fell silent for so long I thought the connection had been broken.

"Father? You still there?"

"Yes. Would you care to explain?" He sounded calm enough. I couldn't tell if he was pissed off, or calculating how to use my mating to his advantage, but knowing him, my money was on the second.

"Zoe's right here," I added. "In the room with me."

"Ah. Please extend my felicitations."

Zoe hadn't moved—or even taken a breath—since Father had spoken.

"Breathe," I mouthed at her, and her lungs heaved.

I gave her an encouraging smile.

"Thanks," I told my father. "I will. When we get back to New York, I'll explain how everything went down, but right now you need to know a few things. First, Tomas Mraz was behind Zaq's kidnapping. He's working with Prima Tremblay."

"You have proof?" He didn't sound surprised. Just resigned.

"He told me himself."

A heavy exhale. "I see. You have a safe connection?"

"Yeah. I'm on a burner phone with a new SIM card."

"Good. Tell me everything you've learned."

I brought my father up to date on everything that had happened in Paris: Tomas's visit to my cell, Victorine and Philippe's complicity, the phone call Zoe had made to Zaq.

It turned out that he already knew some of this, including that Tomas was likely our mole. And of course, he'd suspected Victorine and Philippe as soon as he'd realized that Zaq had been kidnapped in Paris; that was why he'd sent me to Montreal in the first place. He even knew that Zaq had escaped—or been released from—Philippe's lair, and he had people searching for him.

What he didn't know was that Zaq had been brainwashed into believing that he—my father—was behind the kidnapping.

"They told him that you'd embedded a slayer in Gabriel's staff, and that I'd be next if Zaq didn't stake you first. And they sent a slayer with him to make sure it happens."

"So this is why he is hiding from me," my father said. Still very calm, but I knew that had to hurt.

"Tell him they gave Zaq a week," Zoe broke in. "And that was two days ago. Whatever happens, it's going to be soon."

"I heard," said Father.

"There's more," I said. "Tomas said he's planted information that will turn you against Gabriel. And I'm supposedly going to disappear after giving key intel to Prima Victorine."

"What sort of intel?"

"The location of all the Kral covens."

Father said something dark in Slovak. "The S.O.B. hasn't missed a trick, has he?"

"No," I said.

"Anything else?"

"Just that Zoe and I are going to be all over social media—the Tremblay Princess and the Dark Angel. We did it as a preemptive strike against Victorine, but maybe Zaq will see it, too."

"All right, here's what I want you to do—leave France as soon as you can. We can talk more when you get to New York. Do you need money? Passports?"

"No, we're good. We're in a safe place. We'll leave France tomorrow evening. It's too late to catch a flight out now—Zoe has to travel at night."

"Very well."

"We'll fly into JFK. First class—we're not hiding that we're together. I'll text you with the flight info."

"I'll have a limo pick you up."

"Thanks." I hesitated, then added, "Don't be too hard on Zaq, okay? He's been brainwashed into thinking you're the enemy. That you set him up in Paris, and you've arranged things so that the slayers can take out me and Gabriel, too."

"I understand," he said and ended the call.

Zoe got off my lap and stood looking at me. "He's not happy, is he?" She rubbed her hands over her arms. "About our mating?"

"I wouldn't say unhappy, exactly, but he doesn't like surprises. I'll make sure he knows exactly what went down. Don't forget, our mating will settle the blood feud, once and for all."

"That's what I told my mother."

I raised my brows. "You tried to convince Victorine to let us mate?"

She grimaced. "I had to try. But she's obsessed with Karoly. She'll never forgive him for staking my father."

"Well, my dad's more practical. After he gets over the shock, he'll see the advantages to my mating with you, starting with that damn blood feud. That should be a point in our favor. He finds that sort of pointless killing wasteful."

"Wasteful," Zoe repeated neutrally.

I moved a shoulder. Like Victorine, my father had a cold side. He was a vampire, after all.

"Now, come here." I dropped the phone on the night table, pulled off my T-shirt and pulled her back on my lap.

I set her hand on my abs and my mouth to the turn of her neck. "That whole time I was talking, you were distracting me. Touching my stomach like that. I was waiting for you to move your hand lower." I took her hand and placed it on my dick, which was pressing against my zipper.

Her breath hitched. She squeezed me through my jeans. "Yeah?"

"Yeah." I slid a hand up her inner thigh.

She widened her legs, allowing me greater access. I stroked her panties over her sex. "Bad girl."

"You like me bad." She pushed against my fingers, but I kept the touch light. Teasing her.

I was getting to know Zoe, and she liked to be teased, even bossed around—in bed, that is. She was a strong, confident woman, but she got turned on by a little dominance, which was how I liked it, too. She was perfect. We were perfect together.

I removed my fingers from between her thighs and jerked the straps of the sexy little dress down her shoulders, forcing her to keep her arms close to her sides. Underneath, she wore a scrap of something filmy and black.

I growled lowly. It was a surprise. A good one. "Mm, I like it."

I caressed her breasts through the material. Then I recalled something. "Philippe gave you these clothes, right?" When she nodded, I said, "Fuck that."

Those days in the cell had left me in a dark, primitive mood. I wanted my woman—a hard, no-holds-bar fuck.

And I sure as hell didn't want her wearing anything Philippe had provided her.

I took out the switchblade and released the blade with a snick.

Her eyes widened, but she held still as I sliced through the band holding the bra cups together. The catch in her breath told me she found it as hot as I did.

Her breasts were bared to me, the tips hard and dusky red. I set the knife on the nightstand and sucked one into my mouth. She closed her eyes and arched her back, wordlessly asking for more. I switched to the other nipple, giving it a few hard sucks as well.

When I glanced up, she was watching me, her honey-colored eyes heavy-lidded with arousal.

I took hold of her jaw and gave her a kiss. "You're so beautiful. I can't get enough of you."

She smiled against my mouth.

I put my hand under her dress again. She rocked her hips up toward my fingers, seeking more pressure.

I lightened my touch. "Beg for it."

She writhed beneath my hand. "You want to hear you're good?"

I cupped her mons, stroked my finger into her panties. She was so wet. So ready.

"That's a start."

"You're good. So damn good."

"Beg." I scraped my teeth over her nipple and she jerked with surprise—and got even wetter. "You know it makes you hot. I can feel it. Here." I slid my finger into her sex. "And through our bond."

She was panting now, her mouth soft, a little open. "I'm...not sure...if I like you...using that against me."

"Goes both ways." I gently bit the other nipple. "I know you feel me, too. And if you want me to stop, you can just say so. But you don't want to, and we both know it. Now beg for it. Or I'll tease you until sunrise."

"Damn you." Her head fell back. "Please."

"Please what?"

"Please fuck me."

"Oh, I will. When I'm ready."

Her eyes narrowed. I laughed and lifted her off my lap and set her on the bed.

She leaned back on her forearms, her long legs open and half off the bed, her pretty breasts bare above the tight black dress, her hair tumbling around her shoulders like dark silk. The opposite of the ladylike, put-together princess the world knew.

And I was the only one who'd ever see her like this.

I reached for the switchblade again.

She pouted up at me. "I like this dress."

"We'll buy you more in New York."

I pulled the dress away from her body and sliced it down the center. Yeah, it was crude, marking-my-territory stuff, but that's how I felt right now.

I spread the pieces apart and peeled them off her along with the remains of the bra, leaving her in the boots and a pair of see-through black panties.

I removed the boots and kissed my way up her smooth golden skin to her panties. Hooking my fingers into the sides, I pulled them down to her knees and put my mouth on her clit. Kissing and licking and sucking.

She was so primed, she started climaxing almost immediately. She widened her legs, stretching the panties at her knees. I left the panties where they were because the visual was so damn erotic—the scrap of filmy black material almost like a bow around her lower thighs.

My present to myself.

I slid a finger inside her and stroked her G-spot.

She moaned. "Please. Oh, Dark Lady. Please, please, please..."

I stayed with her through the orgasm, then shucked my clothes and rolled on a condom. She scooted the rest of the way onto the mattress and lay there, a flush touching her cheekbones, a satiated expression on her face.

I crawled up over her. Edgy. Needy. Knowing I didn't have it in me to be gentle this time. Something about mating her, and all the fuckery of the last few days was riding me.

I kissed her, slow and deep. "Turn over. And get on your knees."

Her mouth rounded. "Oh."

She obeyed. She even went down on her forearms, like she was reading my mind. Maybe she was, a little—or sensing through the bond what I needed.

I caressed her firm ass, gave it a smack. "I love you. So damn much."

"I love you, too." She turned her head and I saw her full red mouth open in surprise and pleasure as I stroked inside.

I pulled out, stroked back in. "So good."

Heat gathered at the base of my spine. I wasn't going to last long.

I pushed in harder. She was so tight around me. So perfect.

But she was almost a virgin. I slowed down, made myself ease off.

"Tell me if it's too much. I want to make it good for you."

She slanted a look up at me. "I want it just like that. Hard and fast. I want to feel you deep inside."

I didn't need to be told twice. I grasped her hips and shoved deeper. Her moans told me she was all in.

I set up a hard, steady rhythm. Reached around her to touch her clit so she'd come with me, but her hand was already there.

"That's it," I said. "Touch yourself."

She was moaning again.

"Come for me, sweetheart." I slammed into her, again and again. My balls were tight, painfully full.

"Rafe." She rasped my name.

But she was holding back. Something was bothering her.

I didn't like it, but I was too far gone to stop now.

I felt her pleasure and mine at the same time. Her inner muscles constricted around me, and I went off like a rocket, emptying myself into the condom—into *her*—until I felt scraped out, sated.

I hung over her, catching my breath, then came down on the mattress and pulled her into my arms. Even as good as the climax had been, the sense that she'd held back made the pleasure fade quickly.

"What's wrong?" I murmured.

She shook her head against my shoulder. "Nothing."

"Zoe."

"I'll tell you. Just not now, okay?"

I sighed and tightened my grip on her. "I love you. You need to get used to that. We're a unit, remember?"

"I'm trying," she said, and kissed the side of my neck.

❧ 25 ❧

ZOE

Saturday night, we caught a jet to London in case the flights from Paris to New York were being watched.

Lainey had posted several photos of me and Rafe. The one of us deep kissing went viral. By the time we landed at Heathrow, it had close to 200K likes on Instagram and was trending on TikTok and Twitter, too.

We exited the plane and Rafe shed his glamour. All around us, heads snapped around.

The youngest Kral Angel was in the house. Lean, dark, and sexy as sin.

I straightened my spine and released my glamour, too. We both wore jeans and T-shirts, a black tee for him and a white one for me. He still looked too thin and the silver burns on his wrists hadn't healed yet, but he'd recovered remarkably fast. Rafe thought it was due to my blood, and maybe it was—some vampires' blood could heal. I didn't know if mine had that power, since it was the first time anyone had drunk from me.

The whispers followed us down the concourse.

"That's them. Rafe and Zoe."

"She's so scary. The Ice Princess. What the hell does he see in her?"

"He can bloody well drink from me anytime he wants."

The attention made me prickly. I didn't mind that most of it was directed at Rafe. What bothered me was all those women undressing him with their eyes.

We'd combined our stuff into the duffel bag and left my suitcase behind in Paris. Rafe shifted the bag to his opposite shoulder and set a hand on my lower back.

"Hey, I don't love it either," he muttered. "But go with it. Right now, publicity is our friend. The more the better."

A young woman pointed a phone at him. He gave her a grin that made her blush and stare back like a lovesick puppy.

"Smile," he told me out of the corner of his mouth.

I gave the human a toothy grin that made her whiten and stumble over her own sneakers in her hurry to get away.

"Zoe." Rafe chuckled and shook his head.

I dropped my sunglasses over my nose. "Ground rules," I informed my sex-god of a mate. "They can look but they can't touch."

"Whatever you say, sweetheart." He pulled me to a halt and met my eyes. "I'm a one-woman man. You're the only one I want. I didn't even want that thrall the other night at Le Sang Bleu."

I touched my fangs to the sweet spot below his jaw. "Just so we understand each other."

His hand moved lower to rest on my ass. He nibbled my earlobe. The crowd of onlookers ate it up—I heard the click of camera phones. Well, most of the crowd, anyway. A few glared at me like they'd like to skewer me with a long silver blade.

We continued walking. "Is that what's wrong?" he asked in an undertone. "You're afraid I'm going to cheat on you? Because Krals don't do that kind of shit."

The hurt in his voice made my chest compress.

"No." I threaded my fingers through his. "I trust you. I feel you through our bond. I'd know if you were unhappy or feeling trapped."

"Then what is it?"

I exhaled. "I'm afraid."

"Of your mother?"

I nodded.

He squeezed my hand. "You'll be safe in Kral territory. She can't touch you there."

"I'm not afraid of that."

"Then what are you afraid of?"

"I'm afraid for you, damn it."

And a part of me was holding back because of it. This couldn't last. Somehow, some way, Victorine would find a way to split us up.

"Me?" He sent me a long look, and then nodded as if he'd figured something out. "We can't talk here. We'll discuss it on the plane."

⁂

The flight to New York took off shortly before midnight. We went first class, with comfortable leather seats and all the amenities, but I couldn't help thinking of that flight to Paris.

I'd been so happy, hell, giddy with possibilities and freedom. I was happy now, of course—happier than I'd ever been—but I didn't trust it.

Somewhere out there, Victorine was waiting for me to resurface. She couldn't contact me yet because I hadn't returned the SIM card to my phone. But I knew I'd be hearing from her as soon as I did— or even if I didn't.

The flight attendant brought Rafe a rare steak. I sipped a red wine and watched him eat. I hated seeing him so thin.

What have you done?

Cold filled my nostrils.

Stop it. You did the only thing you could. Mating with Rafe was the best way to protect him from Victorine.

But what if I'd figured wrong? What if it wasn't enough? Lainey's posts would buy us time—Victorine was too canny to stir up the humans against her—but I knew my mother.

She had the resources and the singlemindedness to take Rafe away from me. We'd always be watching our backs.

I reminded myself that the Tremblay Syndicate would back me, or at least, most of them anyway. Rafe was my true mate, and I'd make sure everyone knew it.

But would it be enough to protect him?

Rafe finished his meal and the attendant cleaned everything way. He reclined the white leather seat and crooked his finger at me. "C'mere."

Really? I shook off my worries and raised a brow.

I probably shouldn't let him get away with that cocky, I'm-in-charge behavior. Although I had to admit, it turned me on.

His cheek creased in that knee-melting smile that had made me fall for him. "Please, sweetheart?"

I shook my head at him. But he had me at *sweetheart*. It would take a while for the newness of that to wear off.

I reclined my seat.

"There you are," he said like it had been days since we'd last seen each other, and drew me into his arms. "I can't wait to get you alone."

"Mm." I snuggled closer and slid my hand under his T-shirt. Loving that I could touch his warm, hard-muscled body whenever I wanted to.

"All right," he said. "Talk. What are we going to do about Victorine?"

I closed my eyes. I didn't want to talk about Victorine. I didn't even what to think about her.

But I had no choice.

"That last night, when she came to tell me we were going back to Montreal, she told me something."

My chest tightened. I still couldn't believe how cold and matter of fact Victorine had been. Like she didn't care about me at all, just my uterus and the fact that I could bear her an heir.

"Go on," he said.

"She informed me," I said, "that she was going to give me to a man of her choosing."

Rafe swore. "The hell she did."

"I tried to reason with her." I swallowed something sharp and painful as a shard of glass. Recalling how my mother had coolly threatened to take my child had brought the hurt and anger flooding back. "But she'd made up her mind."

"But why? She knows that if she forced you to mate with someone else, you might not have a child with a man you hadn't bonded with."

"It was a chance she was willing to take. She knew I'd never agree to mate with anyone but you. That's why when I saw the chance to mate with you, I took it. It was the only way."

"You did the right thing." Rafe's arms curved protectively around me. "That's it," he gritted. "You have to break with her. You know that, don't you?"

"There's more."

"More than forcing you to mate with a man you don't want?"

I nodded. "She said that if and when I had a child, she'd take the baby and raise it herself."

Beneath my hand, Rafe's stomach went rock-solid. "I'd like to see her try," he said, soft and dangerous.

"She won't willingly let me go. But I'm never going back."

"No fucking way." He exhaled through his teeth. "Okay. At least we know what we're up against."

"Yeah," I said miserably.

My stomach churned. Despite everything, Victorine was my mother. I didn't want to do this.

But I knew her. To break free of her and protect Rafe, I'd have to be as ruthless as she was. She'd clearly crossed a line. The other syndicates wouldn't take sides in a blood feud, but they would if they'd heard she'd not only broken the treaty with the Krals, she'd brought in Slayers, Inc., to take out Karoly's heirs.

She'd be ruined.

"I have allies in the Tremblay Syndicate," I said. "I can force her to honor the terms of the treaty with your father."

"How?"

"I'll threaten to go public with the fact that she hired SI to slay your brothers. She'll agree, because otherwise she'll have a rebellion on her hands. And if I have to, I'll send everything we know about your brother's kidnapping to her allies, and your father's allies as well."

"So we go for the jugular." He sounded approving. "Hit her with everything we've got. I like it. We'll run it past my dad, see what he thinks."

"All right."

My muscles tightened. That was the one thing I hadn't considered—I was going to be living in Kral Syndicate territory, under Karoly Kral's power.

The price of safety from Victorine.

Logic told me things had changed. I was Rafe's mate now, not just Victorine Tremblay's spawn. But sometimes logic doesn't cut it. Karoly Kral was the bogeyman, the monster who'd haunted my childhood. The man who'd staked my father and tried to kill me, more than once.

"Hey." Rafe tucked a lock of my hair behind my ear. "It will be okay. I'll be there, remember? Nobody's going to make you do anything you don't want to. But I think you should defect to us."

I heaved a breath. I'd come to the same conclusion myself. I was too valuable to be unaffiliated with a vampire syndicate.

"Your father will accept me?"

"Of course. You're my mate. And besides, you're a strong, smart vampire in your own right. You'll have to prove yourself to him, but you'll see. He'll be happy to have you."

I nodded.

"So we'll start by negotiating," he said. "But if negotiating doesn't work," he added in a steely voice I'd never heard before, "I'll protect you. My father's accepted the mating, which means you're one of the family now even if you don't defect. If Victorine wants to take this to the mat, she'll lose. We're stronger than her. That's why she signed the truce, and that's why when she decided to break it, she went about this underhanded way of doing it."

Something about the way he said he'd protect me made me look at him.

His handsome face was stern, his mouth in a harsh line. When he said *protection*, he meant he'd go after Victorine himself.

I couldn't let that happen. Rafe was tough for a dhampir, stronger even than some vampires I knew, but Victorine was a vampire in her prime.

In fact, that might be her next tactic. If she could somehow get Rafe to attack her, she could stake him and call it self-defense.

I'd set this off myself by mating with Rafe, but things were happening so fast. There were so many unknowns.

We were hurtling toward a showdown with Victorine, and I was terrified that somehow, someway, she'd find a way to tear us apart.

I couldn't lose Rafe.

Not the man who'd brought color into my black-and-white life.

Not the man who'd shown me love isn't a weakness, it's a strength.

That's when I seriously started to consider staking my mother.

⚜

A Kral limo met us at JFK. A dark-skinned female soldier took the bag from Rafe and opened the door for us. Rafe greeted the woman, then straightened back up without getting inside.

Karoly Kral himself looked at us from the interior.

I went rigid.

"Father." Rafe took my hand in a firm grip.

I'd seen photos of the Kral Primus, of course, but we'd never met. He was slim, black-haired, handsome...and all vampire. A powerful presence that emanated a cool control.

The man who wanted me dead.

But things had changed. I was mated to his son now, and if I wanted to keep Rafe, I had to stand my ground. I lifted my chin and waited for him to acknowledge me.

His dark gaze settled on his son. "Rafe," he said. Just that one word, but there was a world of love infused in it.

Envy shafted through me. I couldn't recall anyone ever looking at me like that.

"You've lost weight," Karoly added gruffly.

Rafe shrugged and grinned like it was no big deal. That was one of the things I loved about him—nothing kept him down for long.

"It would've been worse if Zoe hadn't busted me out of there," he told his father.

Karoly turned to me. The warmth cooled, but his nod was grateful. "Princess Zoe. Thank you from the bottom of my heart for saving my son, and welcome to my city."

I inclined my head. "Thank you, Primus Kral."

Rafe pressed my fingers. "He's okay with this," he said out of the side of his mouth. "He knows you're an asset to us."

"I'm listening," his father said dryly.

Rafe grinned. "I know."

A Kral asset? I blinked.

But of course, that was how he'd see it. The Tremblay Princess, defecting to the Kral Syndicate.

Holy bat shit, what had I gotten myself into?

"Shall we go?" Karoly asked and withdrew deeper into the limo's interior.

I took a deep breath and took the seat across from him. Rafe sat next to me, showing by his body language that he was on my side now. And in case his father hadn't gotten the message, he took my hand and interlaced his fingers through mine.

The Kral soldier shut the door and got into the front seat with the chauffeur.

The three of us exchanged a few minutes of small talk, then the men got down to business. Rafe filled his father in on the details of what had happened in Paris.

"You understand what this means?" Rafe finished. "Tomas isn't going to stop with me, Zaq and Gabriel. He's going to go after you. He gave me some crap about doing it for you, but I think he wants to be primus himself."

His father's mouth pressed into a bleak line. "Tomas is a dead man. I have people looking for him in both Paris and New York."

"Just be careful, all right?" Rafe said. "He knows too much about us. About you."

His father inclined his head. "I know."

The conversation shifted to what Rafe had missed in the two weeks since he'd left for Montreal. His oldest brother Gabriel had narrowly missed being staked by first someone in the Kral Syndicate, and then by a slayer embedded in his own staff. More proof that all three Kral brothers had been targeted by Slayers, Inc.

Rafe told his father something I hadn't heard yet—that Tomas had arranged things so it would look like Gabriel had betrayed Karoly.

"Ah." His father tented his long fingers and touched them to his lips. "That, I didn't know. I'll get someone on it right away."

But there was happy news, too. Gabriel had mated with a human named Camila Vittore and taken the risk of turning her into a dhampir. I knew about Camila, of course. The Tremblays maintained files on all the major players in the Kral Syndicate. Gabriel had dated the human for a couple of years, but after she'd left him, we'd stopped keeping tabs on her.

Rafe was thrilled for his brother. "They're mates?" he asked his father.

"Yes. He insisted on taking her as a mate before she went through the transition." Karoly leaned back in his seat. "My sons are hard-headed like that," he told me with a narrow-eyed look at Rafe.

I smiled tentatively, not sure if he was joking.

His youngest son made a scoffing sound. "Like anyone could've talked you out of mating with Mom."

Karoly's cheek creased ever so slightly. "That was different."

"Mom was the best thing that ever happened to him," Rafe said to me, "and he knows it."

His father inclined his head. "She was—and is."

My smile widened, became more genuine. There was love in this family I'd mated into. Maybe, just maybe, some of it would spill over onto me.

Rafe leaned forward in his seat. "Did Mila make it through the transition?"

"We don't know yet. She's still buried. Gabriel hasn't left her side."

I'd never witnessed the transition from human to dhampir

myself, but I knew it was rough, that Camila might not make it through. I set my hand on Rafe's, offering comfort.

He curled his fingers around mine. "I'll call him," he told his father.

Karoly shook his head. "Later in the week, perhaps. He's not himself right now. He mated with her while she was still human. Their fates are intertwined now."

Rafe's throat worked. I squeezed his hand. If Gabriel had formed a mate bond with Camila, her death would devastate him. He might never mate again.

"She'll make it," Rafe said firmly.

He straightened up and drew a breath. "I have something to tell you, sir."

"Go ahead," Karoly said.

"I staked Victorine's lieutenant. The blood feud is back on."

Rafe sat stiff-backed, hand tight on mine, clearly expecting his father to be angry.

"He did it for me—," I started to say, but Karoly spoke at the same time.

"Good. The sonofabitch was part of the group that kidnapped your brother. I'd have staked him myself, but he'd left Paris by the time I got there."

I blinked. Something else Victorine had kept from me. But it made sense; she wouldn't have risked going to Paris herself. Sending Étan was the next best thing.

Beside me, Rafe relaxed. "If I'd known about Zaq, I'd have staked him in Montreal. The bastard was slapping Zoe around."

The two men shared a look. "Then, of course," Karoly agreed in soft tones, "you had to kill him."

The limo crossed the bridge from Queens to Manhattan. A few minutes later, we stopped in front of an eight-story high-rise on the Upper East Side. I knew from the file we kept on Rafe that he had a penthouse in New York, but it turned out he owned the entire building.

Karoly had fallen silent, but now he stirred in his seat. "For now, it's best if you stay in Manhattan. Let people see you two together. I will let Victorine know you're under my protection."

"She's not going to give up," Rafe said. "She told me—and I quote—that she wanted to 'wipe my family from the face of the earth.'"

A chill went down my spine. I hadn't known that.

"I can handle Victorine," his father said. "It's you and Zoe I'm worried about."

"Zoe has an idea about that," Rafe said.

"Go ahead," Karoly told me.

I gave him a rough sketch of my plan. That if my mother didn't agree to give up the vendetta against the Krals, then I'd go public with how she'd hired Slayers, Inc. to kill Karoly's sons and heirs.

"I'm going to upload the evidence to a secret server," I added.

"I'll want backup," Karoly said.

I hesitated. "Of course."

Rafe understood the reason for my hesitation. "Are you sure Tomas is the only mole?"

Karoly's features sharpened into something feral. "No, I'm not sure. Andre Redbone was another traitor. But Gabriel eliminated that little problem."

"Ah," said Rafe. "Redbone was the New Orleans kapitán," he told me.

I nodded.

"I still want backup," Karoly said. "But you would be wise to have a third person—someone neutral—to keep the evidence safe. Just in case."

"Agreed," said Rafe.

"Very well," Karoly said. "We will try this plan. But meanwhile," he added, "take a night for yourself—just the two of you. You're safe for now."

Rafe brought my hand to his lips. "We could use a night to rest up." Behind the cover of my hand, his tongue touched my palm in a sexy lick that made my inner thighs constrict.

His father's black eyes sparked with amusement. "Of course. You must be...exhausted from your ordeal."

His son smirked. "Something like that."

"Zoe." Karoly reached out his hands to me. "My mate would have my head if I didn't wish you welcome to our family."

I swallowed. I was conscious of both men looking at me. I withdrew my fingers from Rafe's grip and took his father's outstretched hands. They were strong and cool.

"Thank you. It's a pleasure to meet you." That was stretching the truth a little, but a part of me actually meant it.

The Kral Primus squeezed my fingers. "And you," he said with a smile that, for a vampire, held real warmth.

Two guards, a male and a female, greeted us in the high-rise's marble-and-wood foyer.

Rafe gave them an easy nod. "This is my mate, Princess Zoe," he said. "She's to be treated like a member of the family. Inform the rest of the staff."

Their eyes widened. "Of course, sir," they murmured.

"We'll be staying in for the rest of the night." He set a hand on my lower back and ushered me into the elevator.

Rafe's penthouse took up the top two floors of the high-rise. I had the impression of hardwood floors and warm colors. The kitchen/dining room was a warm brick-red with touches of turquoise. Rafe urged me through the foyer and into the living room past a lime couch flanked by lipstick-red chairs. The east side was a wall of specially treated dark windows with a view of a river.

Delighted, I pulled him to a halt and looked around me. "I love your place. The colors are so bright, and it feels so homey."

"I'll give you the tour later." He practically dragged me to the stainless steel staircase at the penthouse's center.

I was giggling now. "What's your hurry?"

"What d'you think?" He pulled me, laughing, up the stairs. Then we were in his bedroom, a lush but cozy space with brick walls and a massive bed covered in jade burnout velvet.

His mouth came down on mine. I eagerly kissed him back. He

walked me backward until my thighs hit the velvet-covered bed. I sat down, and he kneed my legs apart so he could stand between them. He framed my face with his hands and gave me another kiss.

Then I was on my back, my booted feet still on the floor, Rafe over me. He put his forearms on either side of my head, his body pressing mine into the mattress.

My nipples prickled. He rocked his hips against mine.

He gave me a slow, toe-curling kiss, then raised up long enough to remove my T-shirt and bra. His fangs scraped my throat.

I tensed, and then my head dropped back. It was submission, but also a kind of power.

Because he couldn't walk away from this thing between us anymore than I could.

An approving growl. "Mine," he said against my skin. "I'll never let you go."

My vampire liked that, because I wasn't letting him go, either.

He dragged his lips down my throat. Kissed each of my nipples through the bra. "I meant it, you know—what I said when we mated. I always wanted you as a mate."

I stroked my hand down his curls. "I do know it. That thing you said to your father about your mom being the best thing that ever happened to him? That's how I feel about you."

He lifted his head and grinned at me. "About time you realized it."

That did it. I grabbed his shoulders and pulled him back up to me. "Kiss me, Kral."

And he did. Hot, wild, very-Rafe kisses.

He'd apparently been holding back, because now he unleashed his full arsenal. When he'd kissed me breathless, he attacked my clothing. My boots came off first, then he tore off my jeans and panties.

He stood up long enough to divest himself of his own clothes, then reached beneath me to pull down the jade bedspread, revealing chocolate-colored sateen sheets.

I shimmied my hips against the smooth sateen. "Mm. Sexy."

He crawled on top of me. Six feet, two inches of aroused, hard-bodied male.

His dark eyes burned into mine. His erection brushed my belly. He combed his fingers though my hair, arranging it on the pillow to his liking.

"You look like a fucking goddess with your gold eyes and your hot little body and your hair spread out like that around your face."

How did he do that? Make me feel like the sexiest woman in the world?

I opened my arms to him. "*Your* goddess."

His eyes flashed blue. "*My* goddess." He stroked his hands over me like an artist learning every curve so he could commit my body to canvas.

I linked my fingers around his nape and tried to pull him down for a kiss, but he resisted and sat up. "Hang on a minute."

"No." I tried to pull him back.

"Trust me, you want this." He dug into the duffel bag for a large white box wrapped in a gold ribbon. "It's a little late, but happy birthday, sweetheart."

The box was from a Paris chocolatier. He must have picked it up that last day when I'd still been asleep.

I sat up and opened the box. Salted caramel truffles.

"Oh." I sucked in my lower lip.

"Your favorite. I told you I remembered."

I nodded, heart full.

"Here." He selected one and brought it to my mouth.

I took a small bite. The flavor exploded on my tongue—the salt of the caramel mixed with the dark chocolate's rich sweetness. I moaned in pleasure.

"More?" He offered me the rest of the truffle.

"Mm-hm." I took it into my mouth and rolled it around on my tongue. Savoring the taste.

Rafe drew a jagged breath. "Those weeks we were in the negotiations? You have no idea what you did to me when you ate one of those. So slowly. I had such nasty thoughts about your mouth and chocolate."

"Oh, I knew what you were thinking." I reached for another truffle. I took a bite out of it but held the piece in my mouth and pushed him back onto the sateen pillows. "Why do you think I played up to you?"

He shook his head in mock-reproof. "You are *so* bad."

"Yep." I grinned and rubbed the melting chocolate up and down his hard length. "Let me see... Were you thinking something like this?"

His swallow was loud in the quiet bedroom. He took my head and guided me to take him into my mouth.

"Sweetheart, you read my mind."

26

RAFE

We spent most of Sunday in bed catching up with our sleep. I woke before Zoe and lay there, looking at her. I was sloppy in love, and I didn't care. She was so beautiful to me.

My dark-haired, golden-skinned vampire princess.

When she finally opened her eyes, we took a shower together. I indulged myself by washing her all over and then taking her against the black granite wall. We were both starving by then, so we went down to the Village and the Ruby Speakeasy, a Kral vampire club where we could feed.

We spent most of the night looking for Zaq in both vampire and human clubs. My brother wasn't good at conjuring a glamour, but he had a way of blending in with humans that was almost as effective. He had to know I was in New York, but if he was here too, as he'd told Zoe, he was hiding, even from me.

It hurt, even though I knew he'd been brainwashed by Philippe and Tomas.

We returned to my penthouse and made love again. Zoe fell asleep at dawn, but I stayed up for another few hours, trying everything I could think of to track down Zaq. I even went looking for him online, although I knew he was too smart to leave digital traces. If he wanted to hide, he'd stay offline and use cash.

My eyelids grew heavy. I ran a hand down my face, then shut my laptop and crawled into bed with Zoe.

Around dusk, the buzzing of my phone woke me. I grabbed it from the nightstand.

It was Father. Zaq had contacted Gabriel.

I snapped awake. "How is he? What did he say?"

"He's okay, as far as Gabriel could tell. But he wants me to call off the hunt."

I rubbed my forehead. "Why?"

"That's all he said, other than that you and Gabriel should be careful, too—that whoever was behind this wanted to bring me to my knees. He told Gabriel that he couldn't talk long, that he was afraid the call would be traced."

I shook my head. "I don't like it."

"He wouldn't have asked if he didn't have a good reason. I want you to stop searching for him. I'm calling off my people, too. For now, we'll play this his way."

I hadn't told Father that I'd been conducting my own search for Zaq, but I wasn't surprised he knew. What bothered me was that he didn't seem to consider Zaq a threat.

I blew out a frustrated breath. "And if he's been fucking brainwashed? What then?"

"I'm on my guard, thanks to you," was the cool reply. "And you're no longer Philippe's prisoner, which gives your brother some breathing room. I believe Zaquiel is doing everything he can to find a way out of this. I'm still alive, aren't I? Now stand down. That's an order," he added.

I swallowed an exasperated growl. "You're the boss."

"I'll be in touch," he said, and cut the connection.

Zoe stirred sleepily. "That was your father?"

"Yeah." I looked at the phone, tempted to throw the damn thing across the room, but there was no point in taking out my frustration on an innocent device. I set it on the nightstand instead. "You heard what he said?"

"I did." She held out her arms to me.

I went into them, and she wrapped them around me. "I'm sorry," she said. "I know how worried you are."

"I just want to talk to him myself. I don't know why the hell he didn't call me, too."

"Maybe he can't. Maybe they're watching him too closely."

"Yeah. Fuck, I wish this was over."

She kissed my temple. "Me, too."

My phone buzzed a second time. I reluctantly pulled out of her arms and reached for it—and realized I'd picked up Zoe's phone, not mine. Before we'd gone to bed, she'd re-inserted her SIM card into it.

The message was from Victorine. I grimaced.

Zoe pushed up on her elbows, and I handed her the phone. We looked at the text together.

Call me.

The mask snapped down over Zoe's face. She set the phone back on the nightstand without responding.

"You don't have to talk to her," I told her. "This is our town, and you're under my father's protection. Hell, you're family. He probably has his own people looking over the shoulders of my security team. She can't get to you here."

Zoe's mask melted. Her eyes took on a suspicious brightness.

My chest constricted. "Hey." I touched her face. "I mean it. You don't want to talk to Victorine, you don't have to."

She shook her head. "It's not that. It's what you said about us being family."

The tightness in my chest eased. "Oh, that."

She scowled at me and swiped at her wet eyes. "Don't say it like that—like it's nothing. Because it's something. It's everything."

I enfolded her in my arms. I was starting to understand why she'd been holding back. She didn't quite trust what we had together, but not because she didn't trust me. She was afraid of losing it. She'd never had a family, not like I had.

"Whatever you need," I said. "It's yours. If you need me to tell you I love you every fucking hour, then I will. If you need me to say

I've got your back, then I will. If you need me to be your family, then I am. Forever. Got it?"

She swallowed hard. "Got it."

"Okay, then." I laid her back on the bed.

She looped an arm around my neck. "I should call Victorine."

"She can fucking wait." I nibbled her full lower lip.

Zoe bent up her knees so I was between them. I took hold of my dick and stroked it through her slickness, coating it with her juices.

She let out a sigh. "It feels so good."

"This?" I rubbed the sensitive head against her clit.

She brushed my hair back from my face. "Yes, that. Everything."

I played with her a little more until she was moaning, her clit plump with arousal, and then I rolled on a condom and slid inside her.

We did it basic this time. Fingers intertwined, staring into each other's eyes.

And then something happened. Something changed deep inside her, like she'd dropped a last, internal barrier.

"Mine," I said and pressed in hard one more time, and when we came, it was together.

And this time, she didn't hold back.

We collapsed onto the bed together, me still inside her, our faces turned toward each other like we were one body and two heads.

She smiled into my eyes. "I love you, Rafael Kral."

I moved closer so our lips touched. "I love you, too, Zoe Tremblay. Forever."

27

ZOE

It was another hour before I called Victorine.

She answered on the first ring. "Zoe. Enough of this foolishness. I want you on the next plane to Montreal. That's an order."

"No." I wasn't going anywhere near Montreal. I wasn't even willing to meet her on neutral territory. I hadn't forgotten that steel box she'd intended to lock me in.

"That's not acceptable. I'm your prima."

I gripped the phone. "No, you're not. Not if you don't accept that Rafe Kral is my mate."

Her breath sucked in. "So it's true? That wasn't just a ruse?"

"Yes. We swore a blood oath to each other."

"With a Kral? I forbid it. You'll have to undo it."

"That's impossible. We've bonded. And even if I could undo it, I wouldn't."

"Undo it," she said in a cold voice, "or you're no longer my daughter."

Rafe and I were both sitting up in bed. I didn't realize how tense I was holding myself until he touched the small of my back. Reminding me he was there.

Reminding me of what was at stake.

"I'm sorry you feel that way," I said. "But Rafe is my true mate. If you can't accept that, I'm defecting to his syndicate."

Silence. The kind of silence that used to make me shrink into myself.

Then she said, "We have to talk."

"Yes." I gripped the phone tighter. I didn't want to do this. But it was clear nothing and no one would change her mind. There was only one sure way to keep Rafe safe. "Come to New York, then."

Rafe leaned closer. "The Hotel Garnet," he said into my phone.

"Did you hear that?" I asked her.

"Of course. But I won't come to Kral territory."

"That's up to you. But I won't meet you anywhere else."

Rafe had his own phone out, texting his father. He spoke into my phone again. "Prima Victorine? My father has granted you a safe conduct pass for the next twenty-four hours."

"The Hotel Garnet. Midnight tomorrow," I told her and ended the call.

My phone buzzed again. My mother calling back.

I powered the phone down and dropped it on the nightstand, then lay back, an arm over my face.

"It's the best way," Rafe said. "You're right, we can't hide from her forever."

"No," I agreed without looking at him.

He didn't know what I'd decided to do. He still believed the game plan was to threaten Victorine with exposure.

And that was still my first move. I'd give her one more chance, but if that failed, I was going to stake her.

I hadn't told Rafe, because if I did, I was pretty sure he'd feel he had to tell his father, and I wasn't going to put the Krals in the position of offering her safe conduct so she could be killed.

Rafe sensed my turmoil, even if he didn't know the real reason for it. He pressed a kiss to my sternum.

"You've got this, babe. And I'll be with you every step of the way."

My heart squeezed. By the Dark Lady, I loved this man. His cockiness, his smiles, the way he'd go to the wall for his brothers.

The way he'd go to the wall for me.

I lifted my arm from my face. "I love you, so much."

"Right back at you, sweetheart." He rolled on top of me and gave me a slow, achingly sweet kiss.

And when we made love, it was even sweeter.

Afterward, he settled next to me, his head on my breast. I played with his curly dark hair, full of an aching sort of love.

Tomorrow, I told myself, it would be over. One way or another.

⚜

The Hotel Garnet was an exclusive vampire hotel in Greenwich Village. Karoly had ordered the restaurant to be closed so we could meet in private.

Rafe and I entered through a brick courtyard filled with potted topiaries. Overhead, swags of tiny fairy lights lit the way to the restaurant door.

My heels clicked against the bricks. I flashed back to my meeting in the hotel with Rafe two years ago.

My first strike for freedom, and it had been a spectacular failure.

This time is different. This time, Victorine doesn't have all the power.

But my stomach was balled up so tight it felt like it was pressing on my lungs.

I smoothed my hands down the new dress I'd bought at a boutique near Rafe's penthouse. A bright, spring-green dress splashed with sunflowers that Rafe had insisted I buy it when I'd fingered it longingly before turning to the black dresses.

Beneath the pleated skirt, a silver dagger was strapped to my thigh.

I drew back my shoulders, took a breath.

Strong, in control.

The fine hairs on my nape stirred, and Victorine appeared from the shadows in a wave of Opium. She was dressed in a short sheath in her signature power red.

Cold fingers clamped around my upper arm. "Come, Zoe." She tried to steer me back the way we'd entered.

My skin iced, then heated. I jerked free. "No."

Rafe hooked an arm around my waist and hauled me close so we faced her as one. "She's not going anywhere."

Victorine's mouth turned down. She looked at me. "Are you going to let that dhampir order you around?" she demanded.

My lungs squeezed. Everything I'd pushed down, penned up, held in, pressed into my throat, fighting to fly out at my mother.

My right hand flexed. Almost, I drew my dagger.

Strong, in control. And suddenly, I was.

Things really were different this time, because this time, I had Rafe at my side. And Karoly Kral and his people backing me up.

Because that's what family did.

"That dhampir is *my mate*," I gritted out, "and he's not ordering me around, he's defending me. What's more, you're in his father's territory. I'd be polite if I were you."

As if on cue, four flinty-eyed vampires dropped out of the shadows.

Victorine took them in—and whipped a thin silver blade from her bra. She lunged past me at Rafe.

I'd expected that. I stepped in front of him. She came close to skewering me, but stopped herself in time, the point hovering above my chest.

Behind me, Rafe said, "What the hell, Zoe?" He tried to move me aside, but I held up a hand.

"Trust me," I said, my eyes on my mother.

An angry flush tinged her cheekbones. "Step aside. I'm ordering you as your prima."

Our gazes locked. Victorine's will beat against mine. Even with my newfound confidence, she was still dominant to me. Give her enough time, and she could force me to obey. But I only required enough time to explain why she'd better make sure Rafe lived a long and healthy life.

"You're not going to stake Rafe," I said. "Here's why. We've uploaded a file with everything we know to a secret server. In twenty-four hours, unless we both enter our individual passwords, that evidence is going to every major primus and prima in the world. Everyone will know that you're secretly working with Slayers, Inc., including the Tremblay Syndicate. And in case you manage to somehow hack into the server and delete the evidence, Prince Brien has the same information. His instructions are to send it to both his parents and Primus Kral if he doesn't hear from me by tomorrow."

"You dare?"

"Oh, yes." My smile was sharp as the blade in her hand. "And I mean everything, including the photo of Zaquiel Kral in that cell in Philippe's basement. I've included an attachment explaining that both you and Philippe were working with Slayers, Inc. to kidnap and kill Karoly Kral's sons. The other syndicates will believe it, coming from your own daughter. And we'll plaster social media with the information, too. You won't be able to finesse this one. It's over, Victorine."

She brought the knife back to her side. "Why?" She seemed almost bewildered.

"Because I love Rafe. I'll do anything to keep him. You of all people should understand what it's like when you find your true mate."

Her mouth formed a hard scarlet line. "No. I forbid it."

"You can't. One thing you had right—I was your best choice for your next lieutenant. Without me, the Tremblay Syndicate is going to be embroiled in a series of challenges. But you're going to have to choose someone else, because I'm defecting to the Kral Syndicate."

Her face contorted. "Like Hades you are. You're *mine*. My spawn. My only heir."

"It's not your decision. You may be my prima, but I have the right to choose my own mate."

I reached for Rafe's hand. It was right there. He moved up beside me and together, we faced Victorine down.

"We're true mates," Rafe said. "Kill me, and she'll probably never have a child. She might even die herself from the shock."

The blade in Victorine's hand waved. "No," she rasped. "You're lying. I don't believe it."

"It's true." Karoly strolled up from wherever he'd been lurking.

"I can sense their bond. If you weren't so prejudiced against my son, you'd sense it, too."

She bared her fangs at him.

His men stepped closer, but he held them off with a look. "You've lost, Victorine," he said. "Either negotiate with us or go home."

Her gaze snapped to Rafe. "Thrice-damned viper's spawn. I should've staked you two years ago when I had the chance. Why should I accept you as my daughter's mate? A dhampir, when she could've had Étan, the strongest vampire in my syndicate."

"Because I love her," he growled back. "Étan just wanted to use her."

She curled her lip. "What do you know about it?"

"I know Étan would never have taken her side against you. Is that the kind of mate you wanted her to have?"

"Étan would've made her a fine mate."

"No. He might have been a good lieutenant, but he wouldn't have made Zoe a good mate. But it's done. We've bonded. You can't undo it."

Karoly held out a hand. "The knife, Victorine."

The guards moved closer and surrounded the four of us like a noose tightening. Victorine looked at me, as if even now, she expected me to help her.

I stared back. "You heard Primus Kral. You want to negotiate, fine. Otherwise, that information is going out to the world."

Victorine drew herself up to her full height, eyes glittering like an outraged cobra.

"The knife," Karoly repeated.

I readied myself to pull out my dagger. But she gave a tight nod and handed it over.

"Wise choice," Karoly said. He jerked his chin at his people. "Check her for weapons."

A male and a female moved forward. Victorine hissed and flashed her fangs.

Karoly flicked up a single black brow. "You have a problem?"

Her glare should've fried him where he stood. "No," she said between her teeth.

The two vampires patted her down. My mother tolerated it, stiff-backed, her mouth white around the edges.

"She's clean," the man told Karoly, and they stepped back.

Karoly waved a hand, indicating the restaurant door. "After you, Prima Tremblay."

We went inside along with two of the guards. The other pair remained on guard outside. The restaurant was elegant but cozy, with dim lighting, tomato-red tablecloths and a distressed wood floor.

The tall, brown-haired guard remained by the front door. The other took a stance by the only other exit, the door to the kitchen.

A server in black pants and a crisp white shirt ushered us to a round table. Karoly took one side, and my mother the opposite. Rafe and I sat together with Karoly next to Rafe and Victorine next to me.

The server bought us each a glass of blood-wine, then left us alone in the room except for the guards.

Victorine had composed herself, but I was growing tenser by the second. I knew my mother. Her stillness was the contained pressure of a volcano about to blow.

Karoly sat back in his chair. "Why don't we lay our cards on the table?"

She inclined her head. "Please."

"You broke the truce," he said. My mother started to object, but he raised a staying hand. "There's no use denying it. Your own daughter has shown me the evidence."

She went so rigid I was surprised her spine didn't snap. "This is true?" she asked me.

I gazed back calmly. "Yes."

"Philippe is no longer part of your scheme," Karoly continued. "In fact, Primus de Froulay has reprimanded Philippe for his part in detaining my sons, and stripped him of his rank as enforcer. I think you'll find you won't be welcome in Paris for a long, long time. If you persist on this path, your allies will know it. Your own daughter is willing to shout it to the world. You've lost. Admit it."

My mother looked like she'd sucked on a lemon. "Very well. What do you propose?"

Karoly's long fingers toyed with his wine glass. "We have interests in common, you and I. And now my son and your daughter have mated. Surely we can put this feud behind us once and for all?"

"Easy for you to say. Your mate survived the feud. Mine didn't."

"And I was responsible." Karoly studied his wine. "But why was Romanov in Maryland, I wonder? In my own home."

I stilled. That wasn't how I'd heard the story. Victorine had always said Karoly had vowed he wouldn't stop until he'd killed everyone in her immediate family—her, my father, and me.

My mother opened her mouth. Shut it.

"Say it." The Kral Primus set down the glass with a soft thunk. "He was there to stake my boys."

I darted a glance at Rafe. He looked as stunned as me.

"No," I croaked.

"It's true," Karoly told me. "Rafael was still an infant, and my other boys were barely more than toddlers. Your father compelled a human servant to let him in the house. He was nearly to the nursery when I caught him."

My chest seized. I turned to Victorine. "Is this true?"

She dipped her chin.

"You sent Mikhail, didn't you?" ask Karoly.

"Yes," she admitted.

"What do you mean?" I looked from my mother to Karoly. "What's he talking about?"

Victorine's expression appeared to have turned to marble. "We argued about it. Your father thought a treaty was the best way to end the feud. But I didn't trust Karoly to keep his word. I convinced him that if we didn't strike first, we'd lose you."

"So," I said between numb lips, "it's your own fault Father was staked."

"It was a mutual decision, but yes, I convinced him." A trace of animation returned to her features. "The blood feud was bound to end with either me or you—or both of us—dead. Mikhail knew that. He did it to protect us. At the time, Karoly wasn't willing to consider a peace treaty." The look she sent him dripped venom.

"The hell I wasn't," he growled.

Rafe set a hand on my lower back and smoothly redirected the conversation. "I'm sure we all agree that a peace treaty is in our best interest at this point."

"Yes." I took a deep breath. "I meant what I said in the court-yard. Go after Rafe, and both the vampire and the human worlds will hear about your plot against the Kral brothers."

"Agree," Karoly murmured, "and perhaps we can reopen negotia-tions on that joint venture. I have some other ideas, too. Ideas that could make both syndicates a great deal of money. Think, Victorine. If you persist in this vendetta against my sons, I won't rest until you're in your final grave. But aside from that, the two of them have bonded. Zoe's your only spawn. Kill her mate, and your bloodline will end with her."

"She could mate with another man."

Rafe snarled. "Try it. And you'll see how long you live."

Victorine eyed him coldly. She turned back to me. "You really want this dhampir?" She jerked her chin at Rafe.

I took his hand. "I do."

She shook her head, and then suddenly, she deflated. Lines appeared at the side of her mouth. She looked every single one of her two-hundred-plus years.

"You'll live in Montreal," she said. "Both of you. Enough of this talk of defecting."

My heart skipped a beat. I exchanged a look with Rafe.

"You accept Rafe as my mate?" I asked warily.

"Didn't I just say so?" she asked irritably. "I'll expect spawn. More than one. He's a dhampir, after all. At least he can give you more than one child."

"Perhaps," I said. "Someday. But we'll raise them as we see fit. And Karoly will be their primus—not you."

"They're *my* bloodline," she said.

"But I'm their mother," I said. "And Rafe will be their father. You have to prove to both of us that we can trust you again."

Victorine's jaw worked, but this time, she didn't try to force me to obey her.

Maybe she'd stay my prima, and maybe she wouldn't—but either way, the balance of power had shifted in our relationship, and we both knew it. If she disagreed or tried to interfere after my children were born, I'd simply defect to the Krals.

"Agreed," she said through clenched teeth.

"Swear it," I said, hard-voiced. "Swear that you will never hurt Rafael Kral or his brothers by word or deed."

The room went silent. We all watched as she brought her hand to her heart.

"I will never harm Rafael, Zaquiel or Gabriel Kral by word or deed," she said. "Your sons are safe from me," she added with a look at Karoly.

He inclined his head.

It was done. We'd won.

Elation filled me.

"As for Montreal," Rafe said, "we'll see about that, too. You're not my prima, Victorine. For the time being, we'll live in New York. As Zoe said, you'll have to prove we can trust you."

She turned her iciest glare on him.

He responded with his best cocky grin.

Stalemate.

I bit my lip, trying not to smile. Frankly, my money was on my mate. Beneath that handsome face was a tough-as-nails core.

Karoly interrupted the standoff. "A toast," he said to my mother. "To our spawn. May their mating be fruitful."

Victorine lifted her glass. "*Santé.*"

Rafe and I touched our glasses to theirs.

There was a low rumbling from the man guarding the front door. We all turned to look.

A long, lethal dagger gleamed in the guard's hand. He morphed into Tomas Mraz and streaked toward us.

✿ 28 ✿

RAFE

It was like Tomas had tossed a grenade onto the table. The room exploded in a whirlwind of sound and motion.

Father and I dropped our wine glasses and leapt to our feet, our chairs clattering to the floor. Father pulled a dagger from beneath his suitcoat. I grabbed my switchblade and released it.

Zoe was on her feet now, too, and reaching for her dagger. In a blur of motion, Victorine darted around the table and yanked the dagger from her daughter's hand.

"Get the hell out of here," she yelled at Zoe in French.

Tomas zeroed in on me, that death's-head grin on his blunt features. He feinted right and came in low, the dagger aimed at my abdomen from the left, a smooth move I'd see him do it a thousand times in practice sessions. If he'd have connected, I would've been impaled on its long silver blade.

But muscle memory took over. I threw myself to the right, taking Zoe down with me. We rolled over and leapt to our feet. I pulled out another switchblade and tossed it to Zoe.

Tomas stalked toward us. "Stand down, Princess," he told Zoe without taking his cold yellow gaze from me.

I didn't dare take my eyes from Tomas, but I heard the snick as she released the switchblade. Unlike Victorine, I didn't bother telling Zoe to save herself. I knew she'd die for me—as I'd die for her.

So I'd have to make sure we both survived.

"You go left," I muttered in sub-vocal tones. "I'll go right."

Another move I'd learned from Tomas. When it's two against one, split up and divide your opponent's attention.

"Got it." My badass princess circled left, the switchblade in her hand.

Tomas backed toward a wall, keeping an eye on both me and Zoe.

Meanwhile, Father had lunged at Tomas. But Victorine had leapt onto the tabletop, gripping the dagger she'd stolen from Zoe. She swooped off the table like an avenging bat, slamming into Father from the side and taking him down before he reached Tomas.

From the corner of my eye, I saw Victorine rise above my father and stab the knife down toward his heart. Father blocked it with his own blade. Silver clanked against silver.

Father threw Victorine off. She sailed across the restaurant, slamming into the other guard, who'd raced to Father's aid. The soldier plunged his blade toward Victorine's chest, but she rolled away and faded into the shadows quicker than I'd ever seen a vampire disappear. The knife slammed into the wooden floor.

Still, it bought Father the time he needed to rise to his feet.

Tomas's eyes flicked sideways. I saw the moment he realized Victorine had attacked my father. His mouth slackened. His whole body stiffened.

Victorine appeared behind my father, knife raised.

Tomas growled and streaked between me and Zoe, heading straight for my father. He shoved Father out of the way and plunged his dagger into Victorine's chest.

For a sliver of a second, we all stared at him.

Then Zoe gasped. I swore.

Father lunged at Tomas.

Tomas had already pulled out another knife, a switchblade this time. As he pressed the catch, Father slashed out with his knife. The switchblade flew out of Tomas's hand. Blood gushed from his wrist. He backed up, that damned grin on his face, making no move to pick up his weapon.

The other guard gulped. "Holy fuck."

I spun around, but he brought his blade back to his side. "I'm sorry, sirs." He looked from my father to me. "I didn't know it was the lieutenant. I swear, I'm not in on this, whatever it is."

"Good," I snapped. "Now get on the fucking phone and call for back up."

"Yes, sir." He whipped out his cell phone.

Father advanced on Tomas. "What in Hades are you playing at?"

He gave Victorine's dying body a hard look. "You were never the target. That lying bitch promised she wouldn't hurt you."

"So not me. My sons."

"Yes."

Father's jaw tightened. "Were they that much of a threat to you?"

Tomas cradled his bleeding wrist in his left hand. The scent of blood filled the room—his blood, Victorine's. It mixed with the acrid scent of her smoking skin.

"Not a threat," he said. "A weakness. Your weakness."

Father said something sharp in Slovak and bared his fangs. "I don't give a fuck that you saved my life. No one attacks my family, not even you."

"Do it." The big blond man spread his arms. His half-severed hand dangled from his wrist at an odd, scarecrow-like angle, but his grin was as wide as the world. "You always did talk too damn much."

Father was a foot from him now. He lunged, rattlesnake-fast, punching the sharp point through Tomas's sternum and into his heart, a quick, clean kill that the man didn't deserve.

Tomas touched the knife's handle. His grin never wavered. "Zaquiel is ours."

"What do you mean?"

Tomas's hand fell away from the handle. He crumpled to the floor. His skin smoked and turned black.

"You will not find him," he gasped, "until it's too late."

"Tell me, you sonofabitch." Father crouched down and shook his former lieutenant like a rag doll. "Where is he? What have you done to my son?"

"It's over, my friend. Find your true mate. Not…that weak human you made…into a dhampir."

"My true—?" Father released Tomas. "You're insane. The blood madness."

"Not…insane. Smart." Something dark bubbled out of the staked man's mouth. His skin had already blackened and begun flaking off. "Return to your true self. Your vampire self. Or you…will lose it…all."

His lips peeled in a twisted, terrifying facsimile of smile, and then his eyes glazed over as he passed into the light.

Father stood back up. I moved closer, set a tentative hand on his back.

He exhaled slowly through his nose, but didn't speak. Maybe he was as numb as I was.

At our feet, his closest friend began to crumble into soot and ash.

"Damn you." Zoe's shaking voice made me turn from Father. She knelt on the floor next to her mother. "You couldn't just let it go, could you, Moth—" She stopped and shook her head.

I crouched beside Zoe. Victorine's face was tight with agony.

My own mouth twisted.

"I will never harm Rafael, Zaquiel or Gabriel Kral by word or deed."

Technically, she hadn't broken her word. The bitch had probably planned to attack Father all along while Tomas took care of me.

She could barely speak, but her gaze was locked on Zoe. I don't think she even knew I was there. "Say it," she said in a scratchy voice.

"What?" asked Zoe.

"Mother. Say it."

Zoe just stared stonily at her.

Victorine moistened her lips. "Please."

"Why now?"

"Because. Just…because."

Zoe closed her eyes. Pain etched her features.

Then she touched Victorine's hand. "Mother," she whispered.

Victorine's lungs heaved. Her expression smoothed out, and then a fiery puff of smoke came out of her mouth and she went limp.

Zoe's shoulders rose, then fell. I drew her to her feet. She turned into me and burrowed her face into my neck.

"I could never be good enough for her," she said in a flat voice at odds with her shivering body. "No matter how hard I tried."

"Shh, sweetheart." I hugged her to me. "It's over now. It's over."

✵ 29 ✵
ZAQ

Car doors slammed. A half-dozen of the Kral Syndicate's best people pounded into the Hotel Garnet courtyard. The two enforcers who'd been left outside as guards brought them up to date with a few terse sentences.

They spoke in low voices, but I heard every word from where I crouched on the roof in the darkness with the slayer called Reaper.

Tomas Mraz had staked Prima Tremblay, and in retaliation, my father had sent Tomas to his final grave.

Which made no fucking sense, unless what I'd been told was true.

Karoly Kral was purging the Syndicate of some of our best men. First Andre Redbone, the kapitán of the Louisiana Coven. Now Tomas, his lieutenant.

Just as Reaper had warned.

Father emerged from the restaurant alone. He strode into the courtyard, rapping orders at his people.

Where the fuck was Rafe? Ice coated my insides. My fingers tightened on my dagger.

Reaper had said that my brother had escaped Philippe's dungeon, that he'd be at this meeting as well.

He's okay. Somebody would've said something if he'd died.

Ever since Zoe Tremblay's phone call, I hadn't been able to sleep more than a few hours a day. Whenever I closed my eyes, I pictured my younger brother sold into blood slavery. Fed from against his will, as I'd been.

Black crept over my vision.

Reaper nudged me. "Now d'you believe me?" she asked, low-voiced.

I dragged a breath through my teeth.

"Zaq?" She glanced at me.

I shook my head, unsure what to believe.

"If you don't stop Karoly, Rafael and Gabriel are next. If your father hasn't already staked them."

I growled. "You don't give a flying fuck about my brothers."

The skin around her eyes tightened, a small flinch that I caught only because I was coming to know her. You'd think I'd hurt her feelings, which was bullcrap.

Because we both knew the truth.

Slayers, Inc. wanted Karoly Kral in his final grave, and I was the chosen instrument. Me and my brothers were simply collateral damage—or maybe we were the bonus round, I wasn't sure.

Reaper had brought me to New York, but before I acted, I'd insisted on proof. My father could be an ice-cold S.O.B., but he'd strong-armed the Kral Syndicate in to accepting Gabriel, Rafe and me as his heirs. It didn't make sense that he'd try to take us out now.

I swallowed sickly. Damn it, why had I hesitated? If Rafe was dead, I'd never forgive myself.

It didn't matter that when Philippe had released me, I'd been too damn weak to even lift a fork to feed myself. I should've done *something*.

Rafe walked out of the restaurant, an arm around Zoe Tremblay.

Every muscle in my body locked.

He was alive. Thank all the dark gods, he was alive.

"Karoly must have a reason for not killing him yet," Reaper said in an undertone.

"Like what?"

Reaper shrugged and scanned the busy street below, patiently waiting for me to make up my mind. She was good at being patient.

People said I was the nice Kral. The easy-going, bleeding-heart Kral.

I knew better. I had a darkness at my core, and Philippe and his sadistic blood-suckers had poked the beast awake. Now it strained and snapped to be free.

The evidence was mounting that my own father was behind my kidnapping. I should be dead now.

And according to Reaper, Gabriel was next. She'd told me one slayer had already tried and failed to kill Gabriel, something I'd verified myself. But the slayers would just send another, and another, until we were all dead.

The darkness paced edgily. Eager to sink its teeth into the man who'd set Slayers, Inc. on his own sons.

It was time to act. If not, Gabriel and Rafe would die. Reaper had told me that Father had arranged things so we wouldn't even realize he was behind it. And if I tried to warn them, they'd think I was the crazy one, that I'd been brainwashed into believing our own father was trying to kill us.

Reaper shifted, a subtle movement that blended with the street sounds. The woman could give a mouse lessons in stealth. "Well?"

I expelled a breath. "I have to think."

Rafe was still alive. That single, indisputable fact battered at my determination to set in motion the plan to trap Father.

Father could've staked Rafe in the restaurant just now and blamed it on Victorine, but he hadn't.

Why not? What the fuck was he waiting for?

I squeezed my eyes shut. I was exhausted, too tired to think straight.

Time. I needed time.

I turned to leave. Reaper set her hand on my arm. "Where are you going?"

I jerked away from her. "Don't. Touch. Me."

She pressed her lips together. This time her hurt was plain to see.

I scraped a hand down my face. "Sorry."

If not for Reaper, I'd either be dead or still locked in Philippe's dungeon, his vampires' personal chew-toy. She'd convinced Philippe I could be trusted with this mission, then volunteered to accompany me when he would've sent one of his own men.

So I was grateful to her, even if I didn't trust her. I had a bad feeling that if I failed, her orders were to stake me.

"I've seen enough," I said more calmly. "I need to think."

"You're tired." She tilted her head toward the alley behind us. "Let's go back to the squat, talk it over."

❋ 30 ❋

ZOE

We buried my mother's ashes next to my father in the Isle de Minuit garden. The full moon floated above us like a fat silver coin, and the air was drenched with the scent of night-blooming flowers.

All the high-ranking members of Tremblay Syndicate were present, along with Brien and his parents and most of our closest allies including Leo de Froulay, the Paris Primus. I'd refused Philippe's request to attend. I was damned if I'd associate with him any further.

Rafe was there, of course, and Karoly Kral and his dhampir mate Rosemarie had flown in for the day. Karoly and I had agreed his attendance would send a clear signal to the world that not only was the blood feud over, the Tremblays and Krals were now allies.

My mother's passing had sent shock waves throughout the vampire world. With Étan in his final grave as well, a power vacuum had opened. I'd have given half my fortune to walk away from it all for a honeymoon with Rafe, but I'd had no choice but to declare myself the new Tremblay prima.

I liked to believe my mother hadn't intended from the first to slay Karoly when he'd offered her the safe conduct pass to come to

New York. That she'd seen an opportunity when Tomas attacked Rafe, and taken it.

But I'd never know.

She'd left the honor of the Tremblay Syndicate in shambles. Enough of the story behind Rafe and Zaquiel's kidnapping had leaked that I'd have to work my ass off to regain our good name.

But a part of me couldn't help being excited. This is what I'd been born to do, and I was full of ideas I wanted to implement.

My first act as the new prima was to appoint Rafe as a special liaison between the Tremblays and Krals. I'd offered him a position with my syndicate, but he'd gently turned me down.

"I'm a Kral, sweetheart," he said. "A made enforcer. I'm not sure Father would let me leave anyway."

My second act was to elevate Jean-Michel to lieutenant. I needed people around me with experience, and I trusted him to be honest with me. I didn't hold his refusal to help me and Rafe in Paris against him. In fact, he'd proved his trustworthiness in refusing to break his oath to Victorine, and he hadn't hesitated to swear a new oath to me.

My third act was to order the cams removed from both my tower on Midnight Isle and my apartment in the Old City mansion. I kept the cams elsewhere—Rafe and I would always need security —but in my own rooms, I'd finally be free of prying eyes.

My fourth deed as the new prima had been conducted earlier tonight. With Rafe, Rosemarie and Jean-Michel as witnesses, Karoly and I had signed a new treaty—in blood. Even our offspring would find it close to impossible to break a blood treaty.

The long feud was finally over.

The clock tower struck three a.m. The darkest hour, when the Lady was at her most powerful.

The priestess and priest blessed the urn holding my mother's ashes. I took the smooth ebony jar and placed it in the hole next to Father's urn. The bronze fountain sent plumes of water into the night sky as the assembled vampires came forward one at a time to throw a handful of dirt into the small grave.

The priestess spoke the benediction. "Ashes to ashes."

"Ashes to ashes," we responded.

"Bone to bone."

"Bone to bone."

"Blood to blood."

"Blood to blood."

She brought her hands together in prayer. "So may it be."

I stepped forward and poured a vial of my own blood on the dirt, sanctifying the spot for all eternity.

There would be no gravestone; vampires don't mark their final resting place in the human way. Instead, I'd ordered a weeping cherry planted next to the fountain as a living memorial.

Servers appeared with trays of blood-wine. In the gazebo, a jazz quartet played my mother's beloved French prewar songs.

Karoly Kral and Brien's father strolled off, engaged in an intense, low-voiced conversation. The seven-day deadline had passed but Zaquiel was still missing. I knew Rafe's parents must be frantic with worry, although Karoly appeared cool and urbane as usual, and Rosemarie seemed to take her cue from her mate.

As for me, I went cold with fear whenever I remembered Rafe chained in that cell in Paris. We all knew the danger to Rafe and his brothers hadn't died with Tomas and my mother. I'd beefed up security on the island, including adding a third, higher gate at the causeway entrance so no one else could enter in the shadows as Rafe had. If it were up to me, Rafe and I would never leave, but as he said, that would be letting his enemies win.

Still, the plot against the Krals was out in the open now. Rafe's father had uncovered evidence that Slayers, Inc. had been infiltrated by a secret alliance of humans and vampires who were using the slayers to settle personal vendettas or to take out powerful vampires such as Karoly himself. He'd reached out to his allies, and talks had begun about how best to fight back.

The band played the first notes of "La Vie en Rose." My mother's favorite song.

Sorrow pierced me. I stared down at the patch of bare earth covering her urn, wishing things had been different. That she'd been less of a vampire prima and more of a mother. That I could've been perfect enough for her.

Rafe set a hand on my lower back. "You okay?"

I let myself lean into him, just for a minute. "I've been better, but...yeah."

Prince Brien came up to us and I straightened up.

"Zoe." He took my hands. "I'm so sorry. That it had to happen this way... But congratulations on your ascension to prima."

"Thank you. And before you ask, no, I didn't stake her myself." Apparently, gossip was going around to that effect.

Brien leaned closer. "I believe you," he said in an undertone. "But I won't tell anyone, and if I were you, I'd let that rumor stand. Let them think you're that cold-hearted."

I nodded. I'd thought of that myself.

The niceties over, Brien raked a gaze over my new mate. "Prince Rafael," he said coolly.

"Prince Brien." My mate wrapped an arm around my waist and smiled. Not a nice smile. A hands-off-she's-mine smile that showed a hint of fang.

Brien returned it with an equally toothy grin. It was like seeing two male models—the sleek blond prince and the lean dark sex-god —face off.

"You've got a good woman," he told Rafe. "The best. I hope you know that."

"Brien," I muttered. "Chill out, would you?"

The men flicked a look at me, then went back to glaring at each other.

"I know." Rafe's arm tightened on me. "And yeah, I know she's too good for me. But she's mine."

Brien's brow lifted. There was a taut silence. Then his smile softened, became genuine.

He held out his hand. "Congratulations, Kral."

"Call me Rafe," my mate returned, and they shook hands.

"Congrats to you, too, Zoe," Brien added almost as an afterthought.

"*Merci bien,*" I said wryly.

We chatted for a few minutes. Brien kept glancing around the garden as if looking for someone. Finally, he asked, "What happened to that stylist? The cute one with the silver hair."

"Lainey?"

"Yeah," he said so quickly that I wondered if he'd been pretending he didn't recall her name.

"What about her?"

A faint flush touched his cheeks. I blinked. Was this the same self-assured, perfect Prince Brien I'd known since I was a kid?

"I was wondering," he said, then stopped.

"What's up?" I asked.

He moved a shoulder. "Actually, I'd like her phone number."

Rafe and I exchanged a glance.

"What?" Brien asked.

"Forget it," I said. "She's a slayer."

His brows crawled to his hairline. "You're shitting me."

"No lie," said Rafe.

"That whole stylist persona was just a cover," I added. "She's already shut it down." I'd checked, just to be sure.

"So that's why she went off with Olivier," he muttered. Then he gave an easy smile. "Just wondering," he said, but there was something behind his who-cares attitude—anger, or maybe hunger.

His mother beckoned to him, saying there was someone she wanted him to meet, and he wandered off to make like the Perfect Prince.

Rafe still had his arm around my waist. "I like him," he said in a surprised tone. "He always seemed like an arrogant prick, but there's actually something likeable in there."

I chuckled. "He grows on you."

I glanced at where Karoly and Leo still had their heads together. "I should join them," I told Rafe. A battle was brewing, and the Tremblays would be part of it.

Rosemarie Kral came up on my other side in time to hear me. She was a small, dark-haired force of nature with a New Orleans accent and a hard-to-resist warmth. It was easy to see where Rafe's charm came from.

I hadn't expected to like her. No, to be honest, I'd figured she wouldn't like me, but when I'd told Rafe, he'd looked at me like I was crazy.

"Of course, she will."

I'd grimaced. He didn't understand. His childhood had been so different from mine. To me, his home life sounded unreal, like something out of a sitcom. Family dinners. A big house in the country. A mom who cuddled you and read you stories.

What would a mother like that think of the Tremblay Ice Princess?

"I'm not exactly a family person," I told him. "There's a reason people call me the Ice Princess."

"Zoe." He waited until I met his eyes. "Just be yourself. Mom is used to vampires."

When I shook my head, he said, "She lives with my dad, doesn't she? He's not exactly Mr. Warm-and-Fuzzy. And besides, inside, you're warmer than you think. And I'm not just saying this. I can *feel* it. You don't have to please Victorine anymore. You're free to figure out who you really are."

"Yeah," I said slowly. "I am, aren't I?"

Now, Rosemarie slid an arm around my waist from the other side so I was between her and Rafe. She followed my gaze in the direction of Karoly and Leo. "Let them talk. Tonight, let yourself mourn your mother. Forget that you're the new prima. You'll have time enough for that tomorrow."

"But—"

"I wouldn't argue if I were you." Rafe slanted me a grin. "Just nod and go along with whatever she says. It's easier that way."

Rosemarie's lips twitched. "He's right. Just say, 'Yes, Mom,' and we'll get along fine."

A lump filled my throat. "You want me to call you Mom?"

"Of course." She leaned into me like it was the most natural thing in the world.

The heart that Rafe had already opened gave a hopeful lurch.

"Okay." I took a breath—and gave it a try. "Mom."

She squeezed my waist. "See, that wasn't so hard."

"No," I said. "It wasn't."

My heart expanded a little more. Maybe I could do this family thing after all.

My arms were still at my sides. It felt...wrong. So I slid one around Rafe's waist, and the other around Rosemarie's.

⁂

Dawn approached. A hazy pink line appeared on the horizon, warning that sunrise was on the way. The chateau grounds had emptied until only Rafe and I remained. The human thralls had gone to bed, and our vampire security detail had retired to their bunker in the forest.

The tower clock was striking five a.m. when Rafe pulled me into the ballroom. "Let's dance. We didn't get a chance at your ball."

I counted back. Was it only two weeks since I'd first seen Rafe at the Crimson Ball? It seemed like a lifetime ago.

"No, we didn't." I looped my arms around his neck. "But I have to warn you that I'm not going to last much longer. The day sleep..."

"No worries." His grin sent a hot shiver up my spine. "I'll put you to bed."

"I like how you think, Kral." I pressed myself against his hard, warm body and started humming the Ariana Grande song from that night.

Rafe joined in, a raspy tenor that made me smile. But then, it didn't take much to make me smile these days.

He wrapped his arms more tightly around me. We stopped moving our feet and swayed to the rhythm as we sang the words to each other.

This time no one was watching us, and we didn't have to keep it secret.

Neither of us knew the last verse. We trailed off. The only sound in the ballroom was our two hearts, beating.

I rubbed my cheek against Rafe's. He'd shaved earlier, but black stubble had already sprouted. He smelled of the summer night and his own special male spice.

"I love you," I said.

My Dark Angel. My lover. My mate.

I finally understood Victorine's burning obsession with revenge. She'd waited almost two centuries to find her mate, only to lose him within a dozen years.

That didn't make what she'd done right. But if I lost Rafe to another vampire's blade, maybe I'd go a little crazy, too.

"Love you, too." Rafe's mouth covered mine in a soft, sweet kiss I felt clear to my soul. "Let's go to bed," he said against my lips.

Yes," I said, and together, we walked up the winding steps to my tower.

TAKEN

THE VAMPIRE SYNDICATE

The Dark Angel Trilogy concludes with Zaq and Ridley's story...

RIDLEY

Vampires killed my mother and sent me on the run. Now I'm the
mysterious slayer known as Reaper.
I have one mission. Wipe vampires and their half-human cousins,
the dhampir, from the face of the earth.
My current target? Zaq Kral, one of the famous—and inhumanly
beautiful—Dark Angels.

ZAQ

I may be a Kral Syndicate prince, but I never asked for this life.
Still, I play the game when my vampire father requires it—until the
day another syndicate captures me with Reaper's help.
Vampires chain me to a wall with silver cuffs and feed from me. The
silver eats through my skin, poisoning my body and hardening my
heart. When I finally get free, the people behind this will pay.
Starting with Reaper.
Her, I'm going to keep.

Now available at your favorite bookstore!

ALSO BY REBECCA RIVARD

Thanks so much for reading!

Want to be the first to hear about my vampire romances and other steamy romance books? Sign up for my newsletter: rebeccarivard.com/newsletter

In return, I'll gift you with "Lir's Lady," a sexy short story from my Fada Shapeshifters world.

THE VAMPIRE SYNDICATE

Sexy, twisty vampire mafia romance

Tempted (Prologue)

Pursued

Craved

Taken

Fallen

Hunger

The Vampire Kingpin

VAMPIRE BLOOD COURTESANS

Steamy vampire romance set in Michelle Fox's Blood Courtesans World

Ensnared

Compelled

Learn more: rebeccarivard.com/vampires

THE FADA SHAPESHIFTERS

Dark shifters, seductive fae

Stealing Ula (Prequel)

Seducing the Sun Fae

Claiming Valeria

Tempting the Dryad

Lir's Lady

Shifter's Valentine

Sea Dragon's Hunger

Saving Jace

Charming Marjani

Adric's Heart

Learn more: rebeccarivard.com/shapeshifters

ABOUT REBECCA RIVARD

USA Today bestselling author Rebecca Rivard read way too many romances as a teenager, little realizing she was actually preparing for a career. She now spends her days with vampires, shifters and fae—which has to be the best job ever.

Rivard's writing has received numerous prizes including the prestigious PRISM, the RONE, and the Paranormal Romance Guild Reviewers' Choice Award for both her Vampire Syndicate and Fada Shapeshifters Series. In addition, eight of her books have been awarded *InD'Tale Magazine*'s coveted Crowned Heart Review.

When she's not writing (or reading), she walks and bikes in the Chesapeake Bay area with her guitar-playing, storytelling husband. She loves exploring and is always on the lookout for mysterious castles, eerie cemeteries and other abandoned places that she can use as settings in her novels.